The Searchers

**Center Point
Large Print**

**This Large Print Book carries the
Seal of Approval of N.A.V.H.**

ॐ श्री गणेशाय नमः

The Searchers

Alan LeMay

Center Point Publishing
Thorndike, Maine

This Center Point Large Print edition
is published in the year 2001 by arrangement with
Golden West Literary Agency.

The text of this Large Print edition is unabridged.
In other aspects, this book may vary from the original
edition. Printed in Thailand. Set in 16-point Plantin type by
Bill Coskrey.

ISBN 1-58547-080-5

Library of Congress Cataloging-in-Publication Data

Le May, Alan, 1899-1964.
    The searchers / Alan Le May.-- Center Point large print ed.
        p. cm.
    ISBN 1-58547-080-5 (lib. bdg. : alk. paper)
        1. Large type books. I. Title.

PS3523.E513 S4 2001
813'.52--dc21

00-050911

TO MY GRANDFATHER, OLIVER LE MAY, WHO DIED ON THE PRAIRIE; AND TO MY GRANDMOTHER, KAREN JENSEN LE MAY, TO WHOM HE LEFT THREE SONS UNDER SEVEN.

"*These people had a kind of courage that may be the finest gift of man: the courage of those who simply keep on, and on, doing the next thing, far beyond all reasonable endurance, seldom thinking of themselves as martyred, and never thinking of themselves as brave.*"

1

Supper was over by sundown, and Henry Edwards walked out from the house for a last look around. He carried his light shotgun, in hopes the rest of the family would think he meant to pick up a sage hen or two—a highly unlikely prospect anywhere near the house. He had left his gun belt on its peg beside the door, but he had sneaked the heavy six-gun itself into his waistband inside his shirt. Martha was washing dishes in the wooden sink close by, and both their daughters—Lucy, a grown-up seventeen, and Debbie, just coming ten—were drying and putting away. He didn't want to get them all stirred up; not until he could figure out for himself what had brought on his sharpened dread of the coming night.

"Take your pistol, Henry," Martha said clearly. Her hands were busy, but her eyes were on the holster where it hung empty in plain sight, and she was laughing at him. That was the wonderful thing about Martha. At thirty-eight she looked older than she was in some ways, especially her hands. But in other ways she was a lot younger. Her sense of humor did that. She could laugh hard at things other people thought only a little bit funny, or not funny at all; so that often Henry could see the pretty sparkle of the girl he had married twenty years back.

He grunted and went out. Their two sons were on

the back gallery as he came out of the kitchen. Hunter Edwards, named after Martha's family, was nineteen, and as tall as his old man. He sat on the floor, his head lolled back against the adobe, and his mind so far away that his mouth hung open. Only his eyes moved as he turned them to the shotgun. He said dutifully, "Help you, Pa?"

"Nope."

Ben, fourteen, was whittling out a butter paddle. He jumped up, brushing shavings off his blue jeans. His father made a Plains-Indian sign—a fist pulled downward from in front of his shoulder, meaning "sit-stay." Ben went back to his whittling.

"Don't you forget to sweep them shavings up," Henry said.

"I won't, Pa."

They watched their father walk off, his long, slow-looking steps quiet in his flat-heeled boots, until he circled the corrals and was out of sight.

"What's he up to?" Ben asked. "There ain't any game out there. Not short of the half mile."

Hunter hesitated. He knew the answer but, like his father, he didn't want to say anything yet. "I don't know," he said at last, letting his voice sound puzzled. Within the kitchen he heard a match strike. With so much clear light left outside, it was hard to believe how shadowy the kitchen was getting, within its thick walls. But he knew his mother was lighting a lamp. He called softly, "Ma . . . Not right now."

His mother came to the door and looked at him oddly, the blown-out match smoking in her hand. He

10

met her eyes for a moment, but looked away again without explaining. Martha Edwards went back into the kitchen, moving thoughtfully; and no light came on. Hunter saw that his father was in sight again, very far away for the short time he had been gone. He was walking toward the top of a gentle hill northwest of the ranch buildings. Hunter watched him steadily as long as he was in sight. Henry never did go clear to the top. Instead he climbed just high enough to see over, then circled the contour to look all ways, so that he showed himself against the sky no more than he had to. He was at it a long time.

Ben was staring at Hunter. "Hey. I want to know what—"

"Shut up, will you?"

Ben looked astonished, and obeyed.

From just behind the crest of the little hill, Henry Edwards could see about a dozen miles, most ways. The evening light was uncommonly clear, better to see by than the full glare of the sun. But the faint roll of the prairie was deceptive. A whole squadron of cavalry could probably hide itself at a thousand yards, in a place that looked as flat as a parade ground. So he was looking for little things—a layer of floating dust in the branches of the mesquite, a wild cow or an antelope disturbed. He didn't see anything that meant much. Not for a long time.

He looked back at his house. He had other things, the stuff he worked with—barn, corrals, stacks of wild hay, a shacky bunkhouse for sleeping extra hands. But it was the house he was proud of. Its adobe walls were three and four feet thick, so strong that the first room they had built had for a long time been called the Edwards Fort. They had added on to it since, and made it even more secure. The shake roof looked burnable, but it wasn't, for the shakes were laid upon two feet of sod. The outside doors were massive, and the windows had heavy battle shutters swung inside.

And the house had luxuries. Wooden floors. Galleries—some called them porches, now—both front and back. Eight windows with glass. He had made his family fairly comfortable here, at long last, working patiently with his hands through the years when there was no money, and no market for cows, and nothing to do about it but work and wait.

He could hardly believe there had been eighteen years of that kind of hanging on. But they had come out here that long ago—the same year Hunter had been born—drawn by these miles and miles of good grass, free to anyone who dared expose himself to the Kiowas and Comanches. It hadn't looked so dangerous when they first came, for the Texas Rangers had just punished the Wild Tribes back out of the way. But right after that the Rangers were virtually disbanded, on the thrifty theory that the Federal Government was about to take over the defense. The Federal troops did not come. Henry and Martha held on and prayed. One year more, they told each other again and again . . . just another month . . . only until spring. . . . So the risky years slid by, while no military help appeared. Their nearest neighbors, the Pauleys, were murdered off by a Comanche raid, without survivors except a little boy less than two years old; and they heard of many, many more.

Six years of that. Then, in 1857, Texas gave up waiting, and the Rangers bloomed again. A tough line of forts sprang up—McKavitt, Phantom Hill, Bell's Stockade. The little strongholds were far strung out, all the way from the Salt Fork to the Rio Grande, but they gave reassurance nonetheless. The dark years of danger were over; they had lasted out, won through to years of peace and plenty in which to grow old—or so they thought for a little while. Then the War Between the States drained the fighting men away, and the Kiowas and Comanches rose up singing once more, to take their harvest.

Whole counties were scoured out and set back to wilderness in those war years. But the Edwardses stayed, and the Mathisons, and a few more far-spread, dug-in families, holding the back door of Texas, driving great herds of longhorns to Matagorda for the supply of the Confederate troops. And they waited again, holding on just one year more, then another, and one more yet.

Henry would have given up. He saw no hope that he would ever get a foothold out here again, once he drew out, but he would gladly have sacrificed their hopes of a cattle empire to take Martha and their children to a safer place. It was Martha who would not quit, and she had a will that could jump and blaze like a grass fire. How do you take a woman back to the poverty of the cotton rows against her will? They stayed.

The war's end brought the turn of fortune in which they had placed their faith. Hiring cowboys on

13

promise, borrowing to provision them, Henry got a few hundred head into the very first drive to end-of-track at Abilene. Now, with the war four years past, two more drives had paid off. And this year he and Aaron Mathison, pooling together, had sent north more than three thousand head. But where were the troops that peace should have released to their defense? Bolder, wilder, stronger every year, the Comanches and their Kiowa allies punished the range. Counties that had survived the war were barren now; the Comanches had struck the outskirts of San Antonio itself.

Once they could have quit and found safety in a milder land. They couldn't quit now, with fortune beyond belief coming into their hands. They were as good as rich—and living in the deadliest danger that had overhung them yet. Looking back over the years, Henry did not know how they had survived so long; their strong house and everlasting watchfulness could not explain it. It must have taken miracles of luck, Henry knew, and some mysterious quirks of Indian medicine as well, to preserve them here. If he could have seen, in any moment of the years they had lived here, the endless hazards that lay ahead, he would have quit that same minute and got Martha out of there if he had had to tie her.

But you get used to unresting vigilance, and a perpetual danger becomes part of the everyday things around you. After a long time you probably wouldn't know how to digest right, any more, if it altogether went away. All that was behind could not explain, exactly, the way Henry felt tonight. He didn't believe in

14

hunches, either, or any kind of spirit warnings. He was sure he had heard, or seen, or maybe even smelled some sign so small he couldn't remember it. Sometimes a man's senses picked up dim warnings he didn't even recognize. Like sometimes he had known an Indian was around, without knowing what told him, until a little later the breeze would bring the smell of the Indian a little stronger—a kind of old-buffalo-robe smell—which of course had been the warning before he knew he smelled anything. Or sometimes he knew horses were coming before he could hear their hoofs; he supposed this came by a tremor of the ground so weak you didn't know you felt it, but only knew what it meant.

He became aware that he was biting his mustache. It was a thin blond mustache, trailing downward at the corners of his mouth, so that it gave his face a dour look it didn't have underneath. But it wasn't a chewed mustache, because he didn't chew it. Patiently he studied the long sweep of the prairie, looking steadily at each quadrant for many minutes. He was sorry now that he had let Amos go last night to help the Mathisons chase cow thieves; Amos was Henry's brother and a rock of strength. It should have been enough that he let Martin Pauley go along. Mart was the little boy they had found in the brush, after the Pauley massacre, and raised as their own. He was eighteen now, and given up to be the best shot in the family. The Mathisons hadn't been satisfied anyway. Thought he should send Hunter, too, or else come himself. You can't ever please everybody.

A quarter mile off a bedded-down meadow lark sprang into the air, circled uncertainly, then drifted away. Henry became motionless, except for his eyes, which moved continually, casting the plain. Five hundred yards to the right of the spot where the meadow lark had jumped, a covey of quail went up.

Henry turned and ran for the house.

2

Martin Pauley had found this day a strange one almost from the start. Twelve riders had gathered to trail some cow thieves who had bit into the Mathisons'; and the queer thing about it was that five out of the twelve soon disagreed with all the others as to what they were following.

Aaron Mathison, who owned the run-off cattle, was a bearded, calm-eyed man of Quaker extraction. He had not been able to hold onto the part of his father's faith which forswore the bearing of aims, but he still prayed, and read the Bible every day. Everything about the Mathison place was either scrubbed, or raked, or whitewashed, but the house was cramped and sparely furnished compared to the Edwards'. All the money Aaron could scrape went into the quality of his livestock. Lately he had got his Lazy Lightning brand on ten head of blood bulls brought on from Kansas City. These had been held, by the chase-'em-back method, with a small herd on the Salt Crick Flats. This was the herd that was gone.

16

They picked up the churned trail of the stolen herd shortly after dawn, and followed it briskly, paced by the light-riding Mathison boys on their good horses. Martin Pauley lagged back, dogging it in the early hours. He had a special grouch of his own because he had looked forward to a visit with Laurie Mathison before they set out. Laurie was eighteen, like himself—straight and well boned, he thought, in terms he might have used to judge a filly. Lately he had caught her unwary gray eyes following him, now and then, when he was around the Mathisons'. But not this morning.

Laurie had been flying around, passing out coffee and quick-grab breakfast, with two of the Harper boys and Charlie MacCorry helping her on three sides—all of them clowning, and cutting up, and showing off, till there was no way to get near. Martin Pauley was a quiet boy, dark as an Indian except for his light eyes; he never did feel he cut much of a figure among the blond and easy-laughing people with whom he was raised. So he had hung back, and never did get to talk to Laurie. She ran out to his stirrup, and said, "Hi," hardly looking at him as she handed him a hunk of hot meat wrapped in bread—no coffee—and was gone again. And that was the size of it.

For a while Martin kept trying to think of something cute he might have said. Didn't think of a thing. So he got bored with himself, and took a wide unneedful swing out on the flank. He was casting the prairie restlessly, looking for nothing in particular, when presently he found something that puzzled him and made him uneasy.

17

Mystified, he crossed the trail and swung wide on the other flank to take a look at the ground over there; and here he found Amos, doing the same thing. Amos Edwards was forty, two years older than his brother Henry, a big burly figure on a strong but speedless horse. He was some different from the rest of the Edwards family. His heavy head of hair was darker, and probably would have been red-brown, except that it was unbrushed, without any shine to it. And he was liable to be pulled back into his shell between rare bursts of temper. Just now he was riding lumpily, hands in his pockets, reins swinging free from the horn, while he guided his horse by unnoticeable flankings with the calves of his legs and two-ounce shifts of weight. Martin cleared his throat a few times, hoping Amos would speak, but he did not.

"Uncle Amos," Martin said, "You notice something almighty fishy about this trail?"

"Like what?"

"Well, at the jump-off I counted tracks of twelve, fifteen ponies working this herd. Now I can't find no more than four, five. First I supposed the rest had pushed on ahead, and their trails got tromp out by cows—"

"That's shrewd," Amos snubbed him. "I never would have thunk of it."

"—only, just now I find me a fit-up where two more ponies forked off—and they sure didn't push on ahead. They turned back."

"Why?"

"Why? Gosh, Uncle Amos—how the hell should I

18

know? That's what itches me."

"Do me one thing," Amos said. "Drop this 'Uncle' foolishness."

"Sir?"

"You don't have to call me 'Sir,' neither. Nor 'Grampaw,' neither. Nor 'Methuselah,' neither. I can whup you to a frazzle."

Martin was blanked. "What should I call you?"

"Name's Amos."

"All right. Amos. You want I should mosey round and see what the rest of 'em think?"

"They'll tell you the same." He was pulled back in his shell, fixing to bide his time.

It was straight-up noon, and they had paused to water at a puddle in a coulee, before Amos made his opinion known. "Aaron," he said in tones most could hear, "I'd be relieved to know if all these boys realize what we're following here. Because it ain't cow thieves. Not the species we had in mind."

"How's this, now?"

"What we got here is a split-off from an Indian war party, running wild loose on a raid." He paused a moment, then finished quietly. "Maybe you knowed that already. In case you didn't, you know it now. Because I just told you."

Aaron Mathison rubbed his fingers through his beard and appeared to consider; and some of the others put in while he did that. Old Mose Harper pointed out that none of the thieves had ridden side by side, not once on the trail, as the tracks showed plain. Indians and dudes rode single file—Indians to hide

19

their numbers, and dudes because the horses felt like it—but white men rode abreast in order to gab all the time. So the thieves were either Indians or else not speaking. One t'other. This contribution drew partly hidden smiles from Mose Harper's sons.

Young Charlie MacCorry, a good rough-stock rider whom Martin resented because of his lively attentions to Laurie Mathison, spoke of noticing that the thieves all rode small unshod horses, a whole lot like buffalo ponies. And Lije Powers got in his two cents. Lije was an old-time buffalo hunter, who now lived by wandering from ranch to ranch, "stopping by." He said now that he had "knowed it from the fust," and allowed that what they were up against was a "passel of Caddoes."

Those were all who took any stock in the theory.

Aaron Mathison reasoned in even tones that they had no real reason to think any different than when they had started. The northeasterly trend of the trail said plainly that the thieves were delivering the herd to some beef contractor for one of the Indian Agencies—maybe old Fort Towson. Nothing else made any sense. The thieves had very little start; steady riding should force a stand before sundown tomorrow. They had only to push on, and all questions would soon be answered.

"I hollered for a back track at the start," Amos argued. "Where's the main war party these here forked off from? If they're up ahead, that's one thing. But if they're back where our families be—"

Aaron bowed his head for several moments, as if in

20

prayer; but when his head came up he was looking at Amos Edwards with narrowed eyes. He spoke gently, slipping into Quakerish phrasings; and Martin Pauley, who had heard those same soft tones before, knew the argument was done. "Thee can turn back," Aaron said. "If thee fears what lies ahead or what lies behind, I need thee no more."

He turned his horse and rode on. Two or three hesitated, but ended by following him.

Amos was riding with his hands in his pockets again, letting his animal keep up as it chose; and Martin saw that Amos had fallen into one of his deadlocks. This was a thing that happened to Amos repeatedly, and it seemed to have a close relationship with the shape of his life. He had served two years with the Rangers, and four under Hood, and had twice been up the Chisholm Trail. Earlier he had done other things—bossed a bull train, packed the mail, captained a stage station—and he had done all of them well. Nobody exactly understood why he always drifted back, sooner or later, to work for his younger brother, with never any understanding as to pay.

What he wanted now was to pull out of the pursuit and go back. If he did turn, it could hardly be set down to cowardice. But it would mark him as unreliable and self-interested to an unforgivable degree in the eyes of the other cowmen. A thing like that could reflect on his whole family, and tend to turn the range against them. So Amos sat like a sack of wheat, in motion only because he happened to be sitting on a horse, and the horse was following the others.

21

His dilemma ended unexpectedly.

Brad Mathison, oldest of Aaron's boys, was ranging far ahead. They saw him disappear over the saddle of a ridge at more than two miles. Immediately he reappeared, stopped against the sky, and held his rifle over his head with both hands. It was the signal for "found." Then he dropped from sight beyond the ridge again.

Far behind him, the others put the squeeze to their horses, and lifted into a hard run. They stormed over the saddle of the ridge, and were looking down into a broad basin. Some scattered bunches of red specks down there were cattle grazing loose on their own. Aaron Mathison, with his cowman's eyes, recognized each speck that could be seen at all as an individual animal of his own. Here was the stolen herd, unaccountably dropped and left.

Brad was only about a mile out on the flats, but running his horse full stretch now toward the hills beyond the plain.

"Call in that damn fool," Amos said. He fired his pistol into the air, so that Brad looked back.

Aaron spun his horse in close circles to call in his son. Brad turned reluctantly, as if disposed to argue with his father, but came trotting back. Now Aaron spotted something fifty yards to one side, and rode to it for a closer look. He stepped down, and the others closed in around him. One of the young blood bulls lay there, spine severed by the whack of an axe. The liver had been ripped out, but no other meat taken. When they had seen this much, most of the riders sat and looked at each other. They barely glanced at the moccasin prints, faint in the dust-film upon the baked ground. Amos, though, not only dismounted, but went to his knees; and Martin Pauley stooped beside him, not to look wise, but trying to find out what Amos was looking for. Amos jabbed the carcass with his thumb. "Only nine, ten hours old," he said. Then, to Lije Powers, "Can you tell what moccasins them be?"

Lije scratched his thin beard. "Injuns," he said owlishly. He meant it for a joke, but nobody laughed. They followed Mathison as he loped out to meet his son.

"I rode past five more beef kills," Brad said when they came together. He spoke soberly, his eyes alert upon his father's face. "All these down here are heifers. And all killed with the lance. Appears like the lance wounds drive deep forward from just under the short ribs, clean through to the heart. I never saw that before."

"I have," Lije Powers said. He wanted to square himself for his misfire joke. "Them's Comanche buffler hunters done that. Ain't no others left can handle a lance no more."

Some of the others, particularly the older men, were looking gray and bleak. The last five minutes had taken them ten years back into the past, when every night of the world was an uncertain thing. The years of watchfulness and struggle had brought them some sense of confidence and security toward the last; but now all that was struck away as if they had their whole lives to do over again. But instead of taking ten years off their ages it put ten years on.

"This here's a murder raid," Amos said, sending his words at Aaron like rocks. "It shapes up to scald out either your place or Henry's. Do you know that now?"

Aaron's beard was sunk on his chest. He said slowly, "I see no other likelihood."

"They drove your cattle to pull us out," Amos hammered it home. "We've give 'em free run for the last sixteen hours!"

"I question if they'll hit before moonrise. Not them Comanch." Lije spoke with the strange detachment of one who has seen too much for too long.

"Moonrise! Ain't a horse here can make it by midnight!"

Brad Mathison said through his teeth, "I'll come almighty close!" He wheeled his pony and put it into a lope.

Aaron bellowed, "Hold in that horse!" and Brad pulled down to a slamming trot.

Most of the others were turning to follow Brad, talking blasphemies to their horses and themselves. Charlie MacCorry had the presence of mind to yell, "Which place first? We'll be strung out twenty mile!"

"Mathison's is this side!" Mose Harper shouted. Then to Amos over his shoulder, "If we don't fight there, we'll come straight on!"

Martin Pauley was scared sick over what they might find back home, and Laurie was in his mind too, so that the people he cared about were in two places. He was crazy to get started, as if haste could get him to both places at once. But he made himself imitate Amos, who unhurriedly pulled off saddle and bridle.

24

They fed grain again, judging carefully how much their animals would do best on, and throwing the rest away. The time taken to rest and feed would get them home quicker in the end.

By the time they crossed the saddleback the rest of the riders were far spaced, according to the judgment of each as to how his horse might best be spent. Amos branched off from the way the others took. Miles were important, now, and they could save a few by passing well west of Mathison's. Amos had already made up his mind that he must kill his horse in this ride; for they had more than eighty miles to go before they would know what had happened—perhaps was happening now—to the people they had left at home.

3

Henry Edwards stood watching the black prairie through a loophole in a batten shutter. The quartering moon would rise late; he wanted to see it coming, for he believed now that all the trouble they could handle would be on them with the moon's first light. The dark kitchen in which the family waited was closed tight except for the loopholes. The powder smoke was going to get pretty thick in here if they had to fight. Yet the house was becoming cold. Any gleam of light would so hurt their chances that they had even drawn the coals from the firebox of the stove and drowned them in a tub.

The house itself was about as secure as a house

could be made. The loopholed shutters, strap-hinged on the inside, were heavy enough to stop a 30-30, if not a buffalo slug, and the doors were even better. Nine or ten rifles could hold the place forever against anything but artillery. As few as seven would have their hands full against a strong war party, but should hold.

There lay the trouble and the fear. Henry did not have seven. He had himself, and his two sons, and Martha. Hunter was a deadly shot, and Ben, though only fourteen, would put in a pretty fair job. But Martha couldn't shoot any too well. Most likely she would hold fire until the last scratch, in hopes the enemy would go away. And Lucy . . . Lucy might do for a lookout someplace, but her dread of guns was so great she would be useless even to load. Henry had made her strap on a pistol, but he doubted if she could ever fire it, even to take her own life in event of capture.

And then there was Deborah. The boys had been good shots at eight; but Debbie, though pushing ten, seemed so little to Henry that he hadn't let her touch a weapon yet. You don't see your own children grow unless there's a new one to remind you how tiny they come. In Henry's eyes, Debbie hadn't changed in size since she was brand new, with feet no bigger than a fingertip with toes.

Four rifles, then, or call it three and a half, to hold two doors and eight shuttered windows, all of which could be busted in.

Out in the work-team corral a brood mare gave a long whinny, then another after a moment's pause.

Everyone in the kitchen held his breath, waiting for the mare's call to be answered. No answer came, and after a while, when she whinnied again, Henry drew a slow breath. The mare had told him a whole basket of things he didn't want to know. Strange ponies were out there, probably with stud horses among them; the mare's nose had told her, and the insistence of her reaction left no room for doubt. They were Indian ridden, because loose ponies would have answered, and horses ridden by friends would have been let to answer. The Indians were Comanches, for the Comanches were skillful at keeping their ponies quiet. They wove egg-size knots into their rawhide hackamores, so placed that the pony's nostrils could be pinched if he so much as pricked an ear. This was best done from the ground, so Henry judged that the Comanches had dismounted, leaving their ponies with horse holders. They were fixing to close on foot—the most dangerous way there was.

One thing more. They were coming from more than one side, because none would have approached downwind, where the mare could catch their scent, unless they were all around. A big party, then, or it would not have split up. No more hope, either, that the Comanches meant only to break fence on the far side of the corrals to run the stock off. This was a full-scale thing, with all the chips down, tonight.

Lucy's voice came softly out of the dark. "Debbie?" Then more loudly, with a note of panic, "Debbie! Where are you?" Everyone's voice sounded eery coming out of the unseen.

27

"Here I am." They heard the cover put back on the cookie crock at the far end of the room.

"You get back on your pallet, here! And stay put now, will you?"

Long ago, hide-hunting at the age of eighteen, Henry and two others had fought off more than twenty Kiowas from the shelter of nothing more than a buffalo wallow. They had fought with desperation enough, believing they were done for; but he couldn't remember any such sinking of the heart as he felt now behind these fort-strong walls. Little girls in the house—that's what cut a man's strings, and made a coward of him, every bit as bad as if the Comanches held them hostage already. His words were steady, though, even casual, as he made his irrevocable decision.

"Martha. Put on Debbie's coat."

A moment of silence; then Martha's single word, breathy and uncertain: "Now?"

"Right now. Moon's fixing to light us up directly." Henry went into a front bedroom, and quietly opened a shutter. The sash was already up to cut down the hazard of splintering glass. He studied the night, then went and found Martha and Debbie in the dark. The child was wearing moccasins, and hugged a piece of buffalo robe.

"We're going to play the sleep-out game," he told Debbie. "The one where you hide out with Grandma. Like you know? Very quiet, like a mouse?" He was sending the little girl to her grandmother's grave.

"I know." Debbie was a shy child, but curiously unafraid of the open prairie or the dark. She had never

28

known her grandmother, or seen death, but she had been raised to think the grave on the hill a friendly thing. Sometimes she left little picnic offerings up there for Grandma.

"You keep down low," Henry said, "and you go quietly, quietly along the ditch. Then up the hill to Grandma, and roll up in your robe, all snug and cozy."

"I remember how." They had practiced this before, and even used it once, under a threat that blew over.

Henry couldn't tell from the child's whisper whether she was frightened or not. He supposed she must be, what with the tension that was on all of them. He picked her up in his arms and carried her to the window he had opened. Though he couldn't see her, it was the same as if he could. She had a little triangular kitty-cat face, with very big green eyes, which you could see would be slanting someday, if her face ever caught up to them. As he kissed her, he found tears on her cheek, and she hugged him around the neck so hard he feared he would have to pull her arms away. But she let go, and he lifted her through the window.

"Quiet, now—stoop low—" he whispered in her ear. And he set her on the ground outside.

4

Amos pulled up at the top of a long rise ten miles from home; and here Martin Pauley, with very little horse left under him, presently caught up. On the south horizon a spot of fire was beginning to show. The glow bloomed and brightened; their big stacks of wild hay had caught and were going up in light. The east rim still showed nothing. The raiders had made their choice and left Mathison's alone.

For a moment or two Martin Pauley and Amos Edwards sat in silence. Then Amos drew his knife and cut off the quirt, called a romal, that was braided into his long reins. He hauled up his animal's heavy head; the quirt whistled and snapped hard, and the horse labored into a heavy, rocking run.

Martin stepped down, shaking so hard all over that he almost went to his knees. He reset his saddle, and as he mounted again his beat-out pony staggered, almost pulled over by the rider's weight. Amos was out of sight. Mart got his pony into an uncertain gallop, guiding the placement of its awkwardly slung hoofs by the light of the high moon. It was blowing in a wind-broke roar, and when a patch of foam caught Martin in the teeth he tasted blood in it. Yet the horse came nearer to getting home than Martin could have hoped. Half a mile from the house the animal stumbled in a shallow wash and came down heavily. Twice the long head swung up in an effort to rise, but flailed down again. Martin drew his six-gun and put a bullet in the pony's head, then dragged his carbine from the saddle boot and went on, running hard.

The hay fires and the wooden barn had died down to bright beds of coals, but the house still stood. Its shingles glowed in a dozen smoldering patches where torches had been thrown onto the roof, but the sod beneath them had held. For a moment a great impossible hope possessed Martin, intense as a physical pain. Then, while he was still far out, he saw a light come on in the kitchen as a lamp was lighted inside. Even at the distance he could see that the light came through a broken door, hanging skew-jawed on a single hinge.

Martin slowed to a walk, and went toward the house unwillingly. Little flames still wandered across the embers of the hay stacks and the barn, sending up sparks which hung idly on the quiet air; and the house itself showed against the night in a dull red glow. On the back gallery lay a dead pony, tail to the broken door. Probably it had been backed against the door to break the bar. By the steps Amos' horse was down, knees folded under. The heavy head was nodded lower and lower, the muzzle dipping the dust; it would never get up.

Martin stepped over the legs of the dead Comanche pony and went into the kitchen, walking as though he had never learned to walk, but had to pull each separate string. Near the door a body lay covered by a sheet. Martin drew back the limp muslin, and was looking into Martha's face. Her lips were parted a little, and her open eyes, looking straight up, appeared perfectly clear, as if she were alive. Her light hair was shaken loose, the lamplight picking out the silver in it. Martha had such a lot of hair that it was hardly noticeable, at first, that she had been scalped.

Most of the batten shutters had been smashed in. Hunter Edwards lay in a heap near the splintered hall door, his empty hands still clawed as if grasping the duck gun that was gone. Ben had fallen in a tangled

31

knot by the far window, his gangly legs sprawled. He looked immature and undersized as he lay there, like a skinny small boy.

Martin found the body of Henry Edwards draped on its back across the broad sill of a bedroom window. The Comanche knives had done eery work upon this body. Like Martha, Henry and both boys had been scalped. Martin gently straightened the bodies of Henry, and Hunter, and Ben, then found sheets to put over them, as Amos had done for Martha. Martin's hands were shaking, but he was dry-eyed as Amos came back into the house.

When Martin had got a good look at his foster uncle, he was afraid of him. Amos' face was wooden, but such a dreadful light shone from behind the eyes that Martin thought Amos had gone mad. Amos carried something slim and limp in his arms, clutched against his chest. As Amos passed the lamp, Martin saw that the thing Amos carried had a hand, and that it was Martha's hand. He had not drawn down the sheet that covered Martha far enough to see that the body lacked an arm. The Comanches did things like that. Probably they had tossed the arm from one to another, capering and whooping, until they lost it in the dark.

"No sign of Lucy. Or Deborah," Amos said. "So far as I could find in the lack of light." The words were low and came unevenly, but they did not sound insane.

Martin said, "We used to practice sending Debbie up the hill to Grandma's grave—"

"I been up. They sent her there. I found her bit of buffalo robe. But Debbie's not up there. Not now."

32

"You suppose Lucy—" Martin let the question trail off, but they had worked so much together that Amos was able to answer.

"Can't tell yet if Lucy went up with Debbie to the grave. Not till daylight comes on."

Amos had got out another sheet and was tearing it into strips. Martin knew Amos was making bandages to fix up their people as decently as he could. His hands moved methodically, going through the motions of doing the next thing he ought to do, little as it mattered. But at the same time Amos was thinking about something else. "I want you to walk to the Mathisons'. Get them to hook their buckboard, and bring their women on. . . . Martha should have clean clothes put on."

Probably Amos would have stripped and bathed the body of his brother's wife, and dressed it properly, if there had been no one else to do it. But not if a walk of fifteen miles would get it done a more proper way. Martin turned toward the door without question.

"Wait. Pull off them boots and get your moccasins on. You got a long way to go." Martin obeyed that, too. "Where's them pegs you whittled out? I figure to make coffins out of the shelves."

"Behind the woodbox. Back of the range." Martin started off into the night.

Martin Pauley was eight miles on the way to Mathisons' when the first riders met him. All ten who had ridden the day before were on their way over, riding fresh Mathison horses and leading spares. A buckboard, some distance back, was bringing Mrs. Mathison and Laurie, who must no longer be left alone with a war party on the loose.

The fore riders had been pressing hard, hoping against hope that someone was left alive over there. When they had got the word from Martin, they pulled up and waited with him for the buckboard. Nobody pestered at him for details. Laurie made a place for him beside her on the buckboard seat, and they rode in silence, the team at a good trot.

After a mile or two Laurie whimpered, "Oh, Martie . . . Oh, Martie . . ." She turned toward him, rested her forehead against the shoulder of his brush jacket, and there cried quietly for a little while. Martin sat slack and still, nothing left in him to move him either toward her or away from her. Pretty soon she straightened up, and rode beside him in silence, not touching him any more.

5

Dawn was near when they got to the house. Amos had been hard at work. He had laid out his brother Henry and the two boys in one bedroom, and put their best clothes on them. He had put Martha in another room, and Mrs. Mathison and Laurie took over there. All the men went to work, silently, without having to be told what to do. These were lonely, self-sufficient people, who saw each other only a few times a year, yet they worked together well, each finding for himself the next thing that needed to be done. Some got to work with saw, boxplane, auger, and pegs, to finish the coffins Amos had started, while others made coffee, set up a heavy breakfast, and packed rations for the pursuit. They picked up and sorted out the litter of stuff the Indians had thrown about as they looted, put everything where it had belonged, as nearly as they could guess, scrubbed and sanded away the stains, just as if the life of this house were going to go on.

Two things they found in the litter had a special meaning for Martin Pauley. One was a sheet of paper upon which Debbie had tried to make a calendar a few weeks before. Something about it troubled him, and he couldn't make out what it was. He remembered wishing they had a calendar, and very dimly he recalled Debbie bringing this effort to him. But his mind had been upon something else. He believed he had said, "That's nice," and, "I see," without really seeing what the little girl was showing him. Debbie's calendar had not been hung up; he couldn't remember seeing it again until now. And now he saw why. She had made a mistake, right up at the top, so the whole thing had come out wrong. He turned vaguely to Laurie Mathison, where she was washing her hands at the sink.

"I . . ." he said. "It seems like . . ."

She glanced at the penciled calendar. "I remember that. I was over here that day. But it's all right. I explained to her."

"Explained what? What's all right?"

"She made a mistake up here, so it all—"

"Yes, I see that, but—"

35

"Well, when she saw she had spoiled it, she ran to you. . . ."

Her gray eyes looked straight into his. "You and I had a fight that day. Maybe it was that. But—you were always Debbie's hero, Martie. She was—she's still just a baby, you know. She kept saying—" Laurie compressed her lips.

"She kept saying what?"

"Martie, I made her see that—"

He took Laurie by the arms hard. "Tell me."

"All right. I'll tell you. She kept saying, 'He didn't care at all.' "

Martin let his hands drop. "I wasn't listening," he said. "I made her cry, and I never knew."

He let her take the unlucky sheet of paper out of his hand, and he never saw it again. But the lost day when he should have taken Debbie in his arms, and made everything all right, was going to be with him a long time, a peg upon which he hung his grief.

The other thing he found was a miniature of Debbie. Miniatures had been painted of Martha and Lucy, too, once when Henry took the three of them to Fort Worth, but Martin never knew what became of those. Debbie's miniature, gold-framed in a little plush box, was the best of the three. The little triangular face and the green eyes were very true, and suggested the elfin look that went with Debbie's small size. He put the box in his pocket.

6

They laid their people deep under the prairie sod beside Grandma. Aaron Mathison read from the Bible and said a prayer, while Martin, Amos, and the six others chosen for the pursuit stood a little way back from the open graves, holding their saddled horses.

It wasn't a long service. Daylight had told them that Lucy must have been carried bodily from the house, for they found no place where she had set foot to the ground. Debbie, the sign showed, had been picked up onto a running horse after a pitifully short chase upon the prairie. There was hope, then, that they still lived, and that one of them, or even both, might be recovered alive. Most of Aaron's amazing vitality seemed to have drained out of him, but he shared the cracking strain that would be upon them all so long as the least hope lasted. He made the ritual as simple and as brief as he decently could. "Man that is born of woman . . ."

Those waiting to ride feared that Aaron would get carried away in the final prayer, but he did not. Martin's mind was already far ahead on the trail, so that he heard only the last few words of the prayer, yet they stirred his hair. "Now may the light of Thy countenance be turned away from the stubborn and the blind. Let darkness fall upon them that will not see, that all Thy glory may light the way of those who seek . . . and all Thy wisdom lead the horses of the brave.

37

". . . Amen."

It seemed to Martin Pauley that old Aaron, by the humility of his prayer, had invited eternal damnation upon himself, if only the search for Lucy and Debbie might succeed. His offer of retribution to his God was the only word that had been spoken in accusation or in blame, for the error of judgment that had led the fighting men away.

Amos must have had his foot in the stirrup before the end of the prayer, for he swung into the saddle with the last "Amen," and led off without a word. With Martin and Amos went Brad Mathison, Ed Newby, Charlie MacCorry, Mose Harper and his son Zack, and Lije Powers, who thought his old-time prairie wisdom had now come into its own, whether anybody else thought so or not. Those left behind would put layers of boulders in the graves against digging varmints, and set up the wooden crosses Martin Pauley had sectioned out of the house timbers in the last hours of the dark.

At the last moment Laurie Mathison ran to Martin where he sat already mounted. She stepped up lightly upon the toe of his stirruped boot, and kissed him hard and quickly on the mouth. A boldness like that would have drawn a blast of wrath at another time, but her parents seemed unable to see. Aaron still stood with bowed head beside the open graves; and Mrs. Mathison's eyes were staring straight ahead into a dreadful loneliness. The Edwardses, Mathisons, and Pauleys had come out here together. The three families had sustained each other while the Pauleys lived, and after their massacre the two remaining families had looked to each other in all things. Now only the Mathisons were left. Mrs. Mathison's usually mild and kindly face was bleak, stony with an insupportable fear. Martin Pauley would not have recognized her, even if he had been in a mood to notice anything at all.

He looked startled as Laurie kissed him, but only for a second. He seemed already to have forgotten her, for the time being, as he turned his horse.

7

Out in the middle of a vast, flat plain, a day's ride from anything, lay a little bad-smelling marsh without a name. It covered about ten acres and had cat-tails growing in it. Tules, the Mexicans called the cat-tails; but at that time certain Texans were still fighting shy of Mexican ways. Nowhere around was there a river, or a butte, or any landmark at all, except that nameless marsh. So that was how the "Fight at the Cat-tails" got its foolish-sounding name.

Seven men were still with the pursuit as they approached the Cat-tail fight at sundown of their fifth day. Lije Powers had dropped out on the occasion of his thirty-ninth or fortieth argument over interpretation of sign. He had found a headdress, a rather beautiful thing of polished heifer horns on a browband of black and white beads. They were happy to see it, for it told them that some Indian who still rode was wounded and in bad shape, or he would never have left

39

it behind. But Lije chose to make an issue of his opinion that the headdress was Kiowa, and not Comanche—which made no difference at all, for the two tribes were allied. When they got tired of hearing Lije talk about it, they told him so, and Lije branched off in a huff to visit some Mexican hacienda he knew about somewhere to the south.

They had found many other signs of the punishment the Comanches had taken before the destruction of the Edwards family was complete. More important than other dropped belongings—a beaded pouch, a polished ironwood lance with withered scalps on it—were the shallow stone-piled Indian graves. On each lay the carcass of a horse of the Edwards' brand, killed in the belief that its spirit would carry the Comanche ghost. They had found seven of these burials. Four in one place, hidden behind a hill, were probably the graves of Indians killed outright at the ranch; three more, strung out at intervals of half a day, told of wounded who had died in the retreat. In war, no Indian band slacked its pace for the dying. Squaws were known to have given birth on the backs of traveling ponies, with no one to wait for them or give help. The cowmen could not hope that the wounded warriors would slow the flight of the murderers in the slightest.

Amos kept the beaded pouch and the heifer-born headdress in his saddlebags; they might help identify the Comanche killers someday. And for several days he carried the ironwood lance stripped of its trophies. He was using it to probe the depth of the Indian graves, to see if any were shallow enough so that he could open them without falling too far back. Probably he hoped to find something that would give some dead warrior a name, so that someday they might be led to the living by the unwilling dead. Or so Martin supposed at first.

But he could not help seeing that Amos was changing. Or perhaps he was seeing revealed, a little at a time, a change that had come over Amos suddenly upon the night of the disaster. At the start Amos had led them at a horse-killing pace, a full twenty hours of their first twenty-four. That was because of Lucy, of course. Often Comanches cared for and raised captive white children, marrying the girls when they were grown, and taking the boys into their families as brothers. But grown white women were raped unceasingly by every captor in turn until either they died or were "thrown away" to die by the satiated. So the pursuers spent themselves and their horseflesh unsparingly in that first run; yet found no sign, as their ponies failed, that they had gained ground upon the fast-traveling Comanches. After that Amos set the pace cagily at a walk until the horses recovered from that first all-out effort, later at a trot, hour after hour, saving the horses at the expense of the men. Amos rode relaxed now, wasting no motions and no steps. He had the look of a man resigned to follow this trail down the years, as long as he should live.

And then Amos found the body of an Indian not buried in the ground, but protected by stones in a crevice of a sandstone ledge. He got at this one—and took nothing but the scalp. Martin had no idea what Amos believed about life and death; but the

41

Comanches believed that the spirit of a scalped warrior had to wander forever between the winds, denied entrance to the spirit land beyond the sunset. Amos did not keep the scalp, but threw it away on the prairie for the wolves to find.

Another who was showing change was Brad Mathison. He was always the one ranging farthest ahead, the first to start out each morning, the most reluctant to call it a day as the sun went down. His well-grained horses—they had brought four spares and two pack mules—showed it less than Brad himself, who was turning hollow-eyed and losing weight. During the past year Brad had taken to coming over to the Edwardses to set up with Lucy—but only about once every month or two. Martin didn't believe there had been any overpowering attachment there. But now that Lucy was lost, Brad was becoming more involved with every day that diminished hope.

By the third day some of them must have believed Lucy to be dead; but Brad could not let himself think that. "She's alive," he told Martin Pauley. Martin had said nothing either way. "She's got to be alive, Mart." And on the fourth day, dropping back to ride beside Mart, "I'll make it up to her," he promised himself. "No matter what's happened to her, no matter what she's gone through. I'll make her forget." He pushed his horse forward again, far into the lead, disregarding Amos' cussing.

So it was Brad, again, who first sighted the Comanches. Far out in front he brought his horse to the edge of a rimrock cliff; then dropped from the saddle and led his horse back from the edge. And now once more he held his rifle over his head with both hands, signaling "found."

The others came up on the run. Mart took their horses as they dismounted well back from the edge, but Mose Harper took the leads from Mart's hands. "I'm an old man," Mose said. "Whatever's beyond, I've seen it afore—most likely many times. You go on up."

The cliff was a three-hundred-foot limestone wall, dropping off sheer, as if it might be the shoreline of a vanished sea. The trail of the many Comanche ponies went down this precariously by way of a talus break. Twenty miles off, out in the middle of the flats, lay a patch of haze, shimmering redly in the horizontal light of the sunset. Some of them now remembered the cat-tail marsh that stagnated there, serving as a water-hole. A black line, wavering in the ground heat, showed in front of the marsh haze. That was all there was to see.

"Horses," Brad said. "That's horses, there at the water!"

"It's where they ought to be," Mart said. A faint reserve, as of disbelief in his luck, made the words come slowly.

"Could be buffler," Zack Harper said. He was a shag-headed young man, the oldest son of Mose Harper. "Wouldn't look no different."

"If there was buffalo there, you'd see the Comanche runnin' 'em," Amos stepped on the idea.

"If it's horses, it's sure a power of 'em."

"We've been trailin' a power of 'em."

They were silent awhile, studying the distant pen scratch upon the world that must be a band of livestock. The light was failing now as the sunset faded.

"We better feed out," Brad said finally. He was one of the youngest there, and the veteran plainsmen were usually cranky about bearing advice from the young; but lately they seemed to listen to him anyway. "It'll be dark in an hour and a half. No reason we can't jump them long before daylight, with any kind of start."

Ed Newby said, "You right sure you want to jump all them?"

Charlie MacCorry turned to look Ed over. "Just what in hell you think we come here for?"

"They'll be took unawares," Amos said. "They're always took unawares. Ain't an Indian in the world knows how to keep sentries out once the night goes cold."

"It ain't that," Ed answered. "We can whup them all right. I guess. Only thing . . . Comanches are mighty likely to kill any prisoners they've got, if they're jumped hard enough. They've done it again and again."

Mart Pauley chewed a grass blade and watched Amos. Finally Mart said, "There's another way. . . ."

Amos nodded. "Like Mart says. There's another way." Mart Pauley was bewildered to see that Amos looked happy. "I'm talking about their horses. Might be we could set the Comanch' afoot."

Silence again. Nobody wanted to say much now without considering a long while before he spoke.

"Might be we can stampede them ponies, and run off all the whole bunch," Amos went on. "I don't

44

believe it would make 'em murder anybody—that's still alive."

"This thing ain't going to be too easy," Ed Newby said.

"No," Amos agreed. "It ain't easy. And it ain't safe. If we did get it done, the Comanch' should be ready to deal. But I don't say they'll deal. In all my life, I ain't learned but one thing about an Indian: Whatever you know you'd do in his place—he ain't going to do that. Maybe we'd still have to hunt them Comanches down, by bunches, by twos, by ones."

Something like a bitter relish in Amos' tone turned Mart cold. Amos no longer believed they would recover Lucy alive—and wasn't thinking of Debbie at all.

"Of course," Charlie MacCorry said, his eyes on a grass blade he was picking to shreds, "you know, could be ever last one of them bucks has his best pony on short lead. Right beside him where he lies."

"That's right," Amos said. "That might very well be. And you know what happens then?"

"We lose our hair. And no good done to nobody."

"That's right."

Brad Mathison said, "In God's name, will you try it, Mr. Edwards?"

"All right."

Immediately Brad pulled back to feed his horses, and the others followed more slowly. Mart Pauley still lay on the edge of the rimrock after the others had pulled back. He was thinking of the change in Amos. No deadlock now, no hesitation in facing the worst

45

answer there could be. No hope, either, visible in Amos' mind that they would ever find their beloved people alive. Only that creepy relish he had heard when Amos spoke of killing Comanches.

And thinking of Amos' face as it was tonight, he remembered it as it was that worst night of the world, when Amos came out of the dark, into the shambles of the Edwards' kitchen, carrying Martha's arm clutched against his chest. The mutilation could not be seen when Martha lay in the box they had made for her. Her face looked young, and serene, and her crossed hands were at rest, one only slightly paler than the other. They were worn hands, betraying Martha's age as her face did not, with little random scars on them. Martha was always hurting her hands. Mart thought, "She wore them out, she hurt them, working for us."

As he thought that, the key to Amos' life suddenly became plain. All his uncertainties, his deadlocks with himself, his labors without pay, his perpetual gravitation back to his brother's ranch—they all fell into line. As he saw what had shaped and twisted Amos' life, Mart felt shaken up; he had lived with Amos most of his life without ever suspecting the truth. But neither had Henry suspected it—and Martha least of all.

Amos was—had always been—in love with his brother's wife.

8

Amos held them where they were for an hour after dark. They pulled saddles and packs, fed out the last of their grain, and rubbed down the horses with wads of dry grass. Nobody cooked. The men chewed on cold meat and lumps of hard frying-pan bread left from breakfast. All of them studied the shape of the hills a hundred miles beyond, taking a line on the Comanche camp. That fly speck, so far out upon the plain, would be easy to miss in the dark. When the marsh could no longer be seen they used the hill contours to take sights upon the stars they knew, as each appeared. By the time the hills, too, were swallowed by the night, each had star bearings by which he could find his way.

Mose Harper mapped his course by solemnly cutting notches in the rim of the hat. His son Zack grinned as he watched his father do that, but no one else thought it comical that Mose was growing old. All men grew old unless violence overtook them first; the plains offered no third way out of the predicament a man found himself in, simply by the fact of his existence on the face of the earth.

Amos was still in no hurry as he led off, sliding down the talus break by which the Comanches had descended to the plain. Once down on the flats, Amos held to an easy walk. He wanted to strike the Comanche horse herd before daylight, but when he had attacked he wanted dawn to come soon, so they could tell how they had come out, and make a finish. There must be no long muddle in the dark. Given half a chance to figure out what had happened, the war party would break up into singles and ambushes, becoming almost impossible to root out of the short grass.

When the moon rose, very meager, very late, it showed them each other as black shapes, and they could make out their loose pack and saddle stock following along, grabbing jawfuls of the sparse feed. Not much more. A tiny dolloping whisk of pure movement, without color or form, was a kangaroo rat. A silently vanishing streak was a kit fox. About midnight the coyotes began their clamor, surprisingly near, but not in the key that bothered Mart; and a little later the hoarser, deeper howling of a loafer wolf sounded for a while a great way off. Brad Mathison drifted his pony alongside Mart's.

"That thing sound all right to you?"

Mart was uncertain. One note had sounded a little queer to him at one point, but it did not come again. He said he guessed it sounded like a wolf.

"Seems kind of far from timber for a loafer wolf. This time of year, anyway," Brad worried. "Known 'em to be out here, though," he answered his own complaint. He let his horse drop back, so that he could keep count of the loose stock.

After the loafer wolf shut up, a dwarf owl, such as lives down prairie dog holes, began to give out with a whickering noise about a middle distance off. Half a

48

furlong farther on another took it up, after they had left the first one silent behind, and later another as they came abreast. This went on for half an hour, and it had a spooky feel to it because the owls always sounded one at a time, and always nearby. When Mart couldn't stand it any more he rode up beside Amos.

"What you think?" he asked, as an owl sounded again.

Amos shrugged. He was riding with his hands in his pockets again, as Mart had often seen him ride before, but there was no feel of deadlock or uncertainty about him now. He was leading out very straight, sure of his direction, sure of his pace.

"Hard to say," he answered.

"You mean you don't know if that's a real owl?"

"It's a real something. A noise don't make itself."

"I know, but that there is an easy noise to make. You could make it, or—"

"Well, I ain't."

"—or I could make it. Might be anything."

"Tell you something. Every critter you ever hear out here can sometimes sound like an awful poor mimic of itself. Don't always hardly pay to listen to them things too much."

"Only thing," Mart stuck to it, "these here all sound like just one owl, follering along. Gosh, Amos. I question if them things ever travel ten rods from home in their life."

"Yeah. I know. . . . Tell you what I'll do. I'll make 'em stop, being's they bother you." Amos pushed his lips out and sounded an owl cry—not the cry of just any

49

owl, but an exact repeat of the one they had just heard. No more owls whickered that night.

As Mart let his pony drop back, it came almost to a stop, and he realized that he was checking it, unconsciously holding back from what was ahead. He wasn't afraid of the fighting—at least, he didn't think he was afraid of it. He wanted more than anything in the world to come to grips with the Comanches; of that he felt perfectly certain. What he feared was that he might prove to be a coward. He tried to tell himself that he had no earthly reason to doubt himself, but it didn't work. Maybe he had no earthly reason, but he had a couple of unearthly ones, and he knew it. There were some strange quirks inside of him that he couldn't understand at all.

One of them evidenced itself in the form of an eery nightmare that he had had over and over during his childhood. It was a dream of utter darkness, at first, though after a while the darkness seemed to redden with a dim, ugly glow, something like the redness you see through your lids when you look at the sun with closed eyes. But the main thing was the sound—a high, snarling, wailing yammer of a great many voices, repeatedly receding, then rising and swelling again; as if the sound came nearer in search of him, then went past, only to come back. The sound filled him with a hideous, unexplained terror, though he never knew what made it. It seemed the outcry of some weird semihuman horde—perhaps of ghoulish and inimical dead who sought to consume him. This went on and on, while he tried to scream, but could not; until he

50

woke shivering miserably, but wet with sweat. He hadn't had this nightmare in a long time, but sometimes an unnatural fear touched him when the coyotes sung in a certain way far off on the sand hills.

Another loony weakness had to do with a smell. This particularly worried him tonight, for the smell that could bring an unreasoning panic into him was the faintly musky, old-leather-and-fur smell of Indians. The queer thing about this was that he felt no fear of the Indians themselves. He had seen a lot of them, and talked with them in the fragments of sign language he knew; he had even made swaps with some of them—mostly Caddoes, the far-wandering peddlers of the plains. But if he came upon a place where Indians had camped, or caught a faint scent of one down the wind, the same kind of panic could take hold of him as he felt in the dream. If he failed to connect this with the massacre he had survived, it was perhaps because he had no memory of the massacre. He had been carried asleep into the brush, where he had presently wakened lost and alone in the dark; and that was all he knew about it firsthand. Long after, when he had learned to talk, the disaster had been explained to him, but only in a general way. The Edwardses had never been willing to talk about it much.

And there was one more thing that could cut his strings; it had taken him unawares only two or three times in his life, yet worried him most of all, because it seemed totally meaningless. He judged this third thing to be a pure insanity, and wouldn't let himself think about it at all, times it wasn't forced on him

51

without warning.

So now he rode uneasily, dreading the possibility that he might go to pieces in the clutch, and disgrace himself, in spite of all he could do. He began preaching to himself, inaudibly repeating over and over admonishments that unconsciously imitated Biblical forms. "I will go among them. I will prowl among them in the night. I will lay hands upon them; I will destroy them. Though I be cut in a hundred pieces, I will stand against them. . . ." It didn't seem to do any good.

He believed dawn could be no more than an hour off when Brad came up to whisper to him again. "I think we gone past."

Mart searched the east, fearing to see a graying in the sky too soon. But the night was still very dark, in spite of the dying moon. He could feel a faint warm breath of air upon his left cheek. "Wind's shifted to the south," he answered. "What little there is. I think Amos changed his line. Wants to come at 'em up wind."

"I know. I see that. But I think—"

Amos had stopped, and was holding up his hand. The six others closed up on him, stopped their horses and sat silent in their saddles. Mart couldn't hear anything except the loose animals behind, tearing at the grass. Amos rode on, and they traveled another fifteen minutes before he stopped again.

This time, when the shuffle of their ponies' feet had died, a faint sound lay upon the night, hard to be sure of, and even harder to believe. What they were hearing was the trilling of frogs. Now, how did they get way out here? They had to be the little green fellows that can

live anywhere the ground is a little damp, but even so—
either they had to shower down in the rare rains, like
the old folks said, or else this marsh had been here
always, while the dry world built up around.

Amos spoke softly. "Spread out some. Keep in line,
and guide on me. I'll circle close in as I dare."

They spread out until they could just barely see each
other, and rode at the walk, abreast of Amos as he
moved on. The frog song came closer, so close that
Mart feared they would trample on Indians before
Amos turned. And now again, listening hard and
straining their eyes, they rode for a long time. The
north star was on their right hand for a while. Then it
was behind them a long time. Then on their left, then
ahead. At last it was on their right again, and Amos
stopped. They were back where they started. A faint
gray was showing in the east; their timing would have
been perfect, if only what they were after had been
here. Mose Harper pushed his horse in close. "I rode
through the ashes of a farm," he said to Amos. "Did
you know that? I thought you was hugging in awful
close."

"Hush, now," Amos said. "I'm listening for something."

Mose dropped his tone. "Point is, them ashes
showed no spark. Amos, them devils been gone from
here all night."

"Catch up the loose stock," Amos said. "Bring 'em
in on short lead."

"Waste of time," Mose Harper argued. "The boys
are tard, and the Comanches is long gone."

"Get that loose stuff in," Amos ordered again, snapping it this time. I want hobbles on 'em all—and soon!"

Mart was buckling a hobble on a pack mule when Brad dropped on one knee beside him to fasten the other cuff. "Look out yonder," Brad whispered. "When you get a chance."

Mart stood up, following Brad's eyes. A faint grayness had come evenly over the prairie, as if rising from the ground, but nothing showed a shadow yet. Mart cupped his hands over his eyes for a moment, then looked again, trying to look beside, instead of straight at, an unevenness on the flat land that he could not identify. But now he could not see it at all.

He said, "For a minute I thought—but I guess not."

"I swear something showed itself. Then took down again."

"A wolf, maybe?"

"I don't know. Something funny about this, Mart. The Comanch' ain't been traveling by night nor laying up by day. Not since the first hundred miles."

Now followed an odd aimless period, while they waited, and the light imperceptibly increased. "They're out there," Amos said at last. "They're going to jump us. There's no doubt of it now." Nobody denied it, or made any comment. Mart braced himself, checking his rifle again and again. "I got to hold fast," he kept telling himself. "I got to do my share of the work. No matter what." His ears were beginning to ring. The others stood about in loose meaningless positions, not huddled, not restless, but motionless, and very watchful.

When they spoke they held their voices low.

Then Amos' rifle split the silence down the middle, so that behind lay the quiet night, and ahead rose their hour of violence. They saw what Amos had shot at. A single file of ten Comanches on wiry buffalo ponies had come into view at a thousand yards, materializing out of the seemingly flat earth. They came on at a light trot, ignoring Amos' shot. Zack Harper and Brad Mathison fired, but weren't good enough either at the range.

"Throw them horses down!" Amos shouted. "Git your backs to the marsh and tie down!" He snubbed his pony's muzzle back close to the horn, picked up the off fetlock, and threw the horse heavily. He caught one kicking hind foot, then the other, and pig-tied them across the fore cannons. Some of the others were doing the same thing, but Brad was in a fight with his hot-blood animal. It reared eleven feet tall, striking with fore hoofs, trying to break away. "Kill that horse!" Amos yelled. Obediently Brad drew his six-gun, put a bullet into the animal's head under the ear, and stepped from under as it came down.

Ed Newby still stood, his rifle resting ready to fire across the saddle of his standing horse. Mart lost his head enough to yell, "Can't you throw him? Shall I shoot him, Ed?"

"Leave be! Let the Comanch' put him down."

Mart went to the aid of Charlie MacCorry, who had tied his own horse down all right and was wrestling with a mule. They never did get all of the animals down, but Mart felt a whole lot better with something for his hands to do. Three more of the Comanche single-file columns were in sight now, widely spread, trotting well in hand. They had a ghostly look at first, of the same color as the prairie, in the gray light. Then detail picked out, and Mart saw the bows, lances bearing scalps like pennons, an occasional war shield carried for the medicine in its painted symbols as much as for the bullet-deflecting function of its iron-tough hide. Almost half the Comanches had rifles. Some trader, standing on his right to make a living, must have taken a handsome profit putting those in Comanche hands.

Amos' rifle banged again. One of the lead ponies swerved and ran wild as the rider rolled off into the grass. Immediately, without any other discernible signal, the Comanches leaned low on their ponies and came on at a hard run. Two or three more of the cowmen fired, but without effect.

At three hundred yards the four Comanche columns cut hard left, coming into a single loose line that streamed across the front of the defense. The cowmen were as ready as they were going to be; they had got themselves into a ragged semicircle behind their tied-down horses, their backs to the water. Two or three sat casually on their down horses, estimating the enemy.

"May as well hold up," Mose Harper said. His tone was as pressureless as a crackerbox comment. "They'll swing plenty close, before they're done."

"I count thirty-seven," Ed Newby said. He was still on his feet behind his standing horse.

56

Amos said, "I got me a scalp out there, when I git time to take it."

"Providin'," Mose Harper tried to sound jocular, "they don't leave your carcass here in the dirt."

"I come here to leave Indian carcasses in the dirt. I ain't made no change of plan."

They could see the Comanche war paint now as the warriors rode in plain sight across their front. Faces and naked bodies were striped and splotched in combinations of white, red, and yellow; but whatever the pattern, it was always pointed up with heavy accents of black, the Comanche color for war, for battle, and for death. Each warrior always painted up the same, but it was little use memorizing the paint patterns, because you never saw an Indian in war paint except when you couldn't lay hands on him. No use remembering the medicine shields, either, for these, treated as sacred, were never out of their deerskin cases until the moment of battle. Besides paint the Comanches wore breech clouts and moccasins; a few had horn or bear-claw headdresses. But these were young warriors, without the great eagle-feather war bonnets that were the pride of old war chiefs, who had tallied scores of coups. The ponies had their tails tied up, and were ridden bareback, guided by a single jaw rein.

Zack Harper said, "Ain't that big one Buffalo Hump?"

"No-that-ain't-Buffler-Hump," his father squelched him. "Don't talk so damn much."

The Comanche leader turned again and circled in. He brought his warriors past the defenders within fifty yards, ponies loosely spaced, racing full out. Suddenly, from every Comanche throat burst the screaming war cry; and Mart was paralyzed by the impact of that sound, stunned and sickened as by a blow in the belly with a rock. The war cries rose in a high unearthly yammering, wailing and snarling, piercing to his backbone to cut off every nerve he had. It was not exactly the eery sound of his terror-dream, but it was the spirit of that sound, the essence of its meaning. The muscles of his shoulders clenched as if turned to stone, and his hands so vised upon his rifle that it rattled, useless, against the saddle upon which it rested. And at the same time every other muscle in his body went limp and helpless.

Amos spoke into his ear, his low tone heavy with authority but unexcited. "Leave your shoulders go loose. Make your shoulders slack, and your hands will take care of theirselves. Now help me git a couple!"

That worked. All the rifles were sounding now from behind the tied-down horses. Mart breathed again, picked a target, and took aim. One Comanche after another was dropping from sight behind his pony as he came opposite the waiting rifles; they went down in order, like ducks in a shooting gallery, shamming a slaughter that wasn't happening. Each Comanche hung by one heel and a loop of mane on the far side of his pony and fired under the neck, offering only one arm and part of a painted face for target. A pony somersaulted, its rider springing clear unhurt, as Mart fired.

The circling Comanches kept up a continuous

58

firing, each warrior reloading as he swung away, then coming past to fire again. This was the famous Comanche wheel, moving closer with every turn, chewing into the defense like a racing grindstone, yet never committing its force beyond possibility of a quick withdrawal. Bullets buzzed over, whispering "Cousin," or howled in ricochet from dust-spouts short of the defenders. A lot of whistling noises were arrows going over. Zack Harper's horse screamed, then went into a heavy continuous groaning.

Another Indian pony tumbled end over end; that was Amos' shot. The rider took cover behind his dead pony before he could be killed. Here and there another pony jerked, faltered, then ran on. A single bullet has to be closely placed to bring a horse down clean.

Amos said loud through his teeth, "The horses, you fools! Get them horses!" Another Comanche pony slid on its knees and stayed down, but its rider got behind it without hurt.

Ed Newby was firing carefully and unhurriedly across his standing horse. The buzzbees made the horse switch its tail, but it stood. Ed said, "You got to get the shoulder. No good to gut-shot' em. You fellers ain't leading enough." He fired again, and a Comanche dropped from behind his running horse with his brains blown out. It wasn't the shot Ed was trying to make, but he said, "See how easy?"

Fifty yards out in front of him Mart Pauley saw a rifle snake across the quarters of a fallen pony. A horn headdress rose cautiously, and the rifle swung to look Mart square in the eve. He took a snap shot, aiming between the horns, which disappeared, and the enemy rifle slid unfired into the short grass.

After that there was a letup, while the Comanches broke circle and drew off. Out in front of the cowmen lay three downed ponies, two dead Comanches, and two live ones, safe and dangerous behind their fallen horses. Amos was swearing softly and steadily to himself. Charlie MacCorry said he thought he goosed one of them up a little bit, maybe, but didn't believe he convinced him.

"Good God almighty," Brad Mathison broke out, "there's got to be some way to do this!"

Mose Harper scratched his beard and said he thought they done just fine that trip. "Oncet when I was a little shaver, with my pa's bull wagons, a couple hundred of 'em circled us all day long. We never did get 'em whittled down very much. They just fin'y went away. . . . You glued to the ground, Zack? Take care that horse!"

Zack got up and took a look at his wounded horse, but didn't seem to know what to do. He stood staring at it, until his father walked across and shot it.

Mart said to Amos. "Tell me one thing. Was they hollering like that the time they killed my folks?"

Amos seemed to have to think that over. "I wasn't there," he said at last. "I suppose so. Hard to get used to, ain't it?"

"I don't know," Mart said shakily, "if I'll ever be able to get used to it."

Amos looked at him oddly for some moments. "Don't you let it stop you," he said.

"It won't stop me."

They came on again, and this time they swept past at no more than ten yards. A number of the wounded Comanche ponies lagged back to the tail of the line, their riders saving them for the final spurt, but they were still in action. The Comanches made this run in close bunches; the attack became a smother of confusion. Both lead and arrows poured fast into the cowmen's position.

Zack whimpered, "My God—there's a million of 'em!" and ducked down behind his dead horse.

"Git your damn head up!" Mose yelled at his son. "Fire into 'em!" Zack raised up and went to fighting again.

Sometime during this run Ed Newby's horse fell, pinning Ed under it, but they had no time to go to him while this burst of the attack continued. An unhorsed Comanche came screaming at Amos with clubbed rifle, and so found his finish. Another stopped at least five bullets as a compadre tried to rescue him in a flying pickup. There should have been another; a third pony was down out in front of them, but nobody knew where the rider had got to. This time as they finished the run the Comanches pulled off again to talk it over.

All choices lay with the Comanches for the time being. The cowmen got their backs into the job of getting nine hundred pounds of horse off Ed Newby. Mose Harper said, "How come you let him catch you, Ed?"

Ed Newby answered through set teeth. "They got my leg—just as he come down—"

61

Ed's leg was not only bullet-broken, but had doubled under him, and got smashed again by the killed horse. Amos put the shaft of an arrow between Ed's teeth, and the arrowwood splintered as two men put their weight into pulling the leg straight.

A party of a dozen Comanches, mounted on the fastest of the Indian ponies, split off from the main bunch and circled out for still another sweep.

"Hold your fire," Amos ordered. "You hear me? Take cover—but let 'em be!"

Zack Harper, who had fought none too well, chose this moment to harden. "Hold hell! I aim to get me another!"

"You fire and I'll kill you," Amos promised him; and Zack put his rifle down.

Most took to the ground as the Comanches swept past once more, but Amos stood up, watching from under his heavy brows, like a staring ox. The Indians did not attack. They picked up their dismounted and their dead; then they were gone.

"Get them horses up!" Amos loosed the pigging string and got his own horse to its feet.

"They'll scatter now," Mose Harper said.

"Not till they come up with their horse herd, they won't!"

"Somebody's got to stay with Ed," Mose reminded them. "I suppose I'm the one to do that—old crip that I be. But some of them Comanch' might circle back. You'll have to leave Zack with me."

"That's all right."

"And I need one fast man on a good horse to get me

62

help. I can't move him. Not with what we got here."

"We all ought to be back," Amos objected, "in a couple of days."

"Fellers follering Comanches don't necessarily ever come back. I got to have either Brad Mathison or Charlie MacCorry."

"You get Mathison, then," Charlie said. "I'm going on."

Brad whirled on Charlie in an unexpected blast of temper. "There's a quick way to decide it," he said, and stood braced, his open hand ready above his holster.

Charlie MacCorry looked Brad in the eye as he spat at Brad's boots and missed. But after that he turned away.

So three rode on, following a plume of dust already distant upon the prairie. "We'll have the answer soon," Amos promised. "Soon. We don't dast let 'em lose us now."

Mart Pauley was silent. He didn't want to ask him what three riders could do when they caught up with the Comanches. He was afraid Amos didn't know.

9

They kept the feather of dust in sight all day, but in the morning, after a night camp without water, they failed to pick it up. The trail of the Comanche war party still led westward, broad and plain, marked at intervals with the carcasses of buffalo ponies wounded at the Cat-tails. They pushed on, getting all they could out of their horses.

This day, the second after the Fight at the Cat-tails, became the strangest day of the pursuit before it was done, because of something unexplained that happened during a period while they were separated.

A line of low hills, many hours away beyond the plain, began to shove up from the horizon as they rode. After a while they knew the Comanches they followed were already into that broken country where pursuit would be slower and more treacherous than before.

"Sometimes it seems to me," Amos said, "them Comanches fly with their elbows, carrying the pony along between their knees. You can nurse a horse along till he falls and dies, and you walk on carrying your saddle. Then a Comanche comes along, and gets that horse up, and rides it twenty miles more. Then eats it."

"Don't we have any chance at all?"

"Yes. . . . We got a chance." Amos went through the motions of spitting, with no moisture in his mouth to spit. "And I'll tell you what it be. An Indian will chase a thing until he thinks he's chased it enough. Then he quits. So the same when he runs. After while he figures we must have quit, and he starts to loaf. Seemingly he never learns there's such a thing as a critter that might just keep coming on."

As he looked at Amos, sitting his saddle like a great lump of rock—yet a lump that was somehow of one piece with the horse—Mart Pauley was willing to believe that to have Amos following you could be a deadly thing with no end to it, ever, until he was dead.

"If only they stay bunched," Amos finished, and it

was a prayer; "if only they don't split and scatter . . . we'll come up to 'em. We're bound to come up."

Late in the morning they came to a shallow sink, where a number of posthole wells had been freshly dug among the dry reeds. Here the trail of the main horse herd freshened, and they found the bones of an eaten horse, polished shiny in a night by the wolves. And there was the Indian smell, giving Mart a senseless dread to fight off during their first minutes in this place.

"Here's where the rest of 'em was all day yesterday," Amos said when he had wet his mouth; "the horse guards, and the stole horses, and maybe some crips Henry shot up. And our people—if they're still alive."

Brad Mathison was prone at a pothole, dipping water into himself with his tin cup, but he dropped the cup to come up with a snap. As he spoke, Mart Pauley heard the same soft tones Brad's father used when he neared an end of words. "I've heard thee say that times enough," Brad said.

"What?" Amos asked, astonished.

"Maybe she's dead," Brad said, his bloodshot blue eyes burning steadily into Amos' face. "Maybe they're both dead. But if I hear it from thee again, thee has chosen me—so help me God!"

Amos stared at Brad mildly, and when he spoke again it was to Mart Pauley. "They've took an awful big lead. Them we fought at the Cat-tails must have got here early last night."

"And the whole bunch pulled out the same hour," Mart finished it.

It meant they were nine or ten hours back—and every one of the Comanches was now riding a rested animal. Only one answer to that—such as it was: They had to rest their own horses, whether they could spare time for it or not. They spent an hour dipping water into their hats; the ponies could not reach the little water in the bottom of the posthole wells. When one hole after another had been dipped dry they could only wait for the slow seepage to bring in another cupful, while the horses stood by. After that they took yet another hour to let the horses crop the scant bunch grass, helping them by piling grass they cut with their knives. A great amount of this work gained only the slightest advantage, but none of them begrudged it.

Then, some hours beyond the posthole wells, they came to a vast sheet of rock, as flat and naked as it had been laid down when the world was made. Here the trail ended, for unshod hoofs left no mark on the barren stone. Amos remembered this reef in the plain. He believed it to be about four miles across by maybe eight or nine miles long, as nearly as he could recall. All they could do was split up and circle the whole ledge to find where the trail came off the rock.

Mart Pauley, whose horse seemed the worst beat out, was sent straight across. On the far side he was to wait, grazing within sight of the ledge, until one of the others came around to him; then both were to ride to meet the third.

Thus they separated. It was while they were apart, each rider alone with his tiring horse, that some strange thing happened to Amos, so that he became a mystery in himself throughout their last twenty-four hours together.

Brad Mathison was first to get around the rock sheet to where Mart Pauley was grazing his horse. Mart had been there many hours, yet they rode south a long way before they sighted Amos, waiting for them far out on the plain.

"Hasn't made much distance, has he?" Brad commented.

"Maybe the rock slick stretches a far piece down this way."

"Don't look like it to me."

Mart didn't say anything more. He could see for himself that the reef ended in a couple of miles.

Amos pointed to a far-off landmark as they came up. "The trail cuts around that hump," he said, and led the way. The trail was where Amos had said it would be, a great welter of horse prints already blurred by the wind. But no other horse had been along here since the Comanches passed long before.

"Kind of thought to see your tracks here," Brad said.

"Didn't come this far."

Then where the hell had he been all this time? If it had been Lije Powers, Mart would have known he had sneaked himself a nap. "You lost a bed blanket," Mart noticed.

"Slipped out of the strings somewhere. I sure ain't going back for it now." Amos was speaking too carefully. He put Mart in mind of a man half stopped in a fist fight, making out he was unhurt so his opponent wouldn't know, and finish him.

"You feel all right?" he asked Amos.

"Sure. I feel fine." Amos forced a smile, and this was a mistake, for he didn't look to be smiling. He looked as if he had been kicked in the face. Mart tried to think of an excuse to lay a hand on him, to see if he had a fever; but before he could think of anything Amos took off his hat and wiped sweat off his forehead with his sleeve. That settled that. A man doesn't sweat with the fever on him.

"You look like you et something," Mart said.

"Don't know what it could have been. Oh, I did come on three-four rattlesnakes." Seemingly the thought made Amos hungry. He got out a leaf of jerky, and tore strips from it with his teeth.

"You sure you feel—"

Amos blew up, and yelled at him. "I'm all right, I tell you!" He quirted his horse, and loped out ahead.

They off-saddled in the shelter of the hump. A northering wind came up when the sun was gone; its bite reminded them that they had been riding deep into the fall of the year. They huddled against their saddles, and chewed corn meal. Brad walked across and stood over Amos. He spoke reasonably.

"Looks like you ought to tell us, Mr. Edwards." He waited, but Amos didn't answer him. "Something happened while you was gone from us today. Was you laid for? We didn't hear no guns, but . . . Be you hiding an arrow hole from us by any chance?"

"No," Amos said. "There wasn't nothing like that."

Brad went back to his saddle and sat down. Mart laid his bedroll flat, hanging on by the upwind edge, and rolled himself up in it, coming out so that his head was on the saddle.

"A man has to learn to forgive himself," Amos said, his voice unnaturally gentle. He seemed to be talking to Brad Mathison. "Or he can't stand to live. It so happens we be Texans. We took a reachin' holt, way far out, past where any man has right or reason to hold on. Or if we didn't, our folks did, so we can't leave off, without giving up that they were fools, wasting their lives, and wasted in the way they died."

The chill striking up through Mart's blankets made him homesick for the Edwards' kitchen, like it was on winter nights, all warm and light, and full of good smells, like baking bread. And their people—Mart had taken them for granted, largely; just a family, people living alone together, such as you never thought about, especially, unless you got mad at them. He had never known they were dear to him until the whole thing was busted up forever. He wished Amos would shut up.

"This is a rough country," Amos was saying. "It's a country knows how to scour a human man right off the face of itself. A Texan is nothing but a human man way out on a limb. This year, and next year, and maybe for a hundred more. But I don't think it'll be forever. Someday this country will be a fine good place to be. Maybe it needs our bones in the ground before that time can come."

Mart was thinking of Laurie now. He saw her in a bright warm kitchen like the Edwards', and he thought how wonderful it would be living in the same house with Laurie, in the same bed. But he was on the empty prairie without any fire—and he had bedded himself on a sharp rock, he noticed now.

"We've come on a year when things go hard," Amos talked on. "We get this tough combing over because we're Texans. But the feeling we get that we fail, and judge wrong, and go down in guilt and shame—that's because we be human men. So try to remember one thing. It wasn't your fault, no matter how it looks. You got let in for this just by being born. Maybe there never is any way out of it once you're born a human man, except straight across the coals of hell."

Mart rolled out to move his bed. He didn't really need that rock in his ribs all night. Brad Mathison got up, moved out of Amos' line of sight, and beckoned Mart with his head. Mart put his saddle on his bed, so it wouldn't blow away, and walked out a ways with Brad on the dark prairie.

"Mart," Brad said when they were out of hearing, "the old coot is just as crazy as a bedbug fell in the rum."

"Sure sounds so. What in all hell you think happened?"

"God knows. Maybe nothing at all. Might be he just plainly cracked. He was wandering around without rhyme or principle when we come on him today."

"I know."

"This puts it up to you and me," Brad said. "You see that, don't you? We may be closer the end than you think."

"What you want to do?"

"My horse is standing up best. Tomorrow I'll start

70

before light, and scout on out far as I can reach. You come on as you can."

"My horse got a rest today," Mart began.

"Keep saving him. You'll have to take forward when mine gives down."

"All right." Mart judged that tomorrow was going to be a hard day to live far behind on a failing pony. Like Brad, he had a feeling they were a whole lot closer to the Comanches than they had any real reason to believe.

They turned in again. Though they couldn't know it, until they heard about it a long time after, that was the night Ed Newby came out of his delirium, raised himself for a long look at his smashed leg, then put a bullet in his brain.

10

By daylight Brad Mathison was an hour gone. Mart hadn't known how Amos would take it, but there was no fuss at all. They rode on in silence, crossing chains of low hills, with dry valleys between; they were beginning to find a little timber, willow and cottonwood mostly along the dusty streambeds. They were badly in need of water again; they would have to dig for it soon. All day long the big tracks of Brad Mathison's horse led on, on top of the many-horse trample left by the Comanche herd; but he was stirring no dust, and they could only guess how far he must be ahead.

Toward sundown Amos must have begun to worry about him, for he sent Mart on a long swing to the north, where a line of sand hills offered high ground, to see what he could see. He failed to make out any sign of Brad; but, while he was in the hills alone, the third weird thing that could unstring him set itself in front of him again. He had a right to be nerve-raw at this point, perhaps; the vast emptiness of the plains had taken on a haunted, evilly enchanted feel since the massacre. And of course they were on strange ground now, where all things seemed faintly odd and wrong, because unfamiliar. . . .

He had dismounted near the top of a broken swell, led his horse around it to get a distant view without showing himself against the sky. He walked around a ragged shoulder—and suddenly froze at sight of what stood on the crest beyond. It was nothing but a juniper stump; not for an instant did he mistake it for anything else. But it was in the form of similar stumps he had seen two or three times before in his life, and always with the same unexplainable effect. The twisted remains of the juniper, blackened and sand-scoured, had vaguely the shape of a man, or the withered corpse of a man; one arm seemed upraised in a writhing gesture of agony, or perhaps of warning. But nothing about it explained the awful sinking of the heart, the terrible sense of inevitable doom, that overpowered him each of the times he encountered this shape.

An Indian would have turned back, giving up whatever he was about; for he would have known the thing for a medicine tree with a powerful spirit in it, either telling him of a doom or placing a doom upon him. And Mart himself more or less believed that the thing was some kind of a sign. An evil prophecy is always fulfilled, if you put no time limit upon it; fulfilled quite readily, too, if you are a child counting little misfortunes as disasters. So Mart had the impression that this mysteriously upsetting kind of an encounter had always been followed by some dreadful, unforeseeable thing.

He regarded himself as entirely mature now, and was convinced that to be filled with cowardice by the sight of a dead tree was a silly and unworthy thing. He supposed he ought to go and uproot that desolate twist of wood, or whittle it down, and so master the thing forever. But even to move toward it was somehow impossible to him, to a degree that such a move was not even thinkable. He returned to Amos feeling shaken and sickish, unstrung as much by doubt of his own soundness as by the sense of evil prophecy itself.

The sun was setting when they saw Brad again. He came pouring off a long hill at four miles, raising a reckless dust. "I saw her!" he yelled, and hauled up sliding. "I saw Lucy!"

"How far?"

"They're camped by a running crick—they got fires going—look, you can see the smoke!" A thin haze lay flat in the quiet air above the next line of hills.

"Ought to be the Warrior River," Amos said. "Water in it, huh?"

"Didn't you hear what I said?" Brad shouted. "I tell you I saw Lucy—I saw her walking through the camp—"

Amos' tone was bleak. "How far off was you?"

"Not over seventy rod. I bellied up a ridge this side the river, and they was right below me!"

"Did you see Debbie?" Mart got in.

"No, but—they got a bunch of baggage; she might be asleep amongst that. I counted fifty-one Comanch'—What you unsaddling for?"

"Good a place as any," Amos said. "Can't risk no more dust like you just now kicked up. Come dark we'll work south, and water a few miles below. We can take our time."

"Time?"

"They're making it easy for us. Must think they turned us back at the Cat-tails, and don't have to split up. All we got to do is foller to their village—"

"Village? You gone out of your mind?"

"Let 'em get back to their old chiefs and their squaws. The old chiefs have gone cagy; a village of families can't run like a war party can. For all they know—"

"Look—look—" Brad hunted desperately for words that would fetch Amos back to reality. "Lucy's there! I saw her—can't you hear? We got to get her out of there!"

"Brad," Amos said, "I want to know what you saw in that camp you thought was Lucy."

"I keep telling you I saw her walk—"

"I heard you!" Amos' voice rose and crackled this time. "*What* did you see walk? Could you see her yellow hair?"

"She had a shawl on her head. But—"

"She ain't there, Brad."

"God damn it, I tell you, I'd know her out of a million—"

"You saw a buck in a woman's dress," Amos said. "They're game to put anything on 'em. You know that."

Brad's sun-punished blue eyes blazed up as they had at the pothole water, and his tone went soft again. "Thee lie," he said. "I've told thee afore—"

"But there's something I ain't told you," Amos said. "I found Lucy yesterday. I buried her in my own saddle blanket. With my own hands, by the rock. I thought best to keep it from you long's I could."

The blood drained from Brad's face, and at first he could not speak. Then he stammered, "Did they—was she—"

"Shut up!" Amos yelled at him. "Never ask me what more I seen!"

Brad stood as if knocked out for half a minute more; then he turned to his horse, stiffly, as if he didn't trust his legs too well, and he tightened his cinch.

Amos said, "Get hold of yourself! Grab him, Mart!" Brad stepped into the saddle, and the gravel jumped from the hoofs of his horse. He leveled out down the Comanche trail again, running his horse as if he would never need it again.

"Go after him! You can handle him better than me."

Mart Pauley had pulled his saddle, vaulted bareback onto the sweaty withers, and in ten jumps opened up all the speed his beat-out horse had left. He gained no ground on Brad, though he used up what horse he had in trying to. He was chasing the better horse—and the better rider, too, Mart supposed. They weighed about the same, and both had been on horses before they could walk. Some small magic that could not be taught or learned, but had been born into Brad's muscles, was what made the difference. Mart was three furlongs back as Brad sifted into the low hills.

Up the slopes Mart followed, around a knob, and onto the down slope, spurring his wheezing horse at every jump. From here he could see the last little ridge, below and beyond as Brad had described it, with the smoke of Comanche campfires plain above it. Mart's horse went to its knees as he jumped it into a steep ravine, but he was able to drag it up.

Near the mouth of the ravine he found Brad's horse tied to a pin-oak scrub; he passed it, and rode on into the open, full stretch. Far up the last ridge he saw Brad climbing strongly. He looked back over his shoulder, watching Mart without slowing his pace. Mart charged through a dry tributary of the Warrior and up the ridge, his horse laboring gamely as it fought the slope. Brad stopped just short of the crest, and Mart saw him tilt his canteen skyward; he drained it unhurriedly, and threw it away. He was already on his belly at the crest as Mart dropped from his horse and scrambled on all fours to his side.

"God damn it, Brad, what you doing?"

"Get the hell out of here. You ain't wanted."

Down below, at perhaps four hundred yards, half a hundred Comanches idled about their business. They had some piled mule packs, a lot of small fires in shallow fire holes, and parts of at least a dozen buffalo down there. The big horse herd grazed unguarded beyond. Most of the bucks were throwing chunks of meat into the fires, to be snatched out and bolted as soon as the meat blackened on the outside. No sign of pickets. The Comanches relied for safety upon their horsemanship and the great empty distances of the prairies. They didn't seem to know what a picket was.

Mart couldn't see any sign of Debbie. And now he heard Brad chamber a cartridge.

"You'll get Debbie killed, you son-of-a-bitch!"

"Get out of here, I said!" Brad had his cheek on the stock; he was aiming into the Comanche camp. He took a deep breath, let it all out, and lay inert, waiting for his head to steady for the squeeze. Mart grabbed the rifle, and wrenched it out of line.

They fought for possession, rolling and sliding down the slope. Brad rammed a knee into Mart's belly, twisted the rifle from his hands, and broke free. Mart came to his feet before Brad, and dived to pin him down. Brad braced himself on one hand, and with the other swung the rifle by the grip of the stock. Blood jumped from the side of Mart's head as the barrel struck. He fell backward, end over end; then went limp, rolled slackly down the hill, and lay still where he came to rest.

Brad swore softly as he settled himself into firing position again. Then he changed his mind and trotted northward, just behind the crest of the ridge.

Mart came to slowly, without memory or any idea of

where he was. Sight did not return to him at once. His hands groped, and found the rocky ground on which he lay; and next he recognized a persistent rattle of gunfire and the high snarling of Comanche war cries, seemingly some distance away. His hands went to his head, and he felt clotting blood. He reckoned he had got shot in the head, and was blind, and panic took him. He struggled up, floundered a few yards without any sense of balance, and fell into a dry wash. The fall knocked the wind out of him, and when he had got his breath back his mind had cleared enough so that he lay still.

Some part of his sight was coming back by the time he heard a soft footstep upon sand. He could see a shadowy shape above him, swimming in a general blur. He played possum, staring straight up with unwinking eyes, waiting to lose his scalp.

"Can you hear me, Mart?" Amos said.

He knew Amos dropped to his knees beside him. "I got a bullet in my brain," Mart said. "I'm blind."

Amos struck a match and passed it before one eye and then the other. Mart blinked and rolled his head to the side. "You're all right," Amos said. "Hit your head, that's all. Lie still till I get back!" He left, running.

Amos was gone a long time. The riflery and the war cries stopped, and the prairie became deathly still. For a while Mart believed he could sense a tremor in the ground that might mean the movement of many horses; then this faded, and the night chill began to work upward out of the ground. But Mart was able to see the winking of the first stars when he heard Amos coming back.

"You look all right to me," Amos said.

"Where's Brad?"

Amos was slow in answering. "Brad fit him a one-man war," he said at last. "He skirmished 'em from the woods down yonder. Now, why from there? Was he trying to lead them off you?"

"I don't know."

"Wha'd you do? Get throwed?"

"I guess."

"Comanches took him for a Ranger company, seemingly. They're long gone. Only they took time to finish him first."

"Was he scalped?"

"Now, what do you think?"

After he had found Mart, Amos had backed off behind a hill and built a signal fire. He slung creosote bush on it, raised a good smoke, and took his time sending puff messages with his saddle blanket.

"Messages to who?"

"Nobody, damn it. No message, either, rightly—just a lot of different-size hunks of smoke. Comanches couldn't read it, because it didn't say nothing. So they upped stakes and rode. It's all saved our hair, once they was stirred up."

Mart said, "We better go bury Brad."

"I done that already." Then Amos added one sad, sinister thing. "All of him I could find."

Mart's horse had run off with the Comanche ponies, but they still had Brad's horse and Amos'. And the Comanches had left them plenty of buffalo meat.

Amos dug a fire pit, narrow but as deep as he could reach, in the manner of the Wichitas. From the bottom of this, his cooking fire could reflect only upon its own smoke, and he didn't put on stuff that made any. When Mart had filled up on buffalo meat he turned wrong side out, but an hour later he tried again, and this time it stuck.

"Feel like you'll be able to ride come daylight?"

"Sure I'll ride."

"I don't believe we got far to go," Amos said. "The Comanch' been acting like they're close to home. We'll come up to their village soon. Maybe tomorrow."

Mart felt much better now. "Tomorrow," he repeated.

11

Tomorrow came and went, and showed them they were wrong. Now at last the Comanche war party split up, and little groups carrying two or three horses to the man ranged off in ten directions. Amos and Mart picked one trail at random and followed it with all tenacity as it turned and doubled, leading them in far futile ways. They lost it on rock ledges, in running water, and in blown sand, but always found it again, and kept on.

Another month passed before all trails became one, and the paired scratches of many travois showed they were on the track of the main village at last. They followed it northeast, gaining ground fast as the trail grew fresh.

"Tomorrow," Amos said once more. "All hell can't keep them ahead of us tomorrow."

That night it snowed.

By morning the prairie was a vast white blank; and every day for a week more snow fell. They made some wide, reaching casts and guesses, but the plains were empty. One day they pushed their fading horses in a two-hour climb, toiling through drifts to the top of a towering butte. At its craggy lip they set their gaunted horses in silence, while their eyes swept the plain for a long time. The sky was dark that day, but near the ground the air was clear; they could see about as far as a man could ride through that clogging snow in a week. Neither found anything to say, for they knew they were done. Mart had not wept since the night of the massacre. Then he had suffered a blinding shock, and an inconsolable, aching grief so great he had never expected to cry again. But now as he faced the emptiness of a world that was supposed to have Debbie in it, yet was blank to its farthest horizons, his throat began to knot and hurt. He faced away to hide from Amos the tears he could no longer hold back; and soon after that he started his horse slowly back down that long, long slope, lest Amos hear the convulsive jerking of his breath and the snuffling of tears that ran down inside his nose.

They made an early, snowbound camp, with no call to hurry any more or stretch the short days. "This don't change anything," Amos said doggedly. "Not in the long run. If she's alive, she's safe by now, and

81

they've kept her to raise. They do that time and again with a little child small enough to be raised their own way. So . . . we'll find them in the end; I promise you that. By the Almighty God, I promise you that! We'll catch up to 'em, just as sure as the turning of the earth!"

But now they had to start all over again in another way.

What Mart had noticed was that Amos always spoke of catching up to "them"—never of finding "her." And the cold, banked fires behind Amos' eyes were manifestly the lights of hatred, not of concern for a lost little girl. He wondered uneasily if there might not be a peculiar danger in this. He believed now that Amos, in certain moods, would ride past the child, and let her be lost to them if he saw a chance to kill Comanches.

They were freezing miserably in the lightweight clothes in which they had started out. Their horses were ribby shells, and they were out of flour, grease, block matches, coffee, and salt. Even their ammunition was running dangerously low. They were always having to shoot something to eat—a scrawny antelope, a jackrabbit all bones and fur; nothing they shot seemed to last all day. And it took two cartridges to light a fire—one to yield a pinch of powder to be mixed with tinder, a second to fire into the tinder, lighting it by gun flash. They needed to go home and start again, but they could not; there was much they could do, and must do, before they took time to go back.

President Grant had given the Society of Friends full charge of the Indian Agencies for the Wild Tribes, which in the Southwest Plains included Indians speaking more than twenty languages. Important in strength or activity were the Cheyennes, Arapahoes, and Wichitas; the Osages, a splinter of the Sioux; and, especially, that most murderous and irreconcilable alliance of all, the Comanches and Kiowas. The gentle and unrequiring administration of the Quakers very quickly attracted considerable numbers of these to the Agencies as winter closed. Besides government hand-outs, this got them a snow-weather amnesty from the trouble stirred up by their summer raids. Traders, Indian Agents, and army officers ransomed captive white children from winter peace-lovers like these every year. Failing this kind of good fortune, the situation still offered the best of opportunities to watch, to listen, and to learn.

Mart and Amos swung south to Fort Concho, where they re-outfitted and traded for fresh horses, taking a bad beating because of the poor shape their own were in. Amos seemed to have adequate money with him. Mart had never known how much money was kept, variously hidden, around the Edwards' place, but during the last two or three years it had probably been a lot; and naturally Amos wouldn't have left any of it in the empty house. The two riders headed up the north fork of the Butterfield Trail, laid out to provide at least one way to El Paso, but abandoned even before the war. Fort Phanton Hill, Fort Griffin, and Fort Belknap—set up to watch the Tonkawas—were in ruins, but still garrisoned by worried little detachments. At these places, and wherever they went, they told their story, pessimistically convinced that information was best come by in unlikely ways, being seldom found where you would reasonably expect it. Amos was posting a reward of a thousand dollars for any clue that would lead to the recovery of Debbie alive. Mart supposed it could be paid out of the family cattle, or something, if the great day ever came when it would be owed.

Laboriously, sweatily, night after night, Mart worked on a letter to the Mathison family, to tell them of the death of Brad and the manner in which he died. For a while he tried to tell the facts in a way that wouldn't make his own part in it look too futile. But he believed that he had failed, perhaps unforgivably, at the Warrior River, and that if he had been any good, Brad would still be alive. So in the end he gave up trying to fix any part of it up, and just told it the way it happened. He finally got the letter "posted" at Fort Richardson—which meant he left it there for some random rider to carry, if any should happen to be going the right way.

At Fort Richardson they struck north and west, clean out of the State of Texas. Deep in Indian Territory they made Camp Wichita, which they were surprised to find renamed Fort Sill—still a bunch of shacks but already heavily garrisoned. They stayed two weeks; then pushed northward again, far beyond Sill to the Anadarko Agency and Old Fort Cobb. By a thousand questions, by walking boldly through the far-strung-out camps of a thousand savages, by piecing together faint implications and guesses, they were trying to find out from what band of Comanches the raiders must have come. But nobody seemed to know much about Comanches—not even how many there were, or how divided. The military at Fort Sill seemed to think there were eight thousand Comanches; the Quaker Agents believed there to be no more than six thousand; some of the old traders believed there to be at least twelve thousand. And so with the bands: there were seven Comanche bands, there were sixteen, there were eleven. When they counted up the names of all the bands and villages they had heard of, the total came to more than thirty.

But none of this proved anything. The Comanches had a custom that forbade speaking the name of a dead person; if a chief died who had given himself the name of his band, the whole outfit had to have a new name. So sometimes a single village had a new name every year, while all the old names still lived on in the speech of Comanches and others who had not got the word. They found reason to think that the River Pony Comanches were the same as the Parka-nowm, or Waterhole People; and the Widyew, Kitsa-Kahna, Titchakenna, and Yapa-eena were probably all names for the Rooteaters, or Yampareka. For a time they heard the Way-ah-nay (Hill Falls Down) Band talked about as if it were comparable to the Pennetecka (Honey-eaters), which some said included six thousand Comanches by itself. And later they discovered that the Way-ah-nay Band was nothing but six or seven families living under a cut-bank.

The Comanches themselves seemed unable, or perhaps unwilling, to explain themselves any more exactly.

Various groups had different names for the same village or band. They never used the name "Comanche" among themselves. That name was like the word "squaw"—a sound some early white man thought he heard an Indian make once back in Massachusetts; the only Indians who understood it were those who spoke English. Comanches called themselves "Nemmenna," which meant "The People." Many tribes, such as the Navajo and Cheyenne, had names meaning the same thing. So the Comanches considered themselves to be the total population by simple definition. Nothing else existed but various kinds of enemies which The People had to get rid of. They were working on it now.

Mart and Amos did learn a few things from the Comanches, mostly in the way of tricks for survival. They saved themselves from frozen feet by copying the Comanche snow boots, which were knee length and made of buffalo hide with the fur turned inside. And now they always carried small doeskin pouches of tinder, made of punkwood scrapings and fat drippings—or lint and kerosene, which worked even better, when they had it. This stuff could be lighted by boring into dry-rotted wood with a spinning stick. But what they did not learn of, and did not recognize until long after, was the mortal danger that had hung over them as they walked through those Comanche camps—such danger as turned their bellies cold, later, when they knew enough to understand it.

Christmas came and went unnoticed, for they spent it in the saddle; they were into another year. Mart was haunted by no more crooked stumps in this period, and the terror-dream did not return. The pain of grief was no longer ever-present; he was beginning to accept that the people to whom he had been nearest were not in the world any more, except, perhaps, for the lost little child who was their reason for being out here. But they were baffled and all but discouraged, as well as ragged and winter-gaunted, by the time they headed their horses toward home, nearly three hundred miles away.

Night was coming on as they raised the lights of the Mathison ranch two hours away. The sunset died, and a dark haze walled the horizon, making the snow-covered land lighter than the sky. The far-seen lights of the ranch house held their warmest promise in this hour, while you could still see the endless emptiness of the prairie in the dusk. Martin Pauley judged that men on horseback, of all creatures on the face of the world, led the loneliest and most frost-blighted lives. He would have traded places with the lowest sodbuster that breathed, if only he could have had four walls, a stove, and people around him.

But as they drew near, Mart began to worry. The Mathisons should have got his letter two months ago, with any luck. But maybe they hadn't got it at all, and didn't even know that Brad was dead. Or if they did know, they might very likely be holding Brad's death against him. Mart turned shy and fearful, and began to dread going in there. The two of them were a sorry sight at best. They had been forced to trade worn-out horses four times, and had taken a worse beating every swap, so now they rode ponies resembling broke-down dogs. Amos didn't look so bad, Mart thought; gaunted though he was, he still had heft and dignity to him. Thick-bearded to the eyes, his hair grown to a great shaggy mane, he looked a little like some wilderness prophet of the Lord. But Mart's beard had come out only a thin and unsightly straggle. When he had shaved with his skinning knife he was left with such a peaked, sore-looking face that all he needed was a running nose to match. His neck was wind-galled to a turkey red, and his hands were so scaly with chap that they looked like vulture's feet. They had no soap in many weeks.

"We're lucky if they don't shoot on sight," he said. "We ain't fitten to set foot in any decent place."

Amos must have agreed, for he gave a long hail from a furlong out, and rode in shouting their names.

The Mathison house was of logs and built in two parts in the manner of the southern frontier. One roof connected what was really two small houses with a wind-swept passage, called a dog-trot, running between. The building on the left of the dog-trot was the kitchen. The family slept in the other, and Mart didn't know what was in there; he had never been in it.

Brad Mathison's two brothers—Abner, who was six-teen, and Tobe, fifteen—ran out from the kitchen to take their horses. As Abner held up his lantern to make sure of them, Mart got a shock. Ab had the same blue eyes as Brad, and the same fair scrubbed-looking skin, to which no dirt ever seemed to stick; so that for a moment Mart thought he saw Brad walking up to him through the dark. The boys didn't ask about their brother, but they didn't mention Mart's letter, either.

Go on in, they said, the heck with your saddles, Pa's holding the door.

Nothing in the kitchen had changed. Mart remembered each thing in this room, as if nothing had been moved while he was gone. His eyes ran around the place anyway, afraid to look at the people. A row of shined-up copper pots and pans hung over the wood range, which could feed a lot of cowhands when it needed to; it was about the biggest in the country. Everything else they had here was homemade, planed or whittled, and pegged together. But the house was plastered inside, the whole thing so clean and bright he stood blinking in the light of the kerosene lamps, and feeling dirty. Actually he smelled mainly of juniper smoke, leather, and prairie wind, but he didn't know that. He felt as though he ought to be outside, and stand downwind.

Then Aaron Mathison had Mart by the hand. He looked older than Mart remembered him, and his sight seemed failing, as his mild eyes searched Mart's face. "Thank thee for the letter thee wrote," Mathison said.

Mrs. Mathison came and put her arms around him, and for a moment held onto him as if he were her son. She hadn't done that since he was able to walk under a table without cracking his head, and to give him a hug she had to kneel on the floor. He vaguely remembered how beautiful and kind she had seemed to him then. But every year since she had gradually become dumpier, and quieter, and less thought about, until she had no more shape or color than a sack of wheat. She still had an uncommonly sweet smile, though, what

89

times it broke through; and tonight as she smiled at Mart there was such wistfulness in it that he almost kissed her cheek. Only he had not been around people enough to feel as easy as that.

And Laurie . . . she was the one he looked for first, and was most aware of, and most afraid to look at. And she was the only one who did not come toward him at all. She stood at the wood range, pretending to get ready to warm something for them; she flashed Mart one quick smile, but stayed where she was.

"I have a letter for you," Aaron said to Amos. "It was brought on and left here by Joab Wilkes, of the Rangers, as he rode by."

"A what?"

"I have been told the news in this letter," Aaron said gravely. "It is good news, as I hope and believe." Amos followed as Aaron retired to the other end of the kitchen, where he fumbled in a cupboard.

Laurie was still at the stove, her back to the room, but her hands were idle. It occurred to Martin that she didn't know what to say, or do, any more than he did. He moved toward her with no clear object in view. And now Laurie turned at last, ran to him, and gave him a peck of a kiss on the corner of his mouth. "Why, Mart, I believe you're growing again."

"And him on an empty stomach," her mother said. "I wonder he doesn't belt you!"

After that everything was all right.

12

They had fresh pork and the first candied yams Mart had seen since a year ago Thanksgiving. Tobe asked Amos how many Comanch' he had converted in the Fight at the Cat-tails.

"Don't know." Amos was at once stolid and uncomfortable as he answered. "Shot at two-three dozen. But the other varmints carried 'em away. Worse scared than hurt, most like."

Tobe said, "I bet you got plenty scalps in your saddle bags!"

"Not one!"

"He just stomp' 'em in the dirt," Mart explained, and was surprised to see Amos' eyes widen in a flash of anger.

"Come morning," Amos said to Mart, wrenching clear of the subject, "I want you borry the buckboard, and run it over to my place. The boys will show you which team. Round up such clothes of mine, or yours, as got overlooked."

That "my place" didn't sound just right to Mart. It had always been "Henry's place" or "my brother's place" every time Amos had ever spoken of it before.

"Load up any food stores that wasn't stole or spoilt. Especially any unbust presarves. And any tools you see. Fetch 'em here. And if any my horses have come in, feed grain on the tail gate, so's they foller you back."

There was that "my" again. "My horses" this time. Amos had owned exactly one horse, and it was dead.

"What about—" Mart had started to ask what he must do about Debbie's horses. Debbie, not Amos, was heir to the Edwards' livestock if she lived. "Nothing," he finished.

When they had eaten, Aaron Mathison and Amos got their heads together again in the far end of the room. Their long conference partly involved tally books, but Mart couldn't hear what was said. Laurie took her sewing basket to a kind of settle that flanked the wood range, and told Mart by a movement of her eyes that she meant him to sit beside her.

"If you're going over—over home," she said in a near whisper, "maybe I ought to tell you about—something. There's something over there. . . . I don't know if you'll understand." She floundered and lost her way.

He said flatly, "You talking about that story, the place is haunted?"

She stared at him.

He told her about the rider they had come on one night, packing up toward the Nations on business unknown. This man had spoken of heading into what he called the "old Edwards place," thinking to bed down for the night in the deserted house. Only, as he came near he saw lights moving around inside. Not like the place was lived in and lighted up. More like a single candle, carried around from room to room. The fellow got the hell out of there, Mart finished, and excuse him, he hadn't meant to say hell.

"What did Amos say?"

"He went in one of his black fits."

"Martie," Laurie said, "you might as well know what he saw. You'll find the burnt-out candle anyway."

"What candle?"

"Well . . . you see . . . it was coming on Christmas Eve. And I had the strongest feeling you were coming home. You know how hard you can know something that isn't so?"

"I sure do," Mart said.

"So . . . I rode over there, and laid a fire in the stove, and dusted up. And I—you're going to laugh at me, Martie."

"No, I ain't."

"Well, I—I made a couple of great gawky bush-holly wreaths, and cluttered up the back windows with them. And I left a cake on the table. A kind of a cake— it got pretty well crumbed riding over. But I reckoned you could see it was meant for a cake. You might as well fetch home the plate."

"I'll remember."

"And I set a candle in a window. It was a whopper— I bet it burned three-four days. That's what your owl-hoot friend saw. I see no doubt of it."

"Oh," said Mart. It was all he could think of to say.

"Later I felt foolish; tried to get over there, and cover my tracks. But Pa locked up my saddle. He didn't like me out so long worrying Ma."

"Well, I should hope!"

"You'd better burn those silly wreaths. Before Amos sees 'em, and goes in a 'black fit.' "

"It wasn't silly," Mart said.

"Just you burn 'em. And don't forget the plate. Ma thinks Tobe busted it and ate the cake."

"It beats me," Mart said honestly. "How come anybody ever to take such trouble. I never see such a thing."

"I guess I was just playing house. Pretty childish. I see that now. But—I just love that old house. I can't bear to think of it all dark and lonely over there."

It came to him that she wanted the old house to be their house to make bright and alive again. This was the best day he had ever had in his life, he supposed, what with the promising way it was ending. So now, of course, it had to be spoiled.

Two rooms opened off the end of the kitchen opposite the dog-trot, the larger being a big wintry storeroom. The other, in the corner nearest the stove, was a cubbyhole with an arrow-slit window and a buffalo rug. This was called the grandmother room, because it was meant for somebody old, or sick, who needed to be kept warm. Nowadays it had a couple of rawhide-strung bunks for putting up visitors without heating the bunkhouse where the seasonal hands were housed.

When the family had retired across the dog-trot, Amos and Mart dragged out a wooden tub for a couple of long-postponed baths. They washed what meager change of clothes they had, and hung the stuff on a line back of the stove to dry overnight. Their baggy long-handled underwear and footless socks seemed indecent, hung out in a room where Laurie lived, but they couldn't help it.

"What kind of letter you get?" Mart asked. The average saddle tramp never got a letter in his life.

Amos shook out a pair of wet drawers, with big holes worn on the insides of the thigh, and hung them where they dripped into the woodbin. "Personal kind," he grunted, finally.

"Serves me right, too. Don't know why I never learn."

"Huh?"

"Nothing."

"I been fixing to tell you," Amos began.

"That ain't needful."

"What ain't?"

"I know that letter ain't none of my business. Because nothing is. I just set on other people's horses. To see they foller along."

"I wasn't studying on no letter. Will you leave a man speak? I say I made a deal with old Mathison."

Mart was silent and waited.

"I got to be pushing on," Amos said, picking his words. Passing out information seemed to hurt Amos worse every day he lived. "I won't be around. So Mathison is going to run my cattle with his own. Being's I can't see to it myself."

"What's he get, the increase?"

"Why?"

"No reason. Seemed the natural thing to ask, that's all. I don't give a God damn what you do with your stock."

"Mathison come out all right," Amos said.

"When do we start?"

"You ain't coming."

Mart thought that over. "It seems to me," he began. His voice sounded thin and distant to himself. He started over too loudly. "It seems to me—"

"What you hollering for?"

"—we started out to look for Debbie," Mart finished.

"I'm still looking for her."

"That's good. Because so am I."

"I just told you—by God, will you listen?" It was Amos' voice raised this time. "I'm leaving you here!"

"No, you ain't."

"What?" Amos stared in disbelief.

"You ain't telling me where I stay!"

"You got to live, ain't you? Mathison's going to leave you stay on. Help out with the work what you can, and you'll know where your grub's coming from."

"I been shooting our grub," Mart said stubbornly. "If I can shoot for two, I can shoot for one."

"That still takes ca-tridges. And a horse."

Mart felt his guts drop from under his heart. All his life he had been virtually surrounded by horses; to ride one, you only had to catch it. Only times he had ever thought whether he owned one or not was when some fine fast animal, like one of Brad's, had made him wish it was his. But Amos was right. Nothing in the world is so helpless as a prairie man afoot.

"I set out looking for Debbie," he said. "I aim to keep on."

"Why?"

Mart was bewildered. "Because she's my—she's—"

96

He had started to say that Debbie was his own little sister. But in the moment he hesitated, Amos cut him down.

"Debbie's my brother's young'n," Amos said. "She's my flesh and blood—not yours. Better you leave these things to the people concerned with 'em, boy. Debbie's no kin to you at all."

"I—I always felt like she was my kin."

"Well, she ain't."

"Our—I mean, her—her folks took me in off the ground. I'd be dead but for them. They even—"

"That don't make 'em any kin."

"All right. I ain't got no kin. Never said I had. I'm going to keep on looking, that's all."

"How?"

Mart didn't answer that. He couldn't answer it. He had his saddle and his gun, because Henry had given him those; but the loads in the gun were Amos', he supposed. Mart realized now that a man can be free as a wolf, yet unable to do what he wants at all.

They went on to bed in silence. Amos spoke out of the dark. "You don't give a man a chance to tell you nothing," he complained. "I want you to know something, Mart—"

"Yeah—you want me to know I got no kin. You told me already. Now shut your God damned head!"

One thing about being in the saddle all day, and every day, you don't get a chance to worry as much as other men do once you lie down at night. You fret, and you fret, and you try to think your way through—for about a minute and a half. Then you go to sleep.

97

13 ──────────────────────

Mart woke up in the blackness before the winter dawn. He pulled on his pants, and started up the fire in the wood range before he finished dressing. As he took down his ragged laundry from behind the stove, he was of a mind to leave Amos' stuff hanging there, but he couldn't quite bring himself to it. He made a bundle of Amos' things, and tossed it into their room. By the time he had wolfed a chunk of bread and some leavings of cold meat, Tobe and Abner were up.

"I got to fetch that stuff Amos wants," he said, "from over—over at his house. You want to show me what team?"

"Better wait while we hot up some breakfast, hadn't you?"

"I et already."

They didn't question it. "Take them little fat bays, there, in the nigh corral—the one with the shelter shed."

"I want you take notice of what a pretty match they be" said Tobe with shining pride. "We call 'em Sis and Bud. And pull? They'll outlug teams twice their heft."

"Sis is about the only filly we ever did bust around here," Abner said. "But they balanced so nice, we just couldn't pass her by. Oh, she might cow-kick a little—"

"A little? She hung Ab on the top bar so clean he just

lay there flappin'."

"Feller doesn't mind a bust in the pants from Sis, once he knows her."

"I won't leave nothing happen to 'em," Mart promised.

He took the team shelled corn, and brushed them down while they fed. He limbered the frosty straps of the harness with his gloved hands, and managed to be hooked and out of there before Amos was up.

Even from a distance the Edwards place looked strangely barren. Hard to think why, at first, until you remembered that the house now stood alone, without its barn, sheds, and haystacks. The snow hid the black char and the ash of the burned stuff, as if it never had been. Up on the hill, where Martha, and Henry, and the boys were, the snow had covered even the crosses he had carved.

Up close, as Mart neared the back gallery, the effect of desolation was even worse. You wouldn't think much could happen to a sturdy house like that in just a few months, but it already looked as if it had been unlived in for a hundred years. Snow was drifted on the porch, and slanted deep against the door itself, unbroken by any tracks. In the dust-glazed windows Laurie's wreaths were ghostly against empty black.

When he had forced the door free of the iced sill, he found a still cold inside, more chilling in its way than the searing wind of the prairie. A thin high music that went on forever in the empty house was the keening of the wind in the chimneys. Almost everything he remembered was repaired and in place, but a gray film of dust lay evenly, in spite of Laurie's Christmas dusting. Her cake plate was crumbless, centering a pattern of innumerable pocket-mouse tracks in the dust upon the table.

He remembered something about that homemade table. Underneath it, an inch or so below the top, a random structural member made a little hidden shelf. Once when he and Laurie had been five or six, the Mathisons had come over for a taffy pull. He showed Laurie the secret shelf under the table, and they stored away some little square-cut pieces of taffy there. Afterward, one piece of taffy seemed to be stuck down; he wore out his fingers for months trying to break it loose. Years later he found out that the stubbornly stuck taffy was really the ironhead of a lag screw that you couldn't see where it was, but only feel with your fingers.

He found some winter clothes he sure could use, including some heavy socks Martha and Lucy had knitted for him. Nothing that had belonged to Martha and the girls was in the closets. He supposed some shut trunks standing around held whatever of their stuff the Comanches had left. He went to a little chest that had been Debbie's, with some idea of taking something of hers with him, as if for company; but he stopped himself before he opened the chest. I got these bands she used to hang onto, he told himself. I don't need nothing more. Except to find her.

He was in no hurry to get back. He wanted to miss supper at the Mathisons for fear he would lash out at Amos in front of the others; so, taking his time about everything he did, he managed to fool away most of the day.

A red glow from the embers in the stove was the only light in the Mathison house as he put away the good little team, but a lamp went up in the kitchen before he went in. Laurie was waiting up, and she was put out with him.

"Who gave you the right to lag out till all hours, scaring the range stock?"

"Amos and me always night on the prairie," he reminded her. "It's where we live."

"Not when I'm waiting up for you." She was wrapped twice around in a trade-blanket robe cinched up with a leather belt. Only the little high collar of her flannel nightgown showed, and a bit of blue-veined instep between her moccasins and the hem. Actually she had no more clothes than he had ever seen her wear in her life; there was no reason for the rig to seem as intimate as it somehow did.

He mumbled, "Didn't go to make work," and went to throw his rag-pickings in the grandmother room.

Amos was not in his bunk; his saddle and everything he had was gone.

"Amos rode on," Laurie said unnecessarily.

"Didn't he leave no word for me?"

"Any word," she corrected him. She shook down the grate and dropped fresh wood in the firebox. "He just said, tell you he had to get on." She pushed him gently backward against a bench, so that he sat down. "I mended your stuff," she said. "Such as could be saved."

He thought of the saddle-worn holes in the thighs of

101

his other drawers. "Goddle mighty," he whispered.

"Don't know what your purpose is," she said, "getting so red in the face. I have brothers, haven't I?"

"I know, but—"

"I'm a woman, Martie." He had supposed that was the very point. "We wash and mend your dirty old stuff for you all our lives. When you're little, we even wash you. How a man can make out to get bashful in front of a woman, I'll never know."

He couldn't make any sense out of it. "You talk like a feller might just as leave run around stark nekkid."

"Wouldn't bother me. I wouldn't try it in front of Pa, was I you, so long as you're staying on." She went to the stove to fix his supper.

"I'm not staying, Laurie. I got to catch up with Amos."

She turned to see if he meant it. "Pa was counting on you. He's running your cattle now, you know, along with his own—"

"Amos' cattle."

"He let both winter riders go, thinking you and Amos would be back. Of course, riders aren't too hard to come by. Charlie MacCorry put in for a job."

"MacCorry's a good fast hand," was all he said.

"I don't know what you think you can do about finding Debbie that Amos can't do." She turned to face him solemnly, her eyes very dark in the uneven light. "He'll find her now, Mart. Please believe me. I know."

He waited, but she went back to the skillet without explanation. So now he took a chance and told her the truth. "That's what scares me, Laurie."

"If you're thinking of the property," she said, "the land, the cattle—"

"It isn't that," he told her. "No, no. It isn't that."

"I know Debbie's the heir. And Amos has never had anything in his life. But if you think he'd let harm come to one hair of that child's head on account of all that, then I know you're a fool."

He shook his head. "It's his black fits," he said; and wondered how he could make a mortal danger sound so idiotic.

"What?"

"Laurie, I swear to you, I've seen all the fires of hell come up in his eyes, when he so much as thinks about getting a Comanche in his rifle sights. You haven't seen him like I've seen him. I've known him to take his knife . . ." He let that drop. He didn't want to tell Laurie some of the things he had seen Amos do. "Lord knows I hate Comanches. I hate 'em like I never knew a man could hate nothin'. But you slam into a bunch of 'em, and kill some—you know what happens to any little white captives they got hold of, then? They get their brains knocked out. It's happened over and over again."

He felt she didn't take any stock in what he was saying. He tried again, speaking earnestly to her back. "Amos is a man can go crazy wild. It might come on him when it was the worst thing could be. What I counted on, I hoped I'd be there to stop him, if such thing come."

She said faintly, "You'd have to kill him."

He let that go without answer. "Let's have it now.

103

Where's he gone, where you're so sure he'll find her?"

She became perfectly still for a moment. When she moved again, one hand stirred the skillet, while the other brought a torn-open letter out of the breast of her robe, and held it out to him. He recognized the letter that had been left with Aaron Mathison for Amos. His eyes were on her face, questioning, as he took it.

"We hoped you'd want to stay on," she said. All the liveliness was gone from her voice. "But I guess I knew. Seems to be only one thing in the world you care about any more. So I stole it for you."

He spread out the single sheet of ruled tablet paper the torn envelope contained. It carried a brief scrawl in soft pencil, well smeared.

Laurie said, "Do you believe in second sight? No, of course you don't. There's something I dread about this, Martie."

The message was from a trader Mart knew about, over on the Salt Fork of the Brazos. He called himself Jerem (for Jeremiah) Futterman—an improbable name at best, and not his own. He wasn't supposed to trade with Indians there any more, but he did, covering up by claiming that his real place of business was far to the west in the Arroyo Blanco, outside of Texas. The note said:

I bougt a small size dress off a Injun. If this here is a peece of yr chiles dress bring reward, I know where they gone.

Pinned to the bottom of the sheet with a horseshoe

nail was a two-inch square of calico. The dirt that grayed it was worn evenly into the cloth, as if it had been unwashed for a long time. The little flowers on it didn't stand out much now, but they were there. Laurie was leaning over his shoulder as he held the sample to the light. A strand of her hair was tickling his neck, and her breath was on his cheek, but he didn't even know.

"Is it hers?"

He nodded.

"Poor little dirty dress . . ."

He couldn't look at her. "I've got to get hold of a horse. I just got to get me a horse."

"Is that all that's stopping you?"

"It isn't stopping me. I'll catch up to him. I got to."

"You've got horses, Martie."

"I—what?"

"You've got Brad's horses. Pa said so. He means it, Martie. Amos told us what happened at the Warrior. A lot of things you left out."

Mart couldn't speak for a minute, and when he could he didn't know what to say. The skillet started to smoke, and Laurie went to set it to the back of the range.

"Most of Brad's ponies are turned out. But the Fort Worth stud is up. He's coming twelve, but he'll out-game anything there is. And the good light gelding— the fast one, with the blaze."

"Why, that's Sweet-face," he said. He remembered Laurie naming that colt herself, when she was thirteen years old. "Laurie, that's your own good horse."

"Let's not get choosey, Bub. Those two are the ones

Amos wanted to trade for and take. But Pa held them back for you."

"I'll turn Sweet-face loose to come home," he promised, "this side Fiddler's Crick. I ought to cross soon after daylight."

"Soon after— By starting when?"

"Now," he told her.

He was already in the saddle when she ran out through the snow, and lifted her face to be kissed. She ran back into the house abruptly, and the door closed behind her. He jabbed the Fort Worth stud, hard, with one spur. Very promptly he was bucked back to his senses, and all but thrown. The stallion conveyed a hard, unyielding shock like no horse Mart had ever ridden, as if he were made all of rocks and iron bands. Ten seconds of squealing contention cleared Mart's head, though he thought his teeth might be loosened a little; and he was on his way.

14

When Laurie had closed the door, she stood with her forehead against it a little while, listening to the violent hammer of hoofs sometimes muffled by the snow, sometimes ringing upon the frozen ground, as the Fort Worth stud tried to put Mart down. When the stud had straightened out, she heard Mart circle back to pick up Sweet-face's lead and that of the waspish black mule he had packed. Then he was gone, but she still stood against the door, listening to the receding hoofs. They made a crunch in the snow, rather than a beat, but she was able to hear it for a long time. Finally even that sound stopped, and she could hear only the ticking of the clock and the winter's-night pop of a timber twisting in the frost.

She blew out the lamp, crossed the cold dog-trot, and crept softly to her bed. She shivered for a few moments in the chill of the flour-sack-muslin sheets, but she slept between two deep featherbeds, and they warmed quite soon. For several years they had kept a big gaggle of geese, especially for making featherbeds. They had to let the geese range free, and the coyotes had got the last of them now; but the beds would last a lifetime almost.

As soon as she was warm again, Laurie began to cry. This was not like her. The Mathison men had no patience with blubbering women, and gave them no sympathy at all, so Mathison females learned early to do without nervous outlets of this kind. But once she had given way to tears at all, she cried harder and harder. Perhaps she had stored up every kind of cry there is for a long time. She had her own little room, now, with a single rifle-slit window, too narrow for harm to come through; but the matched-fencing partition was too flimsy to be much of a barrier to sound. She pressed her face deep into the feathers, and did her best to let no sound escape. It wasn't good enough. By rights, everybody should have been deep asleep long ago, but her mother heard her anyway, and came in to sit on the side of her bed.

Laurie managed to snuffle, "Get under the covers,

Ma. You'll catch you a chill."

Mrs. Mathison got partly into the bed, but remained sitting up. Her work-stiffened fingers were awkward as she tentatively stroked her daughter's hair. "Now, Laurie. . . . Now, Laurie. . . ."

Laurie buried her face deeper in the featherbed. "I'm going to be an old maid!" she announced rebelliously, her words half smothered.

"Why, Laurie!"

"There just aren't any boys—men—in this part of the world. I think this everlasting wind blows 'em away. Scours the whole country plumb clean."

"Come roundup there's generally enough underfoot, seems to me. At least since the peace. Place swarms with 'em. Worse'n ants in a tub of leftover dishes."

"Oh!" Laurie whimpered in bitter exasperation. "Those hoot-owlers!" Her mind wasn't running very straight. She meant owl-hooters, of course—a term applied to hunted men, who liked to travel by night. It was true that the hands who wandered out here to pick up seasonal saddle work were very often wanted. If a Ranger so much as stopped by a chuck wagon, so many hands would disappear that the cattlemen had angrily requested the Rangers to stay away from roundups altogether. But they weren't professional badmen—not bandits or killers; just youngsters, mostly, who had got into some trouble they couldn't bring themselves to face out. Many of the cattlemen preferred this kind, for they drifted on of their own accord, saving you the uncomfortable job of firing good loyal riders who really wanted to stick and work.

And they were no hazard to home girls. They didn't even come into the house to eat, once enough of them had gathered to justify hiring a wagon cook. Most of them had joked with Laurie, and made a fuss over her, so long as she was little; but they had stopped this about the time she turned fifteen. Nowadays they steered clear, perhaps figuring they were already in trouble enough. Typically they passed her, eyes down, with a mumbled, "Howdy, Mam," and a sheepish tug at a ducked hat brim. Soon they were off with the wagon, and were paid off and on their way the day they got back.

Actually, Laurie had almost always picked out some one of them to idolize, and imagine she was in love with, from a good safe distance. After he rode on, all unsuspecting, she would sometimes remember him, and spin daydreams about him, for months and months. But she was in no mood to remember all that now.

Mrs. Mathison sighed. She could not, in honesty, say much for the temporary hands as eligible prospects. "There's plenty others. Like—like Zack Harper. Such a nice, clean boy—"

"That nump!"

"And there's Charlie MacCorry—"

"*Him.*" A contemptuous rejection.

Her mother didn't press it. Charlie MacCorry hung around a great deal more than Mrs. Mathison wished he would, and she didn't want him encouraged. Charlie was full of high spirits and confidence, and might be considered flashily handsome, at least from a little distance off. Up close his good looks seemed somehow exaggerated, almost as in a caricature. What Mrs. Mathison saw in him, or thought she saw, was nothing but stupidity made noisy by conceit. Mentioning him at all had been a scrape at the bottom of the barrel.

She recognized the upset Laurie was going through as an inevitable thing, that every girl had to go through, somewhere between adolescence and marriage. Mrs. Mathison was of limited imagination, but her observation was sound, and her memory clear, so she could remember having gone through this phase herself. A great restlessness went with it, like the disquiet of a young wild goose at the flight season; as if something said to her, "Now, now or never again! Now, or life will pass you by. . . ." No one who knew Mrs. Mathison now could have guessed that at sixteen she had run away with a tinhorn gambler, having met him, in secret, only twice in her life. She could remember the resulting embarrassments with painful clarity, but not the emotions that had made her do it. She thought of the episode with shame, as an unexplainable insanity, from which she was saved only when her father overtook them and snatched her back.

She had probably felt about the same way when she ran off a second time—this time more successfully, with Aaron Mathison. Her father, a conservative storekeeper and a pillar of the Baptist Church, had regarded the Quakers in the Mathison background as benighted and misled, more to be pitied than anything else. But the young shaggy-headed Aaron he considered a dangerously irresponsible wild man, deserving not a whit more confidence than the staved-off gambler—who at least had the sense to run from danger, not at it. He never spoke to his daughter again. Mrs. Mathison forever after regarded this second escapade as a sound and necessary move, regarding which her parents were peculiarly blind and wrong-headed. Aaron Mathison in truth was a man like a great rooted tree, to which she was as tightly affixed as a lichen; no way of life without him was conceivable to her.

She said now with compassion, "Dear heart, dear little girl—Martin will come back. He's bound to come back." She didn't know whether they would ever see Martin Pauley again or not, but she feared the outrageous things—the runaways, the cheap marriages—which she herself had proved young girls to be capable of at this stage. She wanted to give Laurie some comforting hope, to help her bridge over the dangerous time.

"I don't care what he does," Laurie said miserably. "It isn't that at all."

"I never dreamed," her mother said, thoughtfully, ignoring the manifest untruth. "Why, you two always acted like—more like two tomboys than anything. How long has . . . When did you start thinking of Mart in this way?"

Laurie didn't know that herself. Actually, so far as she was conscious of it, it had been about an hour. Mart had been practically her best friend, outside the family, throughout her childhood. But their friendship had indeed been much the same as that of two boys.

Latterly, she recalled with revulsion, she had idiotically thought Charlie MacCorry more fun, and much more interesting. But she had looked forward with a warm, innocent pleasure to having Mart live with them right in the same house. Now that he was suddenly gone—irrecoverably, she felt now—he left an unexpectedly ruinous gap in her world that nothing left to her seemed able to fill. She couldn't explain all that to her mother. Wouldn't know how to begin.

When she didn't answer, her mother patted her shoulder. "It will all seem different in a little while," she said in the futile cliché of parents. "These things have a way of passing off. I know you don't feel that way now; but they do. Time, the great healer . . ." she finished vaguely. She kissed the back of Laurie's head, and went away.

15

After days of thinking up blistering things to say, Mart judged he was ready for Amos. He figured Amos would come at him before they were through. Amos was a respected rough-and-tumble scrapper away from home. "I run out of words," Mart had heard him explain many a tangle. "Wasn't nothing left to do but hit him." Let him try.

But when he caught up, far up the Salt Fork, it was all wasted, for Amos wouldn't quarrel with him. "I done my best to free your mind," Amos said. "Mathison was fixing to step you right into Brad's boots.

Come to think of it, that's a pair you got on. And Laurie—she wanted you."

"Question never come up," Mart said shortly.

Amos shrugged. "Couldn't say much more than I done."

"No, you sure couldn't. Not without landing flat on your butt!" Mart had always thought of Amos as a huge man, perhaps because he had been about knee high to Amos when he knew him first. But now, as Amos for a moment looked him steadily in the eye, Mart noticed for the first time that their eyes were on the same level. Mrs. Mathison had been right about Mart having taken a final spurt of growth.

"I guess I must have left Jerem's letter lying around."

"Yeah. You left it lying around." Mart had meant to ball up the letter and throw it in Amos' face, but found he couldn't now. He just handed it over.

"This here's another thing I tried to leave you out of," Amos said. "Martha put herself out for fifteen years bringing you up. I'll feel low in my mind if I get you done away with now."

"Ain't studying on getting done away with."

" 'Bring the reward,' he says here. From what I know of Jerem, he ain't the man to trust getting paid when he's earned it. More liable to try to make sure."

"Now, he ought to know you ain't carrying the thousand around with you!"

"Ain't I?"

So he was. Amos did have the money with him. Now there's a damn fool thing, Mart considered. Aloud he said, "If he's got robbery in mind, I suppose he won't

113

tell the truth anyway."

"I think he will. So he'll have a claim later in case we slip through his claws."

"You talk like we're fixing to steal bait from a snap trap!"

Amos shrugged. "I'll admit one thing. In a case like this, two guns got about ten times the chance of one."

Mart was flattered. He couldn't work himself up to picking a fight with Amos after that. Things dropped back to what they had been before they went home at all. The snow melted off, and they traveled in mud. Then the weather went cold again, and the wet earth froze to iron. More snow was threatening as they came to Jerem Futterman's stockade, where Lost Mule Creek ran into the Salt Fork. The creek had not always been called the Lost Mule. Once it had been known as Murder River. They didn't know why, nor how the name got changed, but maybe it was a good thing to remember now.

Jerem Futterman was lightly built, but well knit, and moved with a look of handiness. Had he been a cow-horse you might have bought him, if you liked them mean, and later shot him, if you didn't like them treacherous. He faced them across a plank-and-barrel counter in the murk of his low-beamed log trading room, seeming to feel easier with a barrier between himself and strangers. Once he had had another name. Some thought he called himself Futterman because few were likely to suspect a man of fitting such a handle to himself if it wasn't his right one.

"Knew you'd be along," he said. "Have a drink."

114

"Have one yourself." Amos refused the jug, but rang a four-bit piece on the planks.

Futterman hesitated, but ended by taking a swig and pocketing the half dollar. This was watched by four squaws bunkered down against the wall and a flat-faced breed who snoozed in a corner. Mart had spotted four or five other people around the place on their way in, mostly knock-about packers and bull-team men, who made up a sort of transient garrison.

The jug lowered, and they went into the conventional exchange of insults that passed for good humor out here. "Wasn't sure I'd know you standing up," Futterman said. "Last I saw, you were flat on your back on the floor of a saloon at Painted Post."

"You don't change much. See you ain't washed or had that shirt off," Amos said; and decided that was enough politeness. "Let's see the dress!"

A moment of total stillness filled the room before Futterman spoke. "You got the money?"

"I ain't paying the money for the dress. I pay when the child is found—alive, you hear me?"

The trader had a trick of dropping his lids and holding motionless with cocked head, as if listening. The silence drew out to the cracking point; then Futterman left the room without explanation. Mart and Amos exchanged a glance. What might happen next was anybody's guess; the place had an evil, trappy feel. But Futterman came back in a few moments, carrying a rolled-up bit of cloth.

It was Debbie's dress, all right. Amos went over it,

115

inch by inch, and Mart knew he was looking for blood stains. It was singular how often people west of the Cross Timbers found themselves searching for things they dreaded to find. The dress was made with tiny stitches that Amos must be remembering as the work of Martha's fingers. But now the pocket was half torn away, and the square hole where the sample had been knifed out of the front seemed an Indian kind of mutilation, as if the little dress were dead.

"Talk," Amos said.

"A man's got a right to expect some kind of payment."

"You're wasting time!"

"I paid twenty dollars for this here. You lead a man to put out, and put out, but when it comes to—"

Amos threw down a gold piece, and Mart saw Futterman regret that he hadn't asked more.

"I had a lot of other expense, you realize, before—"

"Bull shit," Amos said. "Where'd you get this?"

One more long moment passed while Jerem Futterman gave that odd appearance of listening. This man is careful, Mart thought; he schemes, and he holds back the aces—but he's got worms in his craw where the sand should be.

"A young buck fetched it in. Filched it, naturally. He said it belonged off a young'n—"

"Is she alive?"

"He claimed so. Said she was catched by Chief Scar the tail end of last summer."

"Take care, Jerem! I never heard of no Chief Scar!"

"Me neither." Futterman shrugged. "He's supposed

to be a war chief with the Nawyecky Comanches."

"War chief," Amos repeated with disgust. Among the Comanches any warrior with a good string of coups was called a war chief.

"You want me to shut up, say so," Futterman said testily. "Don't be standing there giving me the lie every minute!"

"Keep talking," Amos said, relaxing a little.

"Scar was heading north. He was supposed to cross the Red, and winter-in at Fort Sill. According to this buck. Maybe he lied."

"And maybe you lie," Amos said.

"In that case, you won't find her, will you? And I won't get the thousand."

"You sure as hell won't," Amos agreed. He stuffed Debbie's dress into the pocket of his sheepskin.

"Stay the night, if you want. You can have your pick of them squaws."

The squaws sat stolidly with lowered eyes. Mart saw that a couple of them, with the light color of mixed blood, were as pretty as any he had seen. Amos ignored the offer, however. He bought a skimpy mule load of corn for another twenty dollars, with only a token argument over the outrageous price.

"I expect you back when you find her," Futterman reminded him, "to pay the money into this here hand." He showed the dirty hand he meant.

"I'll be back if I find her," Amos said. "And if I don't."

Little daylight was left as they struck northward along Lost Mule Creek. The overcast broke, and a full moon rose, huge and red at first, dwindling and paling as it climbed. And within two hours they knew that the lonely prairie was not half lonely enough, from the standpoint of any safety in this night. Mart's stud horse told them first. He began to prick his ears and show interest in something unseen and unheard, off on their flank beyond the Lost Mule. When he set himself to whinny they knew there were horses over there. Mart picked him up sharply, taking up short on the curb, so the uproar the stud was planning on never come out. But the horse fussed and fretted from then on.

Though the stud could be stopped from hollering, their pack mule could not. A little farther on he upped his tail, lifted his head, and whipsawed the night with a bray fit to rouse the world.

"That fool leatherhead is waking up people in Kansas," Mart said. "You want I should tie down his tail? I heard they can't yell at all, failin' they get their tail up."

Amos had never seen it tried, but he figured he could throw off on that one by percentage alone. "That's what I like about you," he said. "Man can tell you any fur-fetched thing comes in his head, and you'll cleave to it for solemn fact from then on."

"Well, then—why don't we split his pack, and stick a prickle pear under his tail, and fog him loose?"

"He'd foller anyway."

"We can tie him. Shoot him even. This here's the same as traveling with a brass band."

Amos looked at him with disbelief. "Give up a fifteen-dollar mule for the likes of Jerem? I guess you don't know me very well. Leave the brute sing."

The thing was that nothing answered the mule from beyond the creek. The stud might have scented a band of mustangs, but mustangs will answer a mule same as a horse. Their animals were trying to call to ridden horses, probably Spanish curbed.

"I see no least reason," Mart said, "why they can't gallop ahead and dry-gulch us any time they want to try."

"How do you know they haven't tried?"

"Because we ain't been fired on. They could pick any time or place they want."

"I ain't led you any kind of place they want. Why you think I swung so far out back there a few miles? That's our big advantage—they got to use a place I pick."

They rode on and on, while the moon shrunk to a pale dime, and crossed the zenith. The mule lost interest, but the stud still fretted, and tried to trumpet. The unseen, unheard stalkers who dogged them were still there.

"This can't run on forever," Mart said.

"Can't it?"

"We got to lose 'em or outrun 'em. Or—"

"What for? So's they can come on us some far place, when we least expect?"

"I can't see 'em giving up," Mart argued. "If this kind of haunting has to go on for days and weeks—"

"I mean to end it tonight," Amos said.

They off-saddled at last in the rough ground from which the Lost Mule rose. Amos picked a dry gully, and they built a big tenderfoot fire on a patch of dry

119

sand. Mart did what Amos told him up to here.

"I figure I got a right to know what you aim to do," he said at last.

"Well, we might make up a couple of dummies out o'—"

Mart rebelled. "If I heard one story about a feller stuffed grass in his blanket and crawled off in the buck brush, I heard a million! Come morning, the blanket is always stuck full of arrows. Dozens of 'em. Never just one arrow, like a thrifty Indian would make do. Now, you know how hard arrows is to make!"

"Ain't studyin' on Indians."

"No, I guess not. I guess it must be crazy people."

"In poker, in war," Amos said, "what you want is a simple, stupid plan. Reason you hear about the old flim-flams so much is they always work. Never try no deep, tricky plan. The other feller can't foller it; it throws him back on his common sense—which is the last thing you want."

"But this here is childish!"

Amos declared that what you plan out never helps much any; more liable to work against you than anything else. What the other fellow had in mind was the thing you wanted to figure on. It was the way you used *his* plan that decided which of you got added to the list of the late lamented. But he said no more of dummies. "You hungry? I believe they'll stand off and wait for us to settle down. We got time to eat, if you want to cook."

"I don't care if I never eat. Not with what's out there in the dark."

Only precaution they took was to withdraw from the

ember-lighted gully, and take cover under a low-hung spruce on the bank. About the first place a killer would look, Mart thought, once he found their camp. Mart rolled up in his blankets, leaving Amos sitting against the stem of the spruce, his rifle in his hands.

"You see, Martie," Amos went back to it, "a man is very liable to see what he's come expecting to see. Almost always, he'll picture it all out in his mind beforehand. So you need give him but very little help, and he'll swindle hisself. Like one time in the Rangers, Cap Harker offered five hundred dollars reward for a feller—"

"Now who ever give the Rangers five hundred dollars? Not the Texas legislature, I guarandamtee."

"—for taking a feller alive, name of Morton C. Pettigrew. Cap got the description printed up on a handbill. Middling size; average weight; hair-colored hair; eye-colored eyes—"

"Now wait a minute!"

"Shut up. Temperment sociable and stand-offish; quiet, peaceable, and always making trouble."

"Never see such a damn man."

"Well, you know, that thing got us more than forty wanted men? Near every settlement in Texas slung some stranger in the calabozo and nailed up the door. We gathered in every size and shape, without paying a cent. A little short red-head Irishman, and a walking skeleton a head taller'n me, and a Chinaman, and any number of renegade Mex. Near every one of 'em worth hanging for something, too, except the Chinaman; we had to leave him go. Cap Harker was strutting up and down Texas, singing 'Bringing home the sheaves,' and speaking of running for governor. But it finished him."

"How?"

"Marshal down at Castlerock grobe a feller said he *was* Morton C. Pettigrew. We sent a man all the way back to Rhode Island, trying to break his story. But it was his right name, sure enough. Finally we had to make up the reward out of our own pants."

Mart asked nervously, "You think they'll try guns, or knives?"

"What? Who? Oh. My guess would be knives. But you let them make the choice. We'll handle whichever, when it comes. Go'n to sleep. I got hold of everything."

All they really knew was that it would come. No doubt of that now. The stud was trumpeting again, and stammering with his feet. Mart was not happy with the probability of the knives. Most Americans would rather be blown to bits than face up to the stab and slice of whetted steel—nobody seems to know just why. Mart was no different. Sleep, the man says. Fine chance, knowing your next act must be to kill a man, or get a blade in the gizzard. And he knew Amos was a whole lot more strung-up than he was willing to let on. Amos hadn't talked so much in a month of Sundays.

Mart settled himself as comfortably as he could for the sleepless wait that was ahead; and was asleep in the next half minute.

The blast of a rifle wakened him to the most confusing ten minutes of his life. The sound had not been the bang that makes your ears ring when a shot is fired

122

beside you, but the explosive howl, like a snarl, that you hear when it is fired toward you from a little distance off. He was rolling to shift his probably spotted position when the second shot sounded. Somebody coughed as the bullet hit, made a brief strangling noise, and was quiet. Amos was not under the spruce; Mart's first thought was that he had heard him killed.

Down in the gully the embers of their fire still glowed. Nothing was going on down there at all; the action had been behind the spruce on the uphill side. He wormed on his belly to the place where he had heard the man hit. Two bodies were there, instead of one, the nearer within twenty feet of the spot where he had slept. Neither dead man was Amos. And now Mart could hear the hoof-drum of a running horse.

From a little ridge a hundred feet away a rifle now spoke twice. The second flash marked for him the spot where a man stood straight up, firing deliberately down their back trail. Mart leveled his rifle, but in the moment he took to make sure of his sights in the bad light, the figure disappeared. The sound of the running horse faded out, and the night was quiet.

Mart took cover and waited; he waited a long time before he heard a soft footfall near him. As his rifle swung, Amos' voice said, "Hold it, Mart. Shootin's over."

"What in all hell is happening here?"

"Futterman held back. He sent these two creeping in. They was an easy shot from where I was. Futterman, though—it took an awful lucky hunk of lead to catch up with that one. He was leaving like a scalded goat."

"What the devil was you doing out there?"

"Walked out to see if he had my forty dollars on him." It wasn't the explanation Mart was after, and Amos knew it. "Got the gold pieces all right. Still in his pants. I don't know what become of my four bits."

"But how come—how did you make out to nail 'em?"

What can you say to a man so sure of himself, so belittling of chance, that he uses you for bait? Mart could have told him something. There had been a moment when he had held Amos clean in his sights, without knowing him. One more pulse-beat of pressure on the hair-set trigger, and Amos would have got his head blown off for his smartness. But he let it go.

"We got through it, anyway," Amos said.

"I ain't so sure we're through it. A thing like this can make trouble for a long, long time."

Amos did not answer that.

As they rode on, a heavy cloud bank came over the face of the lowering moon. Within the hour, snow began to fall, coming down in flakes so big they must have hissed in the last embers of the fire they had left behind. Sunrise would find only three low white mounds back there, scarcely recognizable for what they were under the blanketing snow.

16 _____

Winter was breaking up into slush and sleet, with the usual freezing setbacks, as they reached Fort Sill again. The Indians would begin to scatter as soon as the first pony grass turned green, but for the present there were many more here than had come in with the early snows. Apparently the Wild Tribes who had taken the Quaker Peace Policy humorously at first were fast learning to take advantage of it. Three hundred lodges of Wichitas in their grass beehive houses, four hundred of Comanches in hide tepees, and more Kiowas than both together, were strung out for miles up Cache Creek and down the Medicine Bluff, well past the mouth of Wolf Creek.

Nothing had been seen of the Queherenna, or Antelope Comanches, under Bull Bear, Black Horse, and Wolf-Lying-Down, or the Kotsetaka (Buffalo-followers) under Shaking Hand, all of whom stayed in or close to the Staked Plains. The famous war chief Tabananica, whose name was variously translated as Sound-of-Morning, Hears-the-Sunrise, and Talks-with-Dawn-Spirits, was not seen, but he was heard from: He sent word to the fort urging the soldiers to come out and fight. Still, those in charge were not heard to complain that they hadn't accumulated Indians enough. A far-sighted chief named Kicking Bird was holding the Kiowas fairly well in check, and the Wichitas were quiet, as if suspicious of their luck;

but the Comanches gleefully repaid the kindness of the Friends with arrogance, insult, and disorderly mischief.

Mart and Amos were unlikely to forget Agent Hiram Appleby. This Quaker, a graying man in his fifties, looked like a small-town storekeeper, and talked like one, with never a "thee" nor "thou"; a quiet, unimpressive man, with mild short-sighted eyes, stains on his crumpled black suit, and the patience of the eternal rocks. He had watched the Comanches kill his milch cows, and barbecue them in his dooryard. They had stolen all his red flannel underwear off the line, and paraded it before him as the outer uniform of an improvised society of young bucks. And none of this changed his attitude toward them by the width of a whistle.

Once they watched a Comanche buck put a knife point to Appleby's throat in a demand for free ammunition, and spit in the Agent's face when it didn't work. Appleby simply stood there, mild, fusty looking, and immovable, showing no sign of affront. Amos stared in disbelief, and his gun whipped out.

"If you harm this Indian," Appleby said, "you will be seized and tried for murder, just as soon as the proper authorities can be reached." Amos put away his gun. The Comanche spat in an open coffee bin, and walked out. "Have to make a cover for that," Appleby said.

They would never understand this man, but they could not disbelieve him, either. He did all he could, questioning hundreds of Indians in more than one tribal tongue, to find out what Mart and Amos wanted

126

to know. They were around the Agency through what was left of the winter, while Comanches, Kiowas, and Kiowa Apaches came and went. When at last Appleby told them that he thought Chief Scar had been on the Washita, but had slipped away, they did not doubt him.

"Used to be twelve main bands of Comanches, in place of only nine, like now," Appleby said, with the customary divergence from everything they had been told before. "Scar seems to run with the Wolf Brothers; a Comanche peace chief, name of Bluebonnet, heads them up."

They knew by now what a peace chief was. Among Comanches, some old man in each family group was boss of his descendants and relatives, and was a peace chief because he decided things like when to move and where to camp—anything that did not concern war. When a number of families traveled together, their peace chiefs made up the council—which meant they talked things over, sometimes. There was always one of the lot that the others came to look up to, and follow more or less—kind of tacitly, never by formal election—and this one was *the* peace chief. A war chief was just any warrior of any age who could plan a raid and get others to follow him. Comanche government was weak, loose, and informal; their ideas of acceptable behavior were enforced almost entirely by popular opinion among their kind.

"Putting two and two together, and getting five," Appleby told them, "I get the idea Bluebonnet kind of tags along with different bunches of Nawyeckies. Sometimes one bunch of 'em, sometimes another. Too

127

bad. Ain't any kind of Comanche moves around so shifty as the Nawyecky. One of the names the other Comanches has for 'em means 'Them As Never Gets Where They're Going.' Don't you believe it. What it is, they like to lie about where they're going, and start that way, then double back, and fork off. As a habit; no reason needed. I wouldn't look for 'em in Indian Territory, was I you; nor anyplace else they should rightfully be. I'd look in Texas. I kind of get the notion, more from what ain't said than what they tell me, they wintered in the Pease River breaks. So no use to look there—they'll move out, with the thaw. I believe I'd look up around the different headwaters of the Brazos, if I was doing it."

"You're talking about a hundred-mile spread, cutting crosswise—you know that, don't you? Comes to tracing out all them branches, nobody's going to do that in any one year!"

"I know. Kind of unencouraging, ain't it? But what's a man to say? Why don't you take a quick look at twenty-thirty miles of the Upper Salt? I know you just been there, or nigh to it, but that was months ago. Poke around in Canyon Blanco a little. Then cut across and try the Double Mountain Fork. And Yellow House Crick after, so long as you're up there. If you don't come on some kind of Nawyeckies, some place around, I'll put in with you!"

He was talking about the most remote, troublesome country in the length of Texas, from the standpoint of trying to find an Indian.

Amos bought two more mules and a small stock of

trade goods, which Appleby helped them to select. They took a couple of bolts of cotton cloth, one bright red and one bright blue, a lot of fancy buttons, spools of ribbon, and junk like that. No knives, because the quality of cheap ones is too easily detected, and no axe heads because of the weight. Appleby encouraged them to take half a gross of surplus stock-show ribbons that somebody had got stuck with, and shipped out to him. These were flamboyant sateen rosettes, as big as your hand, with flowing blue, red, or white ribbons. The gold lettering on the ribbons mostly identified winners in various classes of hogs. They were pretty sure the Indians would prize these highly, and wear them on their war bonnets. No notions of comedy or fraud occurred either to Appleby or the greenhorn traders in connection with the hog prizes. A newcomer might think it funny to see a grim-faced war chief wearing a First Award ribbon, Lard-Type Boar, at the temple of his headdress. But those who lived out there very early got used to the stubbornness of Indian follies, and accepted them as commonplace. They gave the savage credit for knowing what he wanted, and let it go at that.

And they took a great quantity of sheet-iron arrowheads, the most sure-fire merchandise ever taken onto the plains. These were made in New England, and cost the traders seven cents a dozen. As few as six of them would sometimes fetch a buffalo robe worth two and a half to four dollars.

So now they set out through the rains and muck of spring, practicing their sign language, and learning

129

their business as they went along. They were traveling now in a guise of peace; yet they trotted the long prairies for many weeks without seeing an Indian of any kind. Sometimes they found Indian signs—warm ashes in a shallow, bowl-like Comanche firepit, the fresh tracks of an unshod pony—but no trail that they could follow out. Searching the empty plains, it was easy to understand why you could never find a village when you came armed and in numbers to destroy it. Space itself was the Comanche's fortress. He seemed to live out his life immune to discovery, invisible beyond the rim of the world; as if he could disappear at will into the Spirit Land he described as lying beyond the sunset.

Then their luck changed, and for a while they found Comanches around every bend of every creek. Mart learned, without ever quite believing, the difference between Comanches on raid and Comanches among their own lodges. Given the security of great space, these wildest of horsemen became amiable and merry, quick with their hospitality. Generosity was the key to prestige in their communal life, just as merciless ferocity was their standard in the field. They made the change from one extreme to the other effortlessly, so that warriors returning with the loot of a ravaged frontier settlement immediately became the poorest men in their village through giving everything away.

Their trading went almost too well for their purposes. Comanche detachments that had wintered in the mountains, on the borders of Piute and Shoshone country, were rich in furs, particularly fox and otter, far more valuable now than beaver plews since the passing of the beaver hat. A general swap, big enough to clean out a village, took several days, the first of which was spent in long silences and casual conversations pretending disinterest in trade. But by the second day the Comanche minds had been made up; and though Mart and Amos raised their prices past the ridiculous, their mules were soon so loaded that they had to cache their loot precariously to keep an excuse for continuing their search.

Once the first day's silences were over, the Indians loved to talk. Caught short of facts they made up stories to suit—that was the main trouble when you wanted information from them. The searchers heard that Debbie was with Woman's Heart, of the Kiowas; with Red Hog, with Wolves-talk-to-him, with Lost Pony in the Palo Duro Canyon. They heard, in a face-blackened ritual of mourning, that she had died a full year before. Later they heard that she had been dead one month. Many Indians spoke of knowing Scar. Though they never knew just where he was, he was most often said to ride with Bluebonnet—a name sometimes translated as "the Flower." Mart and Amos both felt certain that they were closing in.

That was the summer a sub-chief of the Nocona Comanches, named Double Bird, tried to sell them a gaggle of squaws. They didn't know what he was driving at, to begin with. He signed that he had something to show them, and walked them out of his squalid ten-lodge village to the banks of the Rabbit Ear. Suddenly they were looking down at a covey of eight or nine mother-naked Indian girls, bathing in a shallow pool. The girls yipped and sat down in the water as the strangers appeared. Double Bird spoke; slowly the girls stood up again, and went on washing themselves in a self-conscious silence, lathering their short-cropped hair with bear grass.

Double Bird explained in sign language that he found himself long on women, but short of most every-thing else—especially gunpowder. How did they like these? Fat ones. Thin ones. Take and try. Amos told the chief that they didn't have his price with them, but Double Bird saw no obstacle in that. Try now. You like, go get gunpowder, lead; he would like a few dozen breech-loading rifles. Squaw wait.

Some of the young squaws were slim and pretty, and one or two were light-skinned, betraying white blood. Amos looked at Mart, and saw that he was staring with glassy eyes.

"Wake up," Amos said, jabbing him with a thumb like the butt of a lance. "You going to pick some, or not?"

"I know one thing," Mart said, "I got to give up. Either give up and go back, or give up and stay out."

"That's just the trouble. Pretty soon it's too late. Longer you're out, the more you want to go back—only you don't know how. Until you don't fit any place any more. You'll end up a squaw man—you can mark my word. You see why I tried to leave you home?"

During this time Mart had one recurrence of the terror-dream. He had supposed he would never have it any more, now that he had a pretty fair idea of how it

132

had been caused. But the dream was as strong as ever, and in no way changed. The deathly dream voices in the reddish dark were as weird and unearthly as ever, only vaguely like the yammering war cries he had heard at the Cat-tails. Amos shook him out of it, on the theory he must be choking on something, since he made no sound. But he slept no more that night.

Nevertheless, he was steadying, and changing. His grief for his lost people had forked, and now came to him in two ways, neither one as dreadful as the agony of loss he had felt at first. One way was in the form of a lot of little guilt-memories of unkindnesses that he now could never redress. Times when he had talked back to Martha, hadn't had time to read to Debbie, failed to thank Henry for fixing him up a saddle—sometimes these things came back in cruelly sharp detail.

The other way in which his grief returned was in spells of homesickness. Usually these came on him when things were uncomfortable, or went wrong; while they lasted, nothing ahead seemed to offer any hope. He had no home to which he could ever go back. No such thing was in existence any more on this earth. This homesickness, though, was gradually being replaced by a loneliness for Laurie, who could give him worries of another kind, but who at least was alive and real, however far away.

A more immediate frustration was that he could not seem to catch up with Amos in learning Comanche. He believed this to be of the utmost importance. Sign language was adequate, of course, for talking with

Indians, but they wanted to understand the remarks not meant for their ears. Maybe Mart was trying too hard. Few Comanche syllables had anything like the sound of anything in English. But Amos substituted any crude approximate, whereas Mart was trying to get it right and could not.

Then Mart accidentally bought a squaw.

He had set out to buy a fox cape she was wearing, but ran into difficulty. His stubbornness took hold, and he dickered with her whole family for hours. At one point, Amos came and stood watching him curiously, until the stare got on Mart's nerves. "What the devil you gawkin' at? Y'see somepin' green?"

"Kind of branching out, ain't you?"

"Caught holt of a good hunk o' fur—that's all!"

Amos shrugged. "Guess that's one thing to call it." He went away.

Mart fingered the fox skins again. They still looked like prime winter stuff to him. He closed the deal abruptly by paying far too much, impatient to get it over with. And next he was unable to get possession. Amos had already diamond-hitched the mule packs, and it was time to go. But the squaw would only clutch the cape around her, chattering at him. When finally she signed that she would be back at once, and ran off among the lodges, Mart noticed that an uncomfortable number of Comanches were pressed close around him, looking at him very strangely. Bewildered and furious, he gave up, and pushed through them to his horse.

By the time he was set to ride, the young squaw had unexpectedly reappeared, exactly as she had promised.

She was mounted bareback on an old crowbait that evidently belonged to her, and she carried her squaw bag, packed to bulging, before her on the withers. Behind her massed a whole phalanx of her people, their weapons in their hands. Mart sign-talked at the scowling bucks, "Big happy present from me to you," in rude gestures dangerously close to insult; and he led out, wanting only to be away from there.

The Comanche girl and her old plug fell in behind. He ignored her for a mile, but presently was forced to face it: She thought she was going with them. Brusquely he signed to her to turn her pony. She wheeled it obediently in one complete revolution, and fell in behind them again. He signaled more elaborately, unmistakably this time, telling her she must go back. She sat and stared at him.

Amos spoke sharply. "What the hell you doing?"

"Sending her home, naturally! Can't leave her tag along with—"

"What for God's sake you buy her for, if you didn't want her?"

"Buy her?"

"Mean to tell me—" Amos pulled up short and glared at him with disbelief— "You got the guts to set there and say you didn't even know it?"

"Course I didn't know it! You think I—" He didn't finish it. Comprehension of his ridiculous situation overwhelmed him, and he forgot what he had had in mind.

Amos blew up. "You God damned chunkhead!" he yelled, "When in the name of the sweet Christ you

135

going to learn to watch what you're doing?"

"Well, she's got to go back," Mart said sullenly.

"She sure as hell is not going back! Them bastards would snatch our hair off before sundown, you flout 'em like that!"

"Oh, bloody murder," Mart moaned. "I just as lief give up and—"

"Shut up! Fetch your God damned wife and come along! What we need is distance!"

Wife. This here can't be happening, Mart thought. Man with luck like mine could never last. Not even this far. Should been killed long ago. And maybe I was—that's just what's happened. This horse ain't carrying a thing but a haunted saddle. . . .

He paid no more attention to her, but when they camped by starlight she was there, watering and picketing their animals, building their fire, fetching water. They wouldn't let her cook that night, but she watched them attentively as they fried beans and antelope steak, then made coffee in the same frying pan. Mart saw she was memorizing their motions, so that she would someday be able to please them. He furtively looked her over. She was quite young, a stocky little woman, inches less than five feet tall. Her face was broad and flat, set woodenly, for the time being, in a vaguely pleasant expression. Like most Comanche women, her skin was yellowish, of a lighter color than that of the males, and her hair was cropped short, in accordance with Comanche custom. Her long, entirely unlearnable name, when Amos questioned her about it, sounded like T'sala-ta-komal-ta-nama. "Wants you to call her Mama," Amos interpreted it, and guffawed as Mart answered obscenely. Now that he was over his mad, Amos was having more fun out of this than anything Mart could remember. She tried to tell them in sign language what her name meant without much success. Apparently she was called something like "Wild-Geese-Fly-Over-in-the-Night-Going-Honk," or, maybe, "Ducks-Talk-All-Night-in-the-Sky." In the time that she was with them Mart never once pronounced her name so that she recognized it; he usually began remarks to her with "Look—" which she came to accept as her new name. Amos, of course, insisted on calling her Mrs. Pauley.

Time came to turn in, in spite of Mart's efforts to push it off as long as he could. Amos rolled into his blankets, but showed no sign of dozing; he lay there as bright-eyed as a sparrow, awaiting Mart's next embarrassment with relish. Mart ignored the little Comanche woman as he finally spread out his blankets, hoping that she would let well enough alone if he would. No such a thing. Her movements were shy, deferential, yet completely matter-of-fact, as she laid her own blankets on top of his. He had braced himself against this, and made up his mind what he must do, lest he arm Amos with a hilarious story about him, such as he would never live down. He did not want this Comanche woman in the least, and dreaded the night with her; but he was determined to sleep with her if it killed him.

He pulled his boots, and slowly, gingerly, doubled the blankets over him. The Comanche girl showed neither eagerness nor hesitation, but only an acceptance of the inevitable, as she crept under the blankets, and snuggled in beside him. She was very clean—a good deal cleaner than he was, for the matter of that. The Comanche women bathed a lot when they had any water—they would break ice to get into the river. And often steeped themselves in sage smoke, particularly following menstruation, when this kind of cleansing was a required ritual. She seemed very small, and a little scared, and he felt sorry for her. For a moment he thought the night was going to be all right. Then, faint, but living, and unmistakable, the smell of Indian. . . . It was not an offensive odor; it had to do, rather, with the smoke of their fires, with the fur and wild-tanned leather they wore, and with the buffalo, without which they did not know how to live. He had supposed he had got used to the smoky air of lodges, and outgrown the senseless fear that had haunted his childhood. But now he struck away the blankets and came to his feet.

"Need water," he said in Comanche. She got up at once, and brought him some. A choking sound came from where Amos lay; Mart had a glimpse of Amos' compressed mouth and reddening face before Amos covered his head, burying the laughter he could not repress. Anger snatched Mart, so violent that he stood shaking for a moment, unable to turn away. When he could, he walked off into the dark in his sock feet; he was afraid he would kill Amos if he stood there listening to that smothered laughter.

He had figured out an excuse to give her by the time he came back. He explained in signs that his power-medicine was mixed up with a taboo, such that he must sleep alone for a period of time that he left indefinite. She accepted this tale readily; it was the kind of thing that would seem logical, and reasonable, to her. He thought she looked mildly relieved.

At their noon stop on the third day, Amos believed they had come far enough to be safe. "You can get rid of her, now, if you want."

"How?"

"You can knock her on the head, can't you? Though, now I think of it, I never seen you show much stomick for anything as practical as that."

Mart looked at him a moment. He decided to assume Amos was fooling, and let it pass without answer. Amos doubled a lead rope, weighted it with a couple of big knots, and tested it with a whistling snap. "Show you another way," he said; and started toward the Comanche girl.

Suddenly Mart was standing in front of him. "Put that thing down before I take it away from you!"

Amos stared. "What the hell's got into you now?"

"It's my fault she's here—not hers. She's done all she possibly could to try to be nice, and make herself helpful, and wanted. I never seen no critter try harder to do right. You want to rough something—I'm in reach, ain't I?"

Amos angered. "I ought to wrap this here around your gullet!"

"Go ahead. But when you pick yourself up, you better be running!"

Amos walked away.

The Comanche girl was with them eleven days,

waiting on them, doing their work, watching them to foresee their needs. At the end of the eleventh day, in the twilight, the girl went after water, and did not come back. They found their bucket grounded in the shallows of the creek, and traced out the sign to discover what they were up against. A single Indian had crossed to her through the water; his buffalo pony had stood in the damp sand while the girl mounted behind the rider. The Indian had been the girl's lover most likely. They were glad to have him take her, but it made their scalps crawl to consider that he must have followed them, without their at all suspecting it, for all that time.

Though he was relieved to be rid of her, Mart found that he missed her, and was annoyed with himself for missing her, for many weeks. After a while he could not remember what had made him leap up, the night she had crept into the blankets with him; he regretted it, and thought of himself as a fool. They never saw her again. Years later Mart thought he heard of her, but he could not be sure. A Comanche woman who died a captive had told the soldiers her name was "Look." Mart felt a strange twinge, as of remorse without reason for remorse, as he remembered how a sad-eyed little Comanche woman had once got that name.

He had realized she had been trying to teach him Comanche, though without letting him notice it any more than she could help. When she talked to him in sign language she pronounced the words that went with the signs, but softly, so that he could ignore the spoken speech, if he wished. She responded to his questions with a spark of hidden eagerness, and with the least encouragement told hour-long stories of wars and heroes, miracles and sorceries, in this way. He wouldn't have supposed he could learn anything in so short a time after beating his skull against the stubborn language for so long. But actually it was a turning point; the weird compounds of Comanche speech began to break apart for him at last. When next he sat among Comanches he became aware that he was able to follow almost everything they said. Amos presently began to turn to him for translations; and before the end of that summer, he was interpreter for them both.

Understanding the Comanches better, Mart began to pick up news, or at least rumors filtered through Indian minds, of what was happening upon the frontier. Most of the Comanches didn't care whether the white men understood their tales of misdeeds or not. The Wild Tribes had as yet been given little reason to think in terms of reprisals. Returning raiders boasted openly of the bloodiest things they had done.

There were enough to tell. Tabananica, having again challenged the cavalry without obtaining satisfaction, crept upon Fort Sill in the night, and got off with twenty head of horses and mules out of the Agency corral. White Horse, of the Kiowas, not to be outdone, took more than seventy head from the temporary stake-and-rider corral at the Fort itself. Kicking Bird, bidding to regain prestige lost in days of peace, went into Texas with a hundred warriors, fought a cavalry troop, and whipped it, himself killing the first trooper with his short lance. Wolf-Lying-Down walked into Sill in all insolence, and sold the Quaker agent a little red-haired boy for a hundred dollars. Fast Bear's young men got similar prices for six children, and the mothers of some of them, taken in a murderous Texas raid. The captives could testify to the wholesale murder of their men, yet saw the killers pick up their money and ride free. The Peace Policy was taking effect with a vengeance—though not quite in the way intended.

Often and often, as that summer grew old, the searchers believed they were close to Debbie; but Blue-bonnet somehow still eluded them, and War Chief Scar seemed a fading ghost. They saw reason to hope, though, in another way. The Comanches held the Peace Policy in contempt, but now leaned on it boldly, since it had proved able to bear their weight. Surely, surely all of them would come in this time, when winter clamped down, to enjoy sanctuary and government rations in the shadow of Fort Sill. For the first time in history, perhaps, the far-scattered bands would be gathered in a single area—and fixed there, too, long enough for you to sort through them all.

So this year they made no plans to go home. As the great buffalo herds turned back from their summer pastures in the lands of the Sioux and the Blackfeet, drifting down-country before the sharpening northers, the two pointed their horses toward Fort Sill. Soon they fell into the trail of a small village—twenty-five or thirty lodges—obviously going to the same place that they were. They followed the double pole scratches of the many travois lazily, for though they were many weeks away from Fort Sill, they were in no great hurry to get there. It took time for the Indians to accumulate around the Agency, and the kind they were looking for came late. Some would not appear until they felt the pinch of the Starving Moons—if they came at all.

Almost at once the fire pits they rode over, and the short, squarish shape of dim moccasin tracks, told them they were following Comanches. A little later, coming to a place where the tracks showed better detail, they were able to narrow that down. Most Comanches wore trailing heel fringes that left faint, long marks in the dust. But one bunch of the Kotsetakas—the so-called Upriver branch—sewed weasel tails to the heels of their moccasins, leaving broader and even fainter marks. That was what they had here, and it interested them, for they had seen no such village in the fourteen months that they had searched.

But still they didn't realize what they were following, until they came upon a lone-hunting Osage, a long way from the range where he belonged. This Indian had an evil face, and seemingly no fear at all. He rode up to them boldly, and as he demanded tobacco they could see him estimating the readiness of their weapons, no doubt wondering whether he could do the two of them in before they could shoot him. Evidently he decided this to be impractical. In place of tobacco he settled for a handful of salt, and a red stock-prize ribbon placing him second in the class for Aged Sows. He repaid them with a cogent and hard-hitting piece of information, conveyed in crisp sign language, since he spoke no Comanche.

The village they were following, he said, was two sleeps ahead. Twenty-four lodges; six hundred horses and mules; forty-six battle-rated warriors. Tribe, Kotsetaka Comanche, of the Upriver Band (which they knew, so that the Osage's statements were given a color of truth); Peace Chief, Bluebonnet; War Chiefs, Gold Concho, Scar; also Stone Wold, Pacing Bear; others.

Amos' signs were steady, casual, as he asked if the village had white captives. The Osage said there were four. One woman, two little girls. One little boy. And two Mexican boys, he added as an afterthought. As for himself, he volunteered, he was entirely alone, and rode in peace. He walked the White Man's Way, and had never robbed anybody in his life.

He rode off abruptly after that, without ceremony; and the two riders went into council. The temptation was to ride hard, stopping for nothing, until they overtook the village. But that was not the sensible way. They would be far better off with troops close at hand, however tied-down they might be. And the gentle Quakers were the logical ones to intercede for the child's release, for they could handle it with less risk of a flare-up that might result in hurt to the child herself. No harm in closing the interval, though. They could just as well pick up a day and a half, and follow the Indians a few hours back to cut down chance of losing them in a mix with other Indians, or even a total change of plans. Anyway, they had to put distance between themselves and that Osage, whose last remarks had convinced both of them that he was a scout from a war party, and would ambush them if they let him.

They made a pretense of going into camp, but set off

again in the first starlight, and rode all night. At sunrise they rested four hours for the benefit of their livestock, then made a wide cast, picked up the trail of the village again, and went on. The weather was looking very ugly. Brutal winds screamed across the prairie, and at midday a blue-black wall was beginning to rise, obscuring the northern sky.

Suddenly the broad trail they were following turned south at a right angle, as if broken square in two by the increasing weight of the wind.

"Are they onto us?" Mart asked; then repeated it in a yell, for the wind so snatched his words away that he couldn't hear them himself.

"I don't think that's it," Amos shouted back. "What they got to fear from us?"

"Well, something turned 'em awful short!"

"They know something! That's for damn sure!"

Mart considered the possibility that the Osages had thrown in with the Cheyennes and Arapahoes, and gone to war in great force. Forty-six warriors could only put their village on the run, and try to get it out of the path of that kind of a combination. He wanted to ask Amos what he thought about this, but speech was becoming so difficult that he let it go. And he was already beginning to suspect something else. This time the apprehension with which he watched developments was a reasoned one, with no childhood ghosts about it. The sky and the wind were starting to tell them that a deadly danger might be coming down on them, of a kind they had no means to withstand.

By mid-afternoon they knew. Swinging low to look

closely at the trail they followed, they saw that it was now the trail of a village moving at a smart lope, almost a dead run. The sky above them had blackened, and was filled with a deep-toned wailing. The power of the wind made the prairie seem more vast, so that they were turned to crawling specks on the face of a shelterless world. Amos leaned close to shout in Mart's ear. "They seen it coming! They've run for the Wichita breaks—that's what they done!"

"We'll never make it by dark! We got to hole up shorter than that!"

Amos tied his hat down hard over his ears with his wool muffler. Mart's muffler snapped itself and struggled to get away, like a fear-crazed thing, as he tried to do the same. He saw Amos twisting in the saddle to look all ways, his eyes squeezed tight against the sear of the wind. He looked like a man hunting desperately for a way of escape, but actually he was looking for their pack mules. Horses drift before a storm, but mules head into it, and keep their hair. For some time their pack animals had shown a tendency to swivel into the wind, then come on again, trying to stay with the ridden horses. They were far back now, small dark marks in the unnatural dusk. Amos mouthed unheard curses. He turned his horse, whipping hard, and forced it back the way they had come.

Mart tried to follow, but the Fort Worth stud reared and fought, all but going over on him. He spurred deep, and as the stud came down, reined high and short with all his strength. "Red, you son-of-a-bitch—" Both man and horse might very easily die out here if

146

the stallion began having his way. The great neck had no more bend to it than a log. And now the stud got his head down, and went into his hard, skull-jarring buck.

Far back, Amos passed the first mule he came to, and the second. When he turned downwind, it was their commissary mule, the one with their grub in his packs, that he dragged along by a death-grip on its cheek strap. The Fort Worth stud was standing immovable in his sull as Amos got back. Both Mart and the stud horse were blowing hard, and looked beat out. Mart's nose had started to bleed, and a bright trickle had frozen on his upper lip.

"We got to run for it!" Amos yelled at him. "For God's sake, get a rope on this!"

With his tail to the wind, the stud went back to work, grudgingly answering the rein. Mart got a lead rope on the mule, to the halter first, then back to a standing loop around the neck, and through the halter again. Once the lead rope was snubbed to the stud's saddle horn the mule came along, sometimes sitting down, sometimes at a sort of bounding trot, but with them just the same.

It was not yet four o'clock, but night was already closing; or rather a blackness deeper than any natural night seemed to be lowering from above, pressing downward implacably to blot out the prairie. For a time a band of yellow sky showed upon the southern horizon, but this narrowed, then disappeared, pushed below the edge of the world by the darkness. Amos pointed to a dark scratch near the horizon, hardly more

147

visible than a bit of thread laid flat. You couldn't tell just what it was, or how far away; in that treacherous and failing light you couldn't be sure whether you were seeing half a mile or fifteen. The dark mark on the land had better be willows, footed in the gulch of a creek—or at least in a dry run-off gully. If it was nothing but a patch of buckbrush, their chances were going to be very poor. They angled toward it, putting their horses into a high lope.

Now came the first of the snow, a thin lacing of ice needles, heard and felt before they could be seen. The ice particles were traveling horizontally, parallel to the ground, with an enormous velocity. They made a sharp whispering against leather, drove deep into cloth, and filled the air with hissing. This thin bombardment swiftly increased, coming in puffs and clouds, then in a rushing stream. And at the same time the wind increased; they would not have supposed a harder blow to be possible, but it was. It tore at them, snatching their breaths from their mouths, and its gusts buffeted their backs as solidly as thrown sacks of grain. The galloping horses sat back against the power of the wind as into breechings, yet were made to yaw and stumble as they ran. The long hair of their tails whipped their flanks, and wisps of it were snatched away.

In the last moments before they were blinded by the snow and the dark, Mart got a brief glimpse of Amos' face. It was a bloodless gray-green, and didn't look like Amos' face. Some element of force and strength had gone out of it. Most of the time Amos' face had a wooden look, seemingly without expression, but this

148

was an illusion. Actually the muscles were habitually set in a grim confidence, an almost built-in certainty, that now was gone. They pushed their horses closer together, leaning them toward each other so that they continually bumped knees. It was the only way they could stay together, sightless and deafened in the howling chaos.

They rode for a long time, beaten downwind like driven leaves. They gave no thought to direction; the storm itself was taking care of that. It was only when the winded horses began to falter that Mart believed they had gone past whatever they had seen. His saddle was slipping back, dragged toward the stud's kidneys by the resistance of the mule. He fumbled at the latigo tie, to draw up the cinch, but found his hands so stiff with cold he was afraid to loosen it, lest he slip his grip, and lose mule, saddle, horse, and himself, all in one dump. This thing will end soon, he was thinking. This rig isn't liable to stay together long. Nor the horses last, if it does. Nor us either, if it comes to that. . . . His windpipe was raw; crackles of ice were forming up his nose. And his feet were becoming numb. They had thrown away their worn-out buffalo boots last spring, and had made no more, because of their expectations of wintering snugly at Fort Sill.

No sense to spook it, he told himself, as breathing came hard. Nothing more a man can do. We'll fall into something directly. Or else we won't. What the horses can't do for us won't get done. . . .

Fall into it was what they did. They came full stride, without warning, upon a drop of unknown depth.

149

Seemingly they struck it at a slant, for Amos went over first. His horse dropped a shoulder as the ground fell from under, then was gone. Even in the roar of the storm, Mart heard the crack of the pony's broken neck. He pulled hard, and in the same split second tried first to sheer off, and next to turn the stud's head to the drop—neither with the least effect, for the rim crumbled, and they plunged.

Not that the drop was much. The gully was no more than twelve-feet deep, a scarcely noticeable step down, had either horse or man been able to see. The stud horse twisted like a cat, got his legs under him, and went hard to his knees. The mule came piling down on top of the whole thing, with an impact of enormous weight, and a great thrashing of legs, then floundered clear. And how that was done without important damage Mart never knew.

He got their two remaining animals under control, and groped for Amos. They hung onto each other, blind in the darkness and the snow, leading the stud and the mule up the gully in search of better shelter. Within a few yards they blundered upon a good-sized willow, newly downed by the wind; and from that moment they knew they were going to come through. They knew it, but they had a hard time remembering it, in the weary time before they got out of there. They were pinned in that gully more than sixty hours.

In some ways the first night was the worst. The air was dense with the dry snow, but the wind, rushing with hurricane force down a thousand miles of prairie, would not let the snow settle, or drift, even in the crevice where they had taken refuge. No fire was possible. The wind so cycloned between the walls of the gulch that the wood they lighted in the shelter of their coats immediately vanished in a shatter of white sparks. Mart chopped a tub-sized cave into the frozen earth at the side, but the fire couldn't last there, either. Their canteens were frozen solid, and neither dry cornmeal nor their iron-hard jerky would go down without water. They improvised parkas and foot wrappings out of the few furs they had happened to stuff into the commissary pack, and stamped their feet all night long.

Sometime during that night the Fort Worth stud broke loose, and went with the storm. In the howling of the blizzard they didn't even hear him go.

During the next day the snow began rolling in billows across the prairie, and their gully filled. They were better off by then. They had got foot wrappings on their mule, lest his hoofs freeze off as he stood, and had fed him on gatherings of willow twigs. With pack sheet and braced branches they improved their bivouac under the downed willow, so that as the snow covered them they had a place in which a fire would burn at last. They melted snow and stewed horse meat, and took turns staying awake to keep each other from sleeping too long. The interminable periods in which they lay buried alive were broken by sorties after wood, or willow twigs, or to rub the legs of the mule.

But the third night was in some ways the worst of all. They had made snowshoes of willow hoops and frozen horsehide, tied with thongs warmed at the fire; but Mart no longer believed they would ever use them. He

151

had been beaten against the frozen ground by that murderous uproar for too long; he could not hear the imperceptible change in the roar of the churning sky as the blizzard began to die. This nightmare had gone on forever, and he accepted that it would always go on, until death brought the only possible peace.

He lay stiffened and inert in their pocket under the snow, moving sluggishly once an hour, by habit, to prevent Amos from sleeping himself to death. He was trying to imagine what it would be like to be dead. They were so near it, in this refuge so like a grave, he no longer felt that death could make any unwelcome difference. Their bodies would never be found, of course, nor properly laid away. Come thaw, the crows would pick their bones clean. Presently the freshets would carry their skeletons tumbling down the gulch, breaking them up, strewing them piecemeal until they hung in the driftwood, a thighbone here, a rib there, a skull full of gravel half buried in the drying streambed.

People who knew them would probably figure out they had died in the blizzard, though no one would know just where. Mart Pauley? Lost last year in the blizzard . . . Mart Pauley's been dead four years . . . ten years . . . forty years. No—not even his name would be in existence in anybody's mind, anywhere, as long as that.

Amos brought him out of that in a weird way. Mart was in a doze that was dangerously near a coma, when he became aware that Amos was singing—if you could call it that. More of a groaning, in long-held, hoarse tones, from deep in the galled throat. Mart lifted his

head and listened, wondering, with a desolation near
indifference, if Amos had gone crazy, or into a
delirium. As he came wider awake he recognized
Comanche words. The eery sound was a chant.

The sun will pour life on the earth forever . . .
 (I rode my horse till it died.)
The earth will send up new grass forever . . .
 (I thrust with my lance while I bled.)
The stars will walk in the sky forever . . .
 (Leave my pony's bones on my grave.)

It was a Comanche death song. The members of
some warrior society—the Snow Wolf Brotherhood?—
were supposed to sing it as they died.

"God damn it, you stop that!" Mart shouted, and
beat at Amos with numbed hands.

Amos was not in delirium. He sat up grumpily, and
began testing his creaky joints. He grunted, "No ear for
music, huh?"

Suddenly Mart realized that the world beyond their
prison was silent. He floundered out through the great
depth of snow. The sky was gray, but the surface of the
snow itself almost blinded him with its glare. And from
horizon to horizon, nothing on the white earth moved.
The mule stood in a sort of well it had tromped for
itself, six feet deep in the snow. It had chewed the bark
off every piece of wood in reach, but its hoofs were all
right. Mart dragged Amos out, and they took a look at
each other.

Their lips were blackened and cracked, and their

eyes bloodshot. Amos' beard had frost in it now that was going to stay there as long as he lived. But they were able-bodied, and they were free, and had a mule between them.

All they had to do now was to get through a hundred and ten miles of snow to Fort Sill; and they could figure they had put the blizzard behind them.

17

They took so many weeks to make Fort Sill that they were sure Bluebonnet's village would be there ahead of them; but it was not. They were in weakened, beat-down shape, and they knew it. They slept much, and ate all the time. When they went among the Indians they moved slowly, in short hauls, with long rests between. Hard for them to believe that only a year and a half had passed in their search for Debbie. Many thought they had already made a long, hard, incredibly faithful search. But in terms of what they had got done, it wasn't anything, yet.

Living things on the prairie had been punished very hard. The buffalo came through well, even the youngest calves; only the oldest buffalo were winter killed. Things that lived down holes, like badgers, prairie dogs, and foxes, should have been safe. Actually, animals of this habit were noticeably scarcer for the next few years, so perhaps many froze deep in the ground as they slept. The range cattle were hit very hard, and those of improved breeding stood it the worst. Where fences had come into use, whole herds piled up, and died where they stood. Hundreds had their feet frozen off, and were seen walking around on the stumps for weeks before the last of them were dead.

After the blizzard, a period of melt and freeze put an iron crust on the deep snow. A lot of the cattle that had survived the storm itself now starved, unable to paw down to the feed with their cloven hoofs. Horses did considerably better, for their hoofs could smash the crust. But even these were fewer for a long time, so many were strewn bones upon the prairie before spring.

Yet all this devastation had come unseasonably early. After the first of the year the winter turned mild, as if it had shot its wad. Once travel was practicable, more Indians streamed into the sanctuary of Fort Sill than ever before. Their deceptively rugged tepees, cunningly placed, and anchored by crossed stakes driven five feet into the ground, had stood without a single reported loss; and the villages seemed to have plenty of pemmican to feed them until spring. Perhaps they had been awed by the power of the warring wind spirits, so that they felt their own medicine to be at a low ebb.

They were anything but awed, however, by the soldiers, whom the Peace Policy tied down in helplessness, or by the Society of Friends, whose gentle pacifism the Wild Tribes held in contempt, even while they sheltered behind it. Appears-in-the-Sky, Medicine Chief of the Kiowas, who claimed a spirit owl as his familiar, in January moved out a short distance through the snow to murder four Negro teamsters. Two cowboys were killed at Sill's beef corral, barely

155

half a mile from the fort, and a night wrangler was murdered and scalped closer than that. Half a dozen Queherenna, or Antelope Comanches—the military were calling them Quohadas—stole seventy mules out of Fort Sill's new stone corral, and complacently camped twenty miles away, just as safe as upon their mothers' backboards.

Both Kiowas and Comanches were convinced now of the integrity of the Quakers. They pushed into the Quakers' houses, yanked buttons off the Agent's clothes; helped themselves to anything that caught the eye, then stoned the windows as they left. Those Quakers with families were ordered to safety, but few obeyed. Resolute in their faith, they stood implacably between their Indian charges and the troops. It was going to be a hard, rough, chancy year down below in Texas.

Meanwhile Mart and Amos searched and waited, and still Bluebonnet did not come in. As spring came on they bought new horses and mules, replenished their packs and once more went looking for Indians who forever marched and shuffled themselves in the far lost wastes of their range.

18

Most of that second trading summer was like the first. Being able to understand what the Indians said among themselves had proved of very little use, so far as their search was concerned.

They did hear more, though, of what was happening back home, upon the frontier their wanderings had put so far behind. Mart, particularly, listened sharply for some clue as to whether the Mathisons still held, but heard nothing he could pin down.

In Texas the outlying settlers were going through the most dreadful year in memory. At least fourteen people were dead, and nine children captive, before the middle of May. Only a stubbornness amounting to desperation could explain why any of the pioneers held on. Bloody narratives were to be heard in every Comanche camp the searchers found. A party of surveyors were killed upon the Red River, and their bodies left to spoil in a drying pool. The corpses of three men, a woman and a child were reduced to char in a burning ranch house, cheating the raiders of the scalps. Oliver Loving's foreman was killed beside his own corral. By early summer, Wolf-Lying-Down had stolen horses within sight of San Antonio; and Kiowas under Big Bow, crossing into Mexico near Laredo, had killed seventeen vaqueros, and got back across Texas with a hundred and fifty horses and a number of Mexican children.

General Sherman, who habitually took Texan complaints with a grain of salt, finally had a look for himself. He appeared in Texas along about the middle of the summer, with an escort of only fifteen troopers— and at once nearly added himself to a massacre. Near Cox Mountain a raiding party of a hundred and fifty Comanches and Kiowas destroyed a wagon train, killing seven, some by torture. Unfortunately, for it

157

would have been the highlight of his trip, General Sherman missed riding into this event by about an hour and a half. Proceeding to Fort Sill, Sherman supervised the arrest of Satanta, Satank, and Big Tree, showing a cool personal courage, hardly distinguishable from indifference, in the face of immediate mortal danger. He presented the three war chiefs in handcuffs to the State of Texas; and after went away again.

All this, the two riders recognized, was building up to such a deadly, all-annihilating showdown as would be their finish, if they couldn't get their job done first. But for the present they found the Comanches in high and celebrative mood, unable to imagine the whirlwind that was to come. The warriors were arrogant, boastful, full of the high-and-mighty. Yet, luckily, they remained patronizingly tolerant, for the time, of the white men who dared come among them in their own far fastnesses.

During this time the terror-dream of the red night and the unearthly voices came to Mart only once, and he saw no copy of the unexplained death tree at all. Yet the attitudes of the Indians toward such things were beginning to influence him, so that he more than half believed they carried a valid prophecy. The Comanches were supposed to be the most literal-minded of all tribes. There are Indians who live in a poetic world, half of the spirit, but the Comanches were a tough-minded, practical people, who laughed at the religious ceremonies of other tribes as crazy-Indian foolishness. They had no official medicine men, no pantheon of named gods, no ordered theology. Yet they lived very

158

close to the objects of the earth around them, and sensed in rocks, and winds, and rivers, spirits as living as their own. They saw themselves as of one piece with a world in which nothing was without a spirit.

In this atmosphere, almost every Comanche had a special spirit medicine that had come to him in a dream, usually the gift of some wild animal, such as an otter, a buffalo, or a wolf—never a dog or horse. By the time a Comanche was old, he was either a medicine man, believed to know specific magics against certain ills or disasters, or a black-magic sorcerer, feared because he could maim or kill from far away.

You could never learn to understand an Indian's way of thinking, or guess what he was about to think next. If you saw an Indian looking at the sky, you might know why you would be looking at the sky in his place—and be sure the Indian had some different reason. Yet sometimes they ran into a Comanche, usually an old one, who knew something there was no possible way for him to know.

"You speak Nemenna very well," an old Nocona said to Mart once. (The names of the bands were turning themselves over again; in a single year the name "Nawyecky" had fallen into almost total disuse.) Mart supposed the old man had heard of him, for he had not opened his mouth. He pretended not to understand, hoping to discredit a rumor of that kind. But the old Comanche went on, smiling at Mart's effort to dissimulate. "Sometimes you come upon a spirit in the form of a dead tree," he said. "It is blackened; it looks like a withered corpse, struggling to free itself from the earth."

159

Mart stared, startled into acknowledgment that he understood the old man's speech. At this the Comanche grinned derisively, but went on in grave tones. "You do not fear death very much, I think. Last year, maybe; not this year any more. But you will do well to fear the evil tree. Death is a kind and happy thing beside the nameless things beyond the tree."

He sat back. "I tell you this as a friend," he finished. "Not because I expect any kind of gift. I wish you well, and nothing more. I want no gift at all." Which of course meant that he did.

By middle fall the mood of the Comanches had begun to change. Raids were lacing into Texas at an unprecedented pace; Colorado was heavily scourged, and Kansas hurt to the very borders of Nebraska. Almost every village they came to was waiting in brooding quiet for a great war party to return, if it were not whooping up a scalp dance to celebrate a victory, or a glory dance for sending a party out. But now both Texas and the United States Army were fighting back. The Texas Rangers were in the saddle again, losing men in every skirmish, but making the Indians pay three and four lives for one. The Fort Sill garrison was still immobilized, but Fort Richardson, down on the West Fork of the Trinity, was beyond the authority of the Friends. From Richardson rode Colonel Mackenzie with a regiment and a half of yellowlegs; his forced marches drove deep into the land of the Quohadas. Shaking Hand's Kotsetakas got out of his way, and the great Bull Bear of the Antelopes, with such war chiefs under him as Black Horse, Wolf Tail, Little

Crow, and the brilliant young Quanah, threatened briefly in force but drew back.

Old chiefs were losing favorite sons, and you could see black death behind their eyes when they looked at white men. Warrior societies who scalp-danced for victory after victory counted their strength, and found that in the harvest season of their greatest success they were becoming few. The searchers learned to scout a village carefully, to see if it were in mourning for a raiding party decimated or destroyed, before they took a chance on going in. Over and over, white captives were murdered by torture in revenge for losses sustained upon the savage raids. Mart and Amos rode harder, longer, turning hollow-eyed and gaunted. Their time was running out, and very fast; already they might be too late.

Yet their goal, while it still eluded them, seemed always just ahead. They never had come to any point where either one of them could have brought himself to turn back, from the first day their quest had begun.

Then, as the snow came again, they struck the trail they had hunted for so long. It was that of twenty-two lodges led by Bluebonnet himself, and he had a captive white girl in his village, beyond any reasonable doubt. The horse-trampled parallel lines left by the many travois led south and eastward, crossing the high ground between the Beaver and the Canadian; they followed it fast and easily.

"Tomorrow," Amos said once more as they rode. The captive girl had been described to them as smallish, with yellow hair and light eyes. As they went into camp at twilight he said it again, and now for the last time: "Tomorrow. . . ."

19

Mart Pauley woke abruptly, with no notion of what had roused him. Amos breathed regularly beside him. Each slept rolled in his own blankets, but they shared the wagon sheet into which they folded themselves, heads and all, for shelter from the weather. The cold air stiffened the slight moisture in Mart's nostrils as he stuck his head out. Only the lightest of winds whispered across the surface of the snow. The embers of their fire pulsed faintly in the moving air, and by these he judged the time to be after midnight.

At first he heard nothing; but as he held his breath a trick of the wind brought again the sound that must have come to him in his sleep, so faint, so far off, it might have been a whispering of frost in his own ears.

He closed his grip slowly on Amos' arm until he waked. "Whazzamatter?"

"I swear I heard fighting," Mart said, "a long way off."

"Leave the best man win." Amos settled himself to go back to sleep.

"I mean big fighting—an Indian fight. . . . There! . . . Ain't that a bugle way off down the river?"

A few small flakes of snow touched their faces, but the night turned soundless again as soon as Amos sat up. "I don't hear nothing."

Neither did Mart any more. "It's snowing again."

"That's all right. We'll come up with Bluebonnet. Snow can never hide him from us now! It'll only pin him down for us!"

Mart lay awake for a while, listening hard; but no more sound found its way through the increasing snowfall.

Long before daylight he stewed up a frying-pan breakfast of shredded buffalo jerky, and fed the horses. "Today," Amos said, as they settled, joint-stiff, into their icy saddles. It was the first time they had ever said that after all the many, many times they had said "Tomorrow." Yet the word came gruffly, without exultation. The day was cold, and the snow still fell, as they pushed on through darkness toward a dull dawn.

By mid-morning they reached the Canadian, and forded its unfrozen shallows. They turned downstream, and at noon found Bluebonnet's village—or the place it had seen its last of earth.

They came to the dead horses first. In a great bend of the river, scattered over a mile of open ground, lay nearly a hundred head of buffalo ponies, their lips drawing back from their long teeth as they froze. The snow had stopped, but not before it had sifted over the horses, and the blood, and the fresh tracks that must have been made in the first hours of the dawn. No study of sign was needed, however; what had happened here was plain. The cavalry had learned long ago that it couldn't hold Comanche ponies.

Beyond the shoulder of a ridge they came upon the

site of the village itself. A smudge, and a heavy stench of burning buffalo hair, still rose from the wreckage of twenty-two lodges. A few more dead horses were scattered here, some of them the heavier carcasses of cavalry mounts. But here, too, the snow had covered the blood, and the story of the fight, and all the strewn trash that clutters a field of battle. There were no bodies. The soldiers had withdrawn early enough so that the Comanche survivors had been able to return for their dead, and be gone, before the snow stopped.

Mart and Amos rode slowly across the scene of massacre. Nothing meaningful to their purpose was left in the burnt-out remains of the lodges. They could make out that the cavalry had ridden off down the Canadian, and that was about all.

"We don't know yet," Mart said.

"No," Amos agreed. He spoke without expression, allowing himself neither discouragement nor hope. "But we know where the answer is to be found."

It was not too far away. They came upon the bivouacked cavalry a scant eight miles below.

20

Daylight still held as Mart and Amos approached the cavalry camp, but it was getting dark by the time they were all the way in. The troopers on duty were red-eyed, but with a harsh edge on their manners, after the night they had spent. An outlying vedette passed them into a dismounted sentry, who called the corporal of the guard, who delivered them to the sergeant of the guard, who questioned them with more length than point before digging up a second lieutenant who was Officer of the Day. The lieutenant also questioned them, though more briefly. He left them standing outside a supply tent for some time, while he explained them to a Major Kinsman, Adjutant.

The major stuck a shaggy head out between the tent flaps, looked them over with the blank stare of fatigue, and spat tobacco juice into the snow.

"My name," Amos began again, patiently, "is—"

"Huntin' captives, huh?" The shaggy head was followed into the open by a huge frame in a tightly buttoned uniform. "Let's see if we got any you know." Major Kinsman led the way, not to another tent, but to the wagon park. They followed him as he climbed into the wagonbed of a covered ambulance.

Under a wagon sheet, which the adjutant drew back, several bodies lay straight and neatly aligned, ice-rigid in the cold. In the thickening dark inside the ambulance, Mart could see little more than that they were there, and that one or two seemed to be children.

"Have a light here in a minute," Major Kinsman said. "Orderly's filling a lantern."

Mart Pauley could hear Amos' heavy breathing, but not his own; he did not seem able to breathe in here at all. A dreadful conviction came over him, increasing as they waited, that they had come to the end of their search. It seemed a long time before a lighted lantern was thrust inside.

The bodies were those of two women and two little boys. The older of the women was in rags, but the younger and smaller one wore clean clothes that had certainly belonged to her, and shoes that were scuffed but not much worn. She appeared to have been about twenty, and was quite beautiful in a carved-snow sort of way. The little boys were perhaps three and seven.

"Both women shot in the back of the head," Major Kinsman said, objectively. "Flash-burn range. Light charge of powder, as you see. The little boys got their skulls cracked. We think this woman here is one taken from a Santa Fe stagecoach not many days back. . . . Know any of them?"

"Never saw them before," Amos said.

Major Kinsman looked at Mart for a separate reply, and Mart shook his head.

They went back to the supply tent, and the adjutant took them inside. The commanding officer was there, sorting through a great mass of loot with the aid of two sergeants and a company clerk. The adjutant identified his superior as Colonel Russell M. Hannon. They had heard of him, but never seen him before; he hadn't been out here very long. Just now he looked tired, but in high spirits.

"Too bad there wasn't more of 'em," Colonel Hannon said. "That's the only disappointing thing. We were following the river, not their trail. Wichita scouts brought word there must be a million of 'em. What with the snow, and the night march, an immediate attack was the only course permissible."

He said his troops had killed thirty-eight hostiles,

166

with the loss of two men. Comanches, at that. A ratio of nineteen to one, as compared to Colonel Custer's ratio of fourteen to one against Black Kettle at the Battle of the Washita. "Not a bad little victory. Not bad at all."

Mart saw Amos stir, and worried for a moment. But Amos held his tongue.

"Four hundred ninety-two ponies," said Hannon. "Had to shoot 'em, of course. Wild as antelope—no way to hold onto them. Four captives recovered. Unfortunately, the hostiles murdered them, as we developed the village. Now, if some of this junk will only show *what* Comanches we defeated, we'll be in fair shape to write a report. Those Wichita scouts know nothing whatever about anything; most ignorant savages on earth. However—"

"What you had there," said Amos wearily, "was Chief Bluebonnet, with what's left of the Wolf Brothers, along with a few Nawyecky. Or maybe you call 'em Noconas."

"Get this down," the colonel told the clerk.

It was going to take a long time to find out just who had fought and died at the riverbend—and who had got away into the night and the snow, and so still lived, somewhere upon the winter plain. Even allowing for the great number of dead and dying the Comanches had carried away uncounted, somewhere between a third and a half of Bluebonnet's people must have escaped.

They were glad to help sort through the wagonload of stuff hastily snatched up in the gloom of the dawn before the lodges were set on fire. Some of the pouches, quivers, and squill breastplates were decorated with symbols Mart or Amos could connect with Indian names; they found insignia belonging to Stone Wolf, Curly Horn, Pacing Bear, and Hears-the-Wind-Talk. The patterns they didn't know they tried to memorize, in hopes of seeing them again someday.

Especially valued by Colonel Harmon, as exonerating his attack in the dark, was certain stuff that had to be the loot from raided homesteads: a worn sewing basket, an embroidered pillow cover, a home-carved wooden spoon. Hard to see what the Comanches would want with a store-bought paper lamp shade, a wooden seat for a chamber pot, or an album of pressed flowers. But if someone recognized these poor lost things someday, they would become evidence connecting the massacred Comanches with particular crimes. One incriminating bit was a mail pouch known to have been carried by a murdered express rider. The contents were only half rifled; some Comanche had been taking his time about opening all the letters—no man would ever know what for.

But the thing Mart found that hit him hard, and started his search all over again, was in a little heap of jewelry—Indian stuff mostly: Carved amulets, Mexican and Navajo silver work, sometimes set with turquoise; but with a sprinkling of pathetic imitation things, such as frontiersmen could afford to buy for their women. Only thing of interest, at first sight, seemed to be a severed finger wearing a ring which would not pull off. Mart cynically supposed that any stuff of cash value had stayed with the troopers who collected it.

Then Mart found Debbie's locket.

It was the cheapest kind of a gilt-washed metal heart on a broken chain. Mart himself had given it to Debbie on the Christmas when she was three. It wasn't even a real locket, for it didn't open, and had embarrassed him by making a green spot on her throat every time she wore it. But Debbie had hung on to it. On the back it said "Debbie from M," painfully scratched with the point of his knife.

Both officers showed vigorous disinterest as Mart pressed for the circumstances in which the locket had been found. These were professionals, and recognized the question as of the sort leading to full-dress investigations, and other chancy outcomes, if allowed to develop. But Amos came to Mart's support, and presently they found the answer simply by walking down the mess line with the locket in hand.

The locket had been taken from the body of a very old squaw found in the river along with an ancient buck. No, damn it, the colonel explained, of course they had not meant to kill women and children, and watch your damn tongue. All you could see was a bunch of shapeless figures firing on you—nothing to do but cut them down, and save questions for later. But one of the sergeants remembered how these two bodies had come there. The squaw, recognizable in hindsight as the fatter one, had tried to escape through the river on a pony, and got sabered down. The old man had rushed in trying to save the squaw, and got sabered in turn. Nothing was in hand to tell who these people were.

Colonel Hannon saw to it that the locket was properly tagged and returned to the collection as evidence of a solved child stealing. Restitution would be made to the heirs, upon proper application to the Department, with proof of loss.

"She was there," Mart said to Amos. "She was there in that camp. She's gone with them that got away."

Amos did not comment. They had to follow and find the survivors—perhaps close at hand, if they were lucky; otherwise by tracing them to whatever far places they might scatter. This time neither one of them said "Tomorrow."

21

They had been winter-driven that first time they went home, all but out of horseflesh, and everything else besides. But after the "Battle" of Deadhorse Bend they went home only because all leads very soon staled and petered out in the part of the country where they were. Otherwise, they probably would have stayed out and kept on. They had lived on the wild land so long that they needed nothing, not even money, that they did not know how to scratch out of it. It never occured to them that their search was stretching out into a great extraordinary feat of endurance; an epic of hope without faith, of fortitude without reward, of stubbornness past all limits of reason. They simply kept on, doing the next thing, because they always had one more place to go, following out one more forlorn-hope try.

And they had one more idea now. It had been spelled out for them in the loot Colonel Hannon's troopers had picked up in the wreckage of Bluebonnet's destroyed village. Clear and plain, once you thought of it, though it had taken them weeks of thinking back over the whole thing before they recognized it. Amos, at least, believed that this time they could not fail. They would find Debbie now—if only she still lived.

Their new plan would carry them far into the southwest, into country hundreds of miles from any they had ever worked before. And so long as they had to go south, home was not too far out of the way. Home? What was that? Well, it was the place they used to live; where the Mathisons still lived—so far as they knew—and kept an eye on the cattle that now belonged to Debbie. Mart would always think of that stretch of country as home, though nothing of his own was there, nor anybody waiting for him.

As they rode, a sad, dark thing began to force itself upon their attention. When they came to the country where the farthest-west fringe of ranches had been, the ranches were no longer there. Often only a ghostly chimney stood, solitary upon the endless prairie, where once had been a warm and friendly place with people living in it. Then they would remember the time they had stopped by, and things they had eaten there, and the little jokes the people had made. If you hunted

171

around in the brush that ran wild over all, you could usually find the graves. The remembered people were still there, under the barren ground.

More often you had to remember landmarks to locate where a place had been at all. Generally your horse stumbled over an old footing or something before you saw the flat place where the little house had been. Sometimes you found graves here, too, but more usually the people had simply pulled their house down and hauled the lumber away, retreating from a place the Peace Policy had let become too deadly, coming on top of the war. You got the impression that Texas had seen its high tide, becoming little again as its frontier thinned away. Sundown seemed to have come for the high hopes of the Lone Star Republic to which Union had brought only war, weakening blood losses, and the perhaps inevitable neglect of a defeated people.

On the morning of the last day, with Mathison's layout only twenty-odd miles away, they came upon one more crumbling chimney, lonely beside a little stream. Mart's eyes rested upon it contemplatively across the brush at five hundred yards without recognizing it. He was thinking what a dreadful thing it would be if they came to the Mathisons, and found no more than this left of the place, or the people. Then he saw Amos looking at him strangely, and he knew what he was looking at. Surprising that he had not known it, even though he had not been here in a long time. The chimney marked the site of the old Pauley homestead; the place where he had been born. Here the people who had brought him into the world had loved him, and cared for him; here they had built their hopes, and here they had died. How swiftly fade the dead from people's minds, if he could look at this place and not even know it! He turned his horse and rode toward it, Amos following without question.

He had no memory of his own of how this homestead had looked, and no faintest images of his people's faces. He had been taken over this ground, and had all explained to him when he was about eight years old, but no one had ever been willing to talk to him about it, else. And now, except for the chimney, he couldn't locate where anything had been at all. The snow had gone off, but the ground was frozen hard, so that their heels rang metallically upon it as they dismounted to walk around. The little stream ran all year, and it had a fast ripple in it that never froze, where it passed this place; so that the water seemed to talk forever to the dead. This creek was called the Beanblossom; Mart knew that much. And that was about all.

Amos saw his bewilderment. "Your old m— your father wagoned the Santa Fe Trail a couple of times," he said, "before he settled down. Them Santa Fe traders, if any amongst 'em died, they buried 'em ahead in the trail; so every dang ox in the train tromped over the graves. Didn't want the Indians to catch on they were doing poorly. Or maybe dig 'em up. So your father was against markers on graves. Out here, anyways. Knowing that, and after some argument, we never set none up."

Mart had supposed he knew where the graves were anyway. They had been plainly visible when he had been shown, but now neither mound nor depression showed where they were. The brush had advanced, and under the brush the wind and the rain of the years had filled and packed and planed and sanded the sterile earth until no trace showed anywhere of anything having crumbled to dust beneath.

Amos picked a twig and chewed it as he waded into the brush, taking cross-sightings here and there, trying to remember. "Right here," he said finally. "This is where your mother lies." He scraped a line with the toe of his boot, the frozen ground barely taking the mark. "Here's the foot of the grave." He stepped aside, and walked around an undefined space, and made another mark. "And here's the head, here."

A great gawky bunch of chaparral grew in the middle of what must be the side line of the grave. Mart stood staring at the bit of earth, in no way distinguishable from any other part of the prairie surface. He was trying to remember, or to imagine, the woman whose dust was there. Amos seemed to understand that, too.

"Your mother was a beautiful girl," he said. Mart felt ashamed as he shoved out of his mind the thought that whatever she looked like, Amos would have said that same thing of the dead. "Real thin," Amos said, mouthing his twig, "but real pretty just the same. Brown eyes, almost what you'd call black. But her hair. Red-brown, and a lot of it. With a shine in it, like a gold kind of red, when the light struck through it right. I never seen no prettier hair."

He was silent a few moments, as if to let Mart think for a decent interval about the mother he did not

174

remember. Then Amos got restless, and measured off a long step to the side. "And this here's Ethan—your father," he said. "You favor him, right smart. He had a black-Welsh streak; marked his whole side of the family. It's from him you got your black look and them mighty-near crockery eyes. He was just as dark, with the same light eyes."

Amos turned a little, and chewed the twig, but didn't bother to pace off the locations of the others. "Alongside lies my brother—mine and Henry's brother. The William you've heard tell of so many, many times. I don't know why, but in the family, we never once did call him Bill. . . . William was the best of us. The best by far. Good looking as Henry, and strong as me. And the brains of the family—there they lie, right there. He could been governor, or anything. Except he was less than your age—just eighteen. . . ." Mart didn't let himself question the description, even in his mind. You could assume that the first killed in a family of boys was the one who would have been great. It was what they told you always.

"Beyond, the three more—next to William lies Cash Dennison, a young rider, helping out Ethan; then them two bullwhackers that lived out the wagon-train killing, and made it to here. One's name was Caruthers, from a letter in his pocket; I forget the other. Some blamed them for the whole thing—thought the Comanches come down on this place a-chasing them two. But I never thought that. Seems more like the Comanch' was coming here; and it was the wagon train they fell on by accident on their way."

"You got any notion—does anybody know—did they get many of the Comanches? Here, the night of this thing?"

Amos shook his head. "A summer storm come up. A regular cloudburst—you don't see the like twice in twenty year. It washed out the varmints' trail. And naturally they carried off their dead—such as there was. Nobody knows how many. Maybe none."

Waste, thought Mart. Useless, senseless, heartbreaking waste. All these good, fine, happy lives just thrown away. . . .

Once more Amos seemed to answer his thought. "Mart, I don't know as I ever said this to anybody. But it's been a long time; and I'll tell you now what I think. My family's gone now, too—unless and until we find our one last little girl. But we lived free of harm, and the Mathisons too, for full eighteen years before they struck our bunch again. You want to know what I think why? I think your people here bought that time for us. They paid for it with their lives."

"Wha-at?" No matter what losses his people had inflicted on the raiders, Comanches would never be stopped by that. They would come back to even the score, and thus the tragic border war went on forever. But that wasn't what Amos meant.

"I think this was a revenge raid," Amos said. "It was right here the Rangers come through, trailing old Iron Shirt's band. They cut that bunch down from the strongest there was to something trifling, and killed Iron Shirt himself. So the trail the Rangers followed that time had a black history for Comanches. They come down it just once in revenge for their dead—and Ethan's little place was the farthest out on this trail. And it was a whole Indian generation before they come again. That's why I say—your people bought them years the rest of us lived in peace. . . ."

Mart said, "It's been a long time. Do you think my father would mind now if I come and put markers on them graves? Would that be a foolishness after all this while?"

Amos chewed, eating his twig. "I don't believe he'd mind. Not now. Even could he know. I think it would be a right nice thing to do. I'll help you soon's we have a mite of time." He turned toward the horses, but Mart wanted to know one thing more that no one had ever told him.

"I don't suppose"—he said—"well, maybe you might know. Could you show me where I was when Pa found me in the brush?"

"Your Pa? When?"

"I mean Henry. He always stood in place of my own. I heard tell he found me, and picked me up. . . ."

Amos looked all around, and walked into the brush, chewing slowly, and taking sights again. "Here," he said at last. "I'm sure now. Right—exactly—here." The frost in the earth crackled as he ground a heel into the spot he meant. "Of course, then, the brush was cleared back. To almost this far from the house." He stood around a moment to see if Mart wanted to ask anything more, then walked off out of the brush toward the horses.

This place, this very spot he stood on, Mart thought,

177

was where he once awoke alone in such terror as locked his throat, seemingly; they had told him he made no sound. Queer to stand here, in this very spot where he had so nearly perished before he even got started; queer, because he felt nothing. It was the same as when he had stood looking at the graves, knowing that what was there should have meant so much, yet had no meaning for him at all. He couldn't see anything from here that looked familiar, or reminded him of anything.

Of course, that night of the massacre, he hadn't been standing up better than six feet tall in his boots. He had been down in the roots of the scrub, not much bigger than his own foot was now. On an impulse, Mart lay down in the tangle, pressing his cheek against the ground, to bring his eyes close to the roots.

A bitter chill crept along the whole length of his body. The frozen ground seemed to drain the heat from his blood, and the blood from his heart itself. Perhaps it was that, and knowing where he was, that accounted for what happened next. Or maybe scars, almost as old as he was, were still in existence down at the bottom of his mind, long buried under everything that had happened in between. The sky seemed to darken, while a ringing, buzzing sound came into his ears, and when the sky was completely black it began to redden with a bloody glow. His stomach dropped from under his heart, and a horrible fear filled him— the fear of a small helpless child, abandoned and alone in the night. He tried to spring up and out of that, and he could not move; he lay there rigid, seemingly frozen to the ground. Behind the ringing in his ears began to rise the unearthly yammer of the terror-dream—not heard, not even remembered, but coming to him like an awareness of something happening in some unknown dimension not of the living world.

He fought it grimly, and slowly got hold of himself; his eyes cleared, and the unearthly voices died, until he heard only the hammering of his heart. He saw, close to his eyes, the stems of the chaparral; and he was able to move again, stiffly, with his muscles shaking. He turned his head, getting a look at the actual world around him again. Then, through a rift in the brush that showed the creek bank, he saw the death tree.

Its base was almost on a level with his eyes, at perhaps a hundred feet; and for one brief moment it seemed to swell and tower, writhing its corpse-withered arms. His eyes stayed fixed upon it as he slowly got up and walked toward it without volition, as if it were the only thing possible to do. The thing shrunk as he approached it, no longer towering over him twice his size as it had seemed to do wherever he had seen it before. Finally he stood within arm's length; and now it was only a piece of weather-silvered wood in a tormented shape, a foot and a half shorter than himself.

An elongated knot at the top no longer looked like a distorted head, but only a symbol representing the hideous thing he had imagined there. He lashed out and struck it, hard, with the heel of his right hand. The long-rotted roots broke beneath the surface of the soil; and a twisted old stump tottered, splashed in the creek, and went spinning away.

Mart shuddered, shaking himself back together; and he spoke aloud. "I'll be a son-of-a-bitch," he said; and rejoined Amos. If he still looked shaken up, Amos pretended not to notice as they mounted up.

22

Martin Pauley was taken by another fit of shyness as they approached the Mathison ranch. He was a plainsman now, a good hunter, and a first-class Indian scout. But the saddle in which he lived had polished nothing about him but the seat of his leather pants.

"I tried to leave you back," Amos reminded him. "A couple of burr-matted, sore-backed critters we be. You got a lingo on you like a Caddo whiskey runner. You know that, don't you?"

Mart said he knew it.

"Our people never did have much shine," Amos said. "Salt of the earth, mind you; no better anywhere. But no book learning, like is born right into them Mathisons. To us, grammar is nothing but grampaw's wife."

Mart remembered the times Laurie had corrected his speech, and knew he didn't fit with civilized people. Not even as well as before, when he was merely a failure at it. But someway he was finally herded into the Mathison kitchen.

Laurie ran to him and took both his hands. "Where on earth have you been?"

"We been north," he answered her literally. "Looking

around among the Kiowas."

"Why up there?"

"Well . . ." he answered lamely, "she might have been up there."

She said wonderingly, "Martie, do you realize how long you've been on this search? This is the third winter you've been out."

He hadn't thought of the time in terms of years. It had piled up in little pieces—always just one more place to go that would take just a few weeks more. He made a labored calculation, and decided Laurie was twenty-one. That explained why she seemed so lighted up; probably looked the best she ever would in her life. She was at an age when most girls light up, if they're going to; Mexicans and Indians earlier. A look at their mothers, or their older sisters, reminded you of what you knew for certain: All that bright glow would soon go out again. But you couldn't ever make yourself believe it.

Laurie made him follow her around, dealing out facts and figures about Kiowas, while she helped her mother get dinner. He didn't believe she cared a hoot about Kiowas, but he was glad for the chance to have a look at her.

There was this Indian called Scar, he explained to her. Seemed he actually had one on his face. They kept hearing that Scar had taken a little white girl captive. He showed her how the Indians described the scar, tracing a finger in a sweeping curve from hairline to jaw. A well-marked man. Only they couldn't find him. They couldn't even find any reliable person—no

181

trader, soldier, or black hat—who had ever seen an Indian with such a scar. Then Mart had happened to think that the sign describing the scar was a whole lot like the Plains-Indian sign for sheep. The Kiowas had a warrior society called the Sheep, and he got to wondering if all those rumors were hitting around the fact that the Kiowa Sheep Society had Debbie. So they went to see. . . .

"A pure waste of time, and nobody to blame but me. It was me thought of it."

"It was I," she corrected him.

"You?" he fumbled it; then caught it on the bounce. "No, I meant—the blame was on I."

"There's going to be a barn party," she told him. "Mose Harper built a barn."

"At his age?"

"The State of Texas paid for it, mainly; they're going to put a Ranger stopover in part of it, and store their feed there next year—or the year after, when they get around to it. But the party is right away. I bet you knew!"

"No, I didn't."

"Bet you did. Only reason you came home."

He thought it over, and guessed he would give her some real comical answer later; soon as he thought of one.

After supper Aaron Mathison and Amos Edwards got out the herd books and ledgers, as upon their visit before. Aaron's head bent low, eyes close to the pages, so that Mart noticed again the old man's failing sight, much worse than it had been the last time.

And now Mart made his next mistake, rounding out his tally for the day. He set up camp, all uninvited, on the settle flanking the stove where he had sat with Laurie before; and here, while Laurie finished picking up the supper things, he waited hopefully for her to come and sit beside him. He had a notion that all the time he had been gone would melt away, once they sat there again.

But she didn't come and sit there. Had to get her beauty sleep, she said. Great long drive tomorrow; probably no sleep at all tomorrow night, what with the long drive home.

"Harper's is seven miles," Mart said. "Scarcely a real good spit."

"Don't be coarse." She said good night, respectfully to Amos and briskly to Mart, and went off across the dog-trot into that unknown world in the other section of the house, which he had never entered.

Mart wandered to the other end of the room, intending to join Amos and Aaron Mathison. But "G'night" Amos said to him. And Mathison gravely stood up to shake hands.

"It comes to me," Mart said, "I've been a long time away."

"And if we stayed for the damn barn burning," Amos said, "we'd be a long time off the road." Amos believed he knew where he was going now. All that great jackstraw pile of Indian nonsense was straightening itself in his mind. He could add up the hundreds of lies and half truths they had ridden so far to gather, and make them come out to a certain answer at last.

"You be stubborn men," Aaron Mathison said, "both of you.

Mart tried to share Amos' fire of conviction, but he could not. "Man has to live some place," he said, and slung on his coat, for they were to sleep in the bunkhouse this time. The coat was a long-skirted bearskin, slit high for the saddle; it was big enough to keep his horse warm, and smelled like a hog. "The prairie's all I know any more, I guess." He went out through the cold dark to his bed.

23

Mart was up long before daylight. Some internal clockwork always broke him out early nowadays. In summer the first dawn might be coming on, but in the short days he woke in the dark at exactly half-past four. He started a fire in the bunkhouse stove, and set coffee on. Then he went out to the breaking corral into which they had thrown the horses and mules Amos had picked for the next leg of their perpetual trip.

He grained them all, then went back to the bunkhouse. He set the coffee off the fire, and studied Amos for signs of arisal. He saw none, so he went out to the corral again. They carried three mules now, on account of the trading, and a spare saddle horse, in case one should pull up lame when they were in a hurry. Mart picked himself a stocky buckskin, with zebra stripes on his cannons and one down his back.

He snubbed down, saddled, and bucked out this horse with his bearskin coat on; all horses took outrage at this coat, and had to be broke to it fresh every day for a while, until they got used to it.

He laid aside the bearskin to top off the great heavy stock horse he supposed Amos would ride. Its pitch was straight, and easy to sit, but had such a shock to it that his nose bled a little. Finally he got the pack saddles on the mules, and left them standing hump-backed in a sull. By this time the gray bitter dawn was on the prairie, but the white vapor from the lungs of the animals was the only sign of life around the place as yet.

Amos was sitting up on the edge of his bunk in his long-handled underwear, peering at the world through bleary lids and scratching himself.

"Well," Mart said, "we're saddled."

"Huh?"

"I say I uncorked the ponies, and slung the mule forks on."

"What did you do that for?"

"Because it's morning, I suppose—why the hell did you think? I don't see no smoke from the kitchen. You want I should stir up a snack?"

"We're held up," Amos said. "We got to go to that roof-raising."

"Thought you said we had to flog on. Jesus, will you make up your mind?"

"I just done so. By God, will you clean out your ears?"

"Oh, hell," Mart said, and went out to unsaddle.

24

The barn party was just a rough-and-ready gathering of frontier cattle people, such as Mart knew perfectly well. He knew exactly how these people spent every hour of their lives, and he could do everything they knew how to do better than most of them. What bothered him was to see such a raft of them in one place. They filled the big new barn when they all got there. Where had these dozens of scrubbed-looking girls come from, in all shapes and sizes? All this swarming of strangers gave Mart an uncomfortable feeling that the country had filled up solid while he was gone, leaving no room for him here.

Mart had got stuck with the job of bringing along the pack mules, for Amos wanted to get started directly from Harper's without going back. In consequence, Mart hadn't seen any of the Mathison family after they got dressed up until they appeared at the party. Aaron Mathison was patriarchal in high collar and black suit, across his vest the massive gold chain indispensable to men of substance; and Mrs. Mathison was a proper counterpart in a high-necked black dress that rustled when she so much as turned her eyes. They joined a row of other old-timers, a sort of windbreak of respectability along the wall, suggestive of mysteriously inherited book learning and deals with distant banks.

But it was Laurie who took him by shock, and for whom he was unprepared. She had made her own dress, of no prouder material than starched gingham, but it was full-skirted and tight at the waist, and left her shoulders bare, what time she wasn't shawled up against the cold. He would have been better off if he could have seen this rig at the house, and had time to get used to it. He had never seen her bare shoulders before, nor given thought to how white they must naturally be; and now he had trouble keeping his eyes off them. A wicked gleam showed in her eyes as she caught him staring.

"Honestly, Mart—you act as though you came from so far back in the hills the sun must *never* shine!"

"Listen here," he said, judging it was time to take her down a peg. "When I first rode with you, you was about so high, and round as a punkin. And you wore all-overs made of flour sack. I know because I seen a yearling calf stack you wrong end up in a doodle of wild hay, and you said 'Steamboat Mills' right across the bottom."

She giggled. "How do you know I still don't?" she asked him. But her eyes were searching the crowd for somebody else.

He drew off, to remuster according to plan; and when next he tried to go near her, she was surrounded. The whole place was curdled up with lashings of objectionable young jaybirds he had never seen before in his life, and Laurie had rings in the noses of them all. Some of them wore borrowed-looking store clothes, generally either too long in the sleeves or fixing to split out someplace. But more had come in their saddle outfits, like Mart, with clean handkerchiefs on their necks and their shirts washed out by way of celebration. He took them to be common saddle pounders, mostly. But he imagined a knowingness behind their eyes, as if they were all onto something he did not suspect. Maybe they knew what they were doing here—which was more than he could say for himself. Tobe and Abner knew everybody and mixed everywhere, leaving Mart on his own. Brad had been his best friend, but these younger brothers seemed of a different generation altogether; he had nothing in common with them any more.

Some of the boys kept sliding out the back way to the horse lines, and Mart knew jugs were cached out there. He had taken very few drinks in his life, but this seemed a good time for one. He started to follow a group who spoke owlishly of "seeing to the blankets on the team," but Amos cut him off at the door.

"Huh uh. Not this time." Amos had not had a drop, which was odd in the time and place. Mart knew he could punish a jug until its friends cried out in pain, once he started.

"What's the matter now?"

"I got special reasons."

"Something going to bust?"

"Don't know yet. I'm waiting for something."

That was all he would say. Mart went off and holed up in a corner with old Mose Harper, who asked him questions about "present day" Indians, and listened respectfully to his answers—or the first few words of them, anyway. Mose got the bit in his teeth in less than half a minute, and went into the way things used to be, in full detail. Mart let his eyes wander past Mose to follow Laurie, flushed and whirling merrily, all over the place. The country-dance figures kept people changing partners, and Laurie always had a few quick words for each new one, making him laugh, usually, before they were separated again. Mart wondered what on earth she ever found to say.

"In my day," Mose was telling Mart, "when them Tonkawas killed an enemy, they just ate the heart and liver. Either raw or fussy prepared—didn't make no difference. What they wanted was his medicine. Only they never ate a white man's vitals; feared our medicine wouldn't mix with theirs, seemingly, though they respected our weepons. . . ."

Mart more than half expected that Laurie would come around and try to pull him into a dance, and he was determined he wasn't going to let her do it. He was making up speeches to fend her off with, while he pretended to listen to Mose.

"Nowadays," Mose explained, "they've took to eating the whole corpse, as a food. 'Tain't a ceremony, any more, so much as a saving of meat. But they still won't eat a white man. 'Tain't traditional."

Laurie never did come looking for Mart. She made a face at him once, as she happened to whirl close by, and that was all. Holding back became tiresome pretty fast, with no one to insist on anything different. He got into the dance, picking whatever girls caught his eye, regardless of whom they thought they belonged to. He was perversely half hoping for the fight you can sometimes get into that way, but none started.

He had been afraid of the dancing itself, but actually there wasn't anything to it. These people didn't party often enough to learn any very complicated dances. Just simple reels, and stuff like that. Sashay forward, sashay back, swing your lady, drop her slack. You swing mine, and I'll swing yours, and back to your own, and everybody swing. At these family parties, out here on civilization's brittle edge, they didn't even swing their girls by the waist—a dissolute practice to be seen mainly in saloons. Man grabbed his lady by the arms, and they kind of skittered around each other, any way they could. He got hold of Laurie only about once every two hours, but there were plenty of others. The fiddles and the banjos whanged out a rhythm that shook the barn, and the time flew by, romping and stomping.

Through all this Amos stood by, withdrawn into the background and into himself. Sometimes men he had known came to shake hands with him, greeting him with a heartiness Amos did not return. They were full of the questions to be expected of them, but the answers they got were as short as they could civilly be, and conveyed nothing. No conversation was allowed to develop. Amos remained apart, neither alone nor with anybody. Small use speculating on what he might be waiting for. Mart presently forgot him.

It was long after midnight, though nobody but the nodding old folks along the wall seemed to have noticed it, when the Rangers came in. There were three of them, and they made their arrival inconspicuous. They wore no uniforms—the Rangers had none—and their badges were in their pockets. Nobody was turned nervous, and nobody made a fuss over them, either. Rangers were a good thing, and there ought to be more of them. Sometimes you needed a company of them badly. Didn't need any just now. So long as no robbery or bloody murder was in immediate view, Rangers ranked as people. And that was it.

That, and one thing more: Everyone knew at once that they were there. Within less than a minute, people who had never seen any of these three before knew that Rangers had come in and which men they were. Mart Pauley heard of them from a girl he swung but once, and had them pointed out to him by the next girl to whom he was handed on. "Who? *Him?*" The youngest of the three Rangers was Charlie MacCorry.

"He enlisted last year sometime."

As they finished the set, Mart was trying to make up his mind if he should go shake hands with Charlie MacCorry, or leave him be. He never had liked him much. Too much flash, too much swagger, too much to say. But now he saw something else. Amos and one of the older Rangers had walked toward each other on sight. They had drawn off, and were talking secretly and intently, apart from anyone else. Whatever Amos had waited for was here. Mart went over to them.

"This here is Sol Clinton," Amos told Mart. "Lieutenant in the Rangers. I side-rode him once. But that was long ago. I don't know if he remembers."

Sol Clinton looked Mart over without to-do, or any move to shake hands. This Ranger appeared to be in his forties, but he was so heavily weathered that he perhaps looked older than he was. He had a drooping sandy mustache and deep grin lines that seemed to have been carved there, for he certainly wasn't smiling.

"I'm that found boy the Edwards family raised," Mart explained, "name of—"

"Know all about you," Sol Clinton said. His stare lay on Mart with a sort of tired candor. "You look something like a breed," he decided.

"And you," Mart answered, "look something like you don't know what you're talking about."

"Stop that," Amos snapped.

"He's full of snakehead," Mart stood his ground. "I can smell it on him."

"Why, sure," the Ranger conceded mildly. "I've had a snort or two. This is a dance, isn't it? Man can't haul off and dance in cold blood."

"Mind your manners anyway," Amos advised Mart.

"That's all right," Sol said. "You know a trader calls himself Jerem Futterman up the Salt Fork of the Brazos?"

Mart looked at Amos, and Amos answered him. "He knows him, and he knows he's dead."

"Might let him answer for himself, Amos."

"Sol was speaking of us riding to Austin with him," Amos went on stolidly, "to talk it over."

Mart said sharply, "We got no time for—"

"I explained him that," Amos said. "Will you get this through your damn head? This is an invite to a neck-tie party! Now stop butting in."

"Not quite that bad," Clinton said. "Not yet. We hope. No great hurry, either, right this minute. Best of our witnesses broke loose on us; got to catch him again before we put anything together. Most likely, all we'll want of you fellers is to pad out a good long report. Show zeal, you know." He dropped into a weary drawl. "Show we're unrestin'. Get our pay raised—like hell."

"I guarantee Mart Pauley will come back to answer," Amos said, "same as me."

"I guess the same bond will stretch to cover you both," Sol Clinton said. "I'll scratch down a few lines for you to sign."

"It's a wonderful thing to be a former Ranger," Amos said. "It's the way everybody trusts you—that's what gets to a man."

"Especially if you're also a man of property," Clinton agreed in that same mild way. "Amos put up a thousand head of cattle," he explained to Mart, "that says you and him will come on into Austin, soon as you finish this next one trip."

"Aaron Mathison told me about this," Amos said. "I couldn't believe he had it right. I got to believe it now."

"They know about this, then. They knew it all the time. . . ."

"I stayed on to make sure. There's nothing more to wait on now. Go and tell the Mathisons we're leaving."

"Stay on awhile," Sol Clinton suggested. "Have a good time if you want."

Martin Pauley said, "No, thanks," as he turned away.

He went looking for Laurie first. She wasn't dancing, or anywhere in the barn. He went out to the barbecue pit, where some people were still poking around what was left of a steer, but she wasn't there. He wandered down the horse line, where the saddle stock was tied along the length of a hundred-foot rope. He knew some of the women had gone over to Mose Harper's house; a passel of young children had been bedded down over there, for one thing. He had about decided to go butt in there when he found her.

A couple stood in the shadows of a feed shelter. The man was Charlie MacCorry; and the girl in his arms was Laurie Mathison, as Mart somehow knew without needing to look.

Martin Pauley just stood there staring at them, his head down a little bit, like some witless cow-critter half knocked in the head. He stood there as long as they did. Charlie MacCorry finally let the girl go, slowly, and turned.

"Just what the hell do *you* want?"

A weakness came into Mart's belly muscles, and then a knotting up; and he began to laugh, foolishly, sagging against the feed rack. He never did know what he was laughing at.

Charlie blew up. "Now you look here!" He grabbed Mart by the front of the jacket, straightened him up, and slapped his face fit to break his neck. Mart lashed out by reflex, and Charlie MacCorry was flat on his back in the same tenth of a second.

He was up on the bounce, and they went at it. They were at it for some time.

They had no prize ring out in that country; fights were many but unrehearsed. These men were leathery and hard to hurt, but their knuckle brawls were fought by instinct, without the skill they showed with other

194

weapons. Mart Pauley never ducked, blocked, nor gave ground; he came straight in, very fast at first, later more slowly, plodding and following. He swung workman-like, slugging blows, one hand and then the other, putting his back into it. Charlie MacCorry fought standing straight up, circling and sidestepping, watching his chances. He threw long-armed, lacing blows, mostly to the face. Gradually, over a period of time, he beat Mart's head off.

They never knew when Laurie left them. A close circle of men packed in around them, shouting advice, roaring when either one was staggered. Amos Edwards was there, and both of MacCorry's fellow Rangers. These three stood watching critically but impassively in the inner circle, the only silent members of the crowd. Neither fighter noticed them, or heard the yelling. Somewhere along the way Mart took a slam on the side of the face with his mouth open, and the inside of his cheek opened on his own teeth. Daylight later showed frozen splotches of bright red over a surprising area, as if a shoat had been slaughtered. Mart kept on moving in, one eye puffed shut and the other closing; and suddenly this thing was over.

The blow that ended it was no different than a hundred others, except in its luck. Mart had no idea which hand had landed, let alone how he did it. Charlie Mac-Corry went down without notice, as if all strings were cut at once. He fell forward on his face, and every muscle was slack as they turned him over. For a couple of moments Mart stood looking down at him with a stupid surprise, wondering what had happened.

He turned away, and found himself facing Sol Clinton. He spit blood, and said, "You next?"

The Ranger stared at him. "Who? Me? What for?" He stood aside.

A dawn as cheerless as a drunkard's awakening was making a line of gray on the eastern horizon. Mart walked to their mules after passing them once and having to turn back. Any number of hands helped him, and took over from him, as he went about feeding their animals, so he took time to take the handkerchief from his neck, and stuff it into his cheek. The sweat with which it was soaked stung the big cut inside his cheek, but his mouth stopped filling up.

Charlie MacCorry came to him. "You all right?" His nose showed a bright blaze where it had hit the frozen ground as he fell.

"I'm ready to go on with it if you are."

"Well—all right—if you say. Just tell me one thing. What was you laughing at?"

"Charlie, I'll be damned if I know."

Watching him narrowly, Charlie said, "You don't?"

"Don't rightly recall what we was fighting about, when it comes to that."

"Thought maybe you figured I cross-branded your girl."

"I got no girl. Never had."

Charlie moved closer, but his hands were in his pockets. He looked at the ground, and at the cold streak of light in the cast, before he looked at Mart. "I'd be a fool not to take your word," he decided. Charlie stuck out his hand, then drew it back, for it was swollen to double size around broken bones. He offered his left hand instead. "God damn, you got a hard head."

"Need one, slow as I move." He gave Charlie's left hand the least possible shake, and pulled back.

"You don't move slow," Charlie said. "See you in Austin." He walked away.

Amos came along. "Stock's ready."

"Good." Mart tightened his cinch, and they rode. Neither had anything to say. As the sun came up, Amos began to sing to himself. It was an old song from the Mexican War, though scarcely recognizable as Amos sang it. A good many cowboys had replaced forgotten words and turns of tune with whatever came into their heads before the song got to Amos.

> Green grow the rushes, oh,
> Green grow the rushes, oh,
> Only thing I ever want to know
> Is where is the girl I left behind. . . .

Well, it had been sung a good many thousand times before by men who hadn't left anything behind, because they had nothing to leave.

25

They angled southwest at a good swinging pace, their animals fresh and well grained. At Fort Phantom Hill they found the garrison greatly strengthened and full of aggressive confidence for a change. This was surprising enough, but at Fort Concho they saw troop after troop of newly mustered cavalry; and were told that Fort Richardson was swarming with a concentration of much greater strength. Southwest Texas was going to have a real striking force at last. They had prayed for this for a long time, and they welcomed it no less because of a sardonic bitterness in it for those to whom help had come too late.

Beyond the Colorado they turned toward the setting sun, through a country with nothing man-made to be seen in it. So well were they moving that they outrode the winter in a couple of weeks. For once, instead of heading into the teeth of the worst weather they could find, they were riding to meet the spring. By the time they rounded the southern end of the Staked Plains the sun blazed hot by day, while yet the dry-country cold bit very hard at night. The surface of the land was strewn with flints and black lava float; it grew little besides creosote bush, chaparral, and bear grass, and the many, many kinds of cactus. Waterholes were far apart, and you had better know where they were, once you left the wagon tracks behind.

Beyond Horsehead Crossing they rode northwest and across the Pecos, skirting the far flank of the Staked Plains—called Los Llanos Estacados over here. They were reaching for New Mexico Territory, some hundred and fifty miles above, as a horse jogs; a vulture could make it shorter, if he would stop his uncomplimentary circling over the two riders, and line out. Their time for this distance was much worse than a week, for half of which they pushed into a wind so thick with dust that they wore their neckerchiefs up to their eyes.

When finally they crossed the Territory line, they didn't even know it, being unable to tell Delaware Creek from any other dry wash unfed by snows. Dead reckoning persuaded them they must be in New Mexico, but they wouldn't have known it. Where were the señoritas and cantinas, the guitars and tequila, Amos had talked about? He may have confused this lately Mexican country he had never seen with the Old Mexico he knew beyond the lower Rio Grande. Without meaning to, probably, he had made the Southwest sound like a never-never country of song and illicit love, with a streak of wicked bloody murder interestingly hidden just under a surface of ease and mañana. The territory didn't look like that. Nor like anything else, either, at the point where they entered it. There wasn't anything there at all.

But now the wind rested, and the air cleared. The country recovered its characteristic black and white of hard sun and sharp shadows. Mart dug Debbie's miniature out of his saddle bags to see how it had come through the dust. He carried the little velvet box wrapped in doeskin now, and he hadn't opened it for a long time. The soft leather had protected it well; the little portrait looked brighter and fresher in the white desert light than he had ever seen it. The small kitty-cat face looked out of the frame with a life of its own, bright-eyed, eager, happy with the young new world. He felt a twinge he had almost forgotten—she seemed so dear, so precious, and so lost. From this point on he began to pull free from the backward drag of his bad days back home. No, not back home; he had no home. His hopes once more led out down the trail.

For now they were in the land of the Comancheros, toward which they had been pointed by the loot of Deadhorse Bend. Here Bluebonnet must have traded for the silverwork and turquoise in the spoils; here surely he would now seek refuge from the evil that had come upon him in the north.

That name, Comanchero, was a hated one among Texans. Actually the Comancheros were nothing but some people who traded with Comanches, much as Mart and Amos themselves had often done. If you were an American, and traded with Comanches from the United States side, basing upon the forts of West Texas and Indian Territory, you were a trader. But if you were a Mexican, basing in Mexico, and made trading contact with Comanches on the southwest flank of the Staked Plains, you were not called a trader, but a Comanchero.

During the years of armed disagreement with Mexico, the Comancheros had given Texans plenty of reasons for complaint. When thousands of head of Texas horses, mules, and cattle disappeared into the Staked Plains every year, it was the Comancheros who took all that livestock off Indian hands, and spirited it into deep Mexico. And when great numbers of breech-loading carbines appeared in the hands of Comanche raiders, it was the Comancheros who put them there.

Of course, Amos had once traded some split-blocks

of sulphur matches and a bottle of Epsom salts (for making water boil magically by passing your hand over it) for some ornaments of pure Mexican gold no Indian ever got by trading. But that was different.

Mart had always heard the Comancheros described as a vicious, slinking, cowardly breed, living like varmints in unbelievable filth. These were the people who now seemed to hold their last great hope of finding Debbie. The great war chiefs of the Staked Plains Comanches, like Bull Bear, Wild Horse, Black Duck, Shaking Hand, and the young Quanah, never came near the Agencies at all. Well armed, always on the fight, they struck deep and vanished. Amos was certain now that these irreconcilables did business only with the Comancheros—and that the Flower had to be with them.

Somewhere there must be Comancheros who knew every one of them well. Somewhere must be one who knew where Debbie was. Or maybe there isn't, Mart sometimes thought. But they're the best bet we got left. We'll find her now. Or never at all.

First they had to find the Comancheros. Find Comancheros? Hell, first you had to find a human being. That wasn't easy in this country they didn't know. Over and over they followed trails which should have forked together, and led some place, but only petered out like the dry rivers into blown sand. There had to be people here someplace, though, and eventually they began to find some. Some small bunches of Apaches, seen at a great distance, were the first, but these shied off. Then finally they found a village.

This was a cluster of two-dozen, mud-and-wattle huts called jacals, around a mud hole and the ruins of a mission, and its name was Esperanza. Here lived some merry, friendly, singing people in possession of almost nothing. They had some little corn patches, and a few sheep, and understood sign language. How did they keep the Apaches out of the sheep? A spreading of the hands. It was not possible. But the Apaches never took all the sheep. Always left some for seed, so there would be something to steal another year. So all was well, thanks to the goodness of God. Here were some guitars at last, and someone singing someplace at any hour of day or night. Also some warm pulque, which could bring on a sweaty lassitude followed by a headache. No señoritas in evidence, though. Just a lot of fat squawlike women, with big grins and no shoes.

Once they had found one village, the others were much more easily discoverable—never exactly where they were said to be, nor at anything like the distance which was always described either as "Not far" or "Whoo!" But landmarked, so you found them eventually. They made their way to little places called Derecho, Una Vaca, Gallo, San Pascual, San Marco, Plata Negra, and San Philipe. Some of these centered on fortified ranchos, some on churches, others just on waterholes. The two riders learned the provincial Spanish more easily than they had expected; the vocabulary used out here was not very large. And they became fond of these sun-sleepy people who were always singing, always making jokes. They had voluble good manners and an open-handed hospitality. They didn't seem to wash very much, but actually it didn't seem necessary in this dry air. The villages and the people had a sort of friendly, sun-baked smell.

They looked much happier, Mart thought, than Americans ever seem to be. A man built a one-room jacal, or maybe an adobe, if mud was in good supply when he was married. Though he bred a double-dozen children, he never built onto that one room again. As each day warmed up, the master of the house was to be found squatting against the outer wall. All day long he moved around it, following the shade when the day was hot, the sun when the day was cool; and thus painlessly passed his life, untroubled. Mart could envy them, but he couldn't learn from them. Why is it a man can never seem to buckle down and train himself to indolence and stupidity when he can see what sanctuary they offer from toil and pain?

But they found no Comancheros. They had expected a spring burst of fur trading, but spring ran into summer without any sign of anything like that going on. They were in the wrong place for it, obviously. And the real Comanchero rendezvous would be made in the fall at the end of the summer-raiding season. They worked hard to make sure of their Comancheros by the end of the summer—and they didn't learn a thing. The paisanos could retreat into a know-nothing shell that neither cunning nor bribery could break down. A stranger could see their eyes become placidly impenetrable, black and surface-lighted like obsidian; and when he saw that he might as well quit.

Then, at Potrero, they ran into Lije Powers. They remembered him as an old fool; and now he seemed immeasurably older and more foolish than he had been before. But he set them on the right track.

Lije greeted them with whoops and exaggerated grimaces of delight, in the manner of old men who have led rough and lonely lives. He pumped their hands, and stretched eyes and jaws wide in great meaningless guffaws. When that was over, though, they saw that there wasn't so very much of the old man left. His eyes were sunken, his cheeks had fallen in; and his worn clothes hung on a rack of bones.

"You look like holy hell," Amos told him.

"I ain't been too well," Lije admitted. "I been looking for you fellers. I got to talk to you."

"You heard we came out here?"

"Why, sure. Everybody I seen in the last six months knows all about you. Come on in the shade."

Lije took them to a two-by-four cantina without even a sign on it where whiskey was to be had, for a new thing and a wonder.

"I been looking for Debbie Edwards," he told them.

"So have we. We never have quit since we seen you last."

"Me neither," Lije said. He had turned abstemious, sipping his whiskey slowly, as if with care. When it came time to refill the glasses, his was always still more than half full, and he wouldn't toss it off, as others did, but just let the glass be filled up. He didn't seem much interested in hearing what they had tried, or where they had been, or even if they had ever found any clues. Just

204

wanted to tell at great length, with all the detail he could get them to stand for, the entire history of his own long search. He droned on and on, while Mart grew restless, then drunk, then sober again. But Amos seemed to want to listen.

"Guess you heard about the reward I put up," Amos said.

"I don't want the money, Amos," Lije said.

"Just been doing this out of the goodness of your heart, huh?"

"No . . . I'll tell you what I want. I want a job. Not a good job, nor one with too much riding. Bull cook, or like that, without no pay, neither, to speak of. Just a bunk, and a little grub, and a chai' by a stove. A place. But one where I don't never get throwed out. Time comes for me to haul off and die up, I want to be let die in that bunk. Not be throwed out for lack of the space I take up, or because a man on the die don't do much work."

There you had it—the end a prairie man could look forward to. Reaching out to accomplish some one great impossible thing at the last—as your only hope of securing just a place to lie down and die. Mart expected to hear Amos say that Lije was welcome to the bunk in any case.

"All right, Lije," Amos said. But he added, "If you find her."

Lije looked pleased; he hadn't expected anything more, nor been sure of this much. "So now lately, I been talking to these here Comancheros," he said.

"*Talking* to 'em?" Amos butted in.

205

"What's wrong with that? Ain't you been?"

"I ain't even seen one!"

Lije looked at him with disbelief, then with wonder; and finally with pity. "Son, son. In all this time you been in the Territory, I don't believe you've seen one other dang thing else!"

Not that these peons knew much about what they were doing, he admitted. They hired on as trail drivers, or packers, or bullwhackers, when the work was shoved at them. Probably wouldn't want to name their bosses, either, to a stranger who didn't seem to know any of them. You had to find los ricos—the men who ran the long drives down into Old Mexico, too deep for anything ever to be recovered. He named about a dozen of these, and Amos made him go back over some of the names to be sure he would remember them all.

"Old Jaime Rosas—he's the one I'd talk to, was I you." (He pronounced it "Hymie Rosies.") "I swear he knows where Bluebonnet is. And the girl."

"You think she's alive?"

"I figure *he* thinks so. I figure he's seen her. I all but had it out of him. Then I was stopped."

"How stopped? Who stopped you?"

"You did. . . . Jaime got word you was in the territory. He wouldn't deal no more with me. I figure he believed he could do better for himself letting you come to him. Direct."

Find Jaime Rosas. It was all they had to do, and it shouldn't be too hard with the Comanchero willing to deal. He was around this border someplace for a part of every year. Most years, anyway. Find him, and this search is licked. Out of the rattle-brained old fraud of a broke-down buffalo hunter had come the only straight, direct lead they had ever had.

Amos gave Lije forty dollars, and Lije rode off in a different direction than Amos took. Said he wanted to check on some Caddoes he heard was running whiskey in. He always had seemed to have Caddoes on the brain. And Amos and Mart went looking for Jaime Rosas.

26

They did find old Jaime Rosas; or perhaps he had to find them in the end. It was the heart-breaking distances that held them back from coming up with him for so long. You were never in the wrong place without being about a week and a half away from the right one. That country seemed to have some kind of weird spell upon it, so that you could travel in one spot all day long, and never gain a mile. You might start out in the morning with a notched butte far off on your left; and when you camped at nightfall the same notched butte would be right there, in the same place. Maybe it was a good thing that a man and his plodding horse could not see that country from the sky, as the vultures saw it. If a man could have seen the vastness in which he was a speck, the heart would have gone out of him; and if his horse could have seen it, the animal would have died.

Now that they knew the names of the boss

Comancheros, the people were more willing to help them, relaying news of the movements of Jaime Rosas. If they had no news they made up some, and this could prove a costly thing. If a peon wanted to please you he would give you a tale of some kind—never hesitating to send you ninety miles out of your way, rather than disappoint you by telling you he didn't know.

While they were hunting for Jaime Rosas, Martin Pauley's nights became haunted for a while by a peculiar form of dream. The source of the dream was obvious. One blazing day in Los Gatos, where they were held up through the heat of the siesta hours, Mart had wandered into a church, because it looked cool and pleasantly dark within the deep adobe walls. Little candles grouped in several places stood out in bright pinpoints, some of them red where they had burned down in their ruby glasses. Mart sat down, and as his eyes adjusted he began to see the images, life-size and dark-complected mostly, of saints and martyrs, all around him in the gloom. Painted in natural colors, with polished stones for eyes, they looked a lot like people, here in the dark. Except that they were unnaturally still. Not even the candle flames wavered in the quiet air. Mart sat there, fascinated, for a long time.

About a week after that, Mart dreamed of Debbie. In all this time he had never seen her in a dream before; perhaps because he rarely dreamed at all. But this dream was very real and clear. He seemed to be standing in the dark church. The images around him again, like living people, but holding unnaturally still. He could feel their presence strongly, but they seemed neither friendly nor hostile—just there. Directly in front of him a candlelighted shrine began to brighten, and there was Debbie, in the middle of a soft white light. She was littler than when she was lost, littler than in the miniature even, and with a different look and pose than the miniature had—more of a side-face position. She didn't look out at him, or move, any more than the images did, but she was alive—he knew she was alive; she fairly glowed with life, as if made of the light itself.

He stood holding his breath, waiting for her to turn and see him. He could feel the moment when she would turn to him coming nearer, and nearer, until the strain was unbearable, and woke him up just too soon.

The same dream returned to him on other nights, sometimes close together, sometimes many days apart, perhaps a dozen times. The whole thing was always as real and clear as it had been the first time; and he always woke up just before Debbie turned. Then, for no reason, he quit having that dream, and he couldn't make it come back.

Rumors found their way to them from Texas, most of them fourth- or fifth-hand tales of things that had happened months before. Yet there was enough substance to what they heard to tell that the smoldering frontier was blazing up into open war. A chief usually called Big Red Food, but whose name Mart translated as Raw Meat, charged a company of infantry close to Fort Sill, broke clean through it, and rode away. Wolf Tail drummed up a great gathering of warriors from many bands, dragging Quanah into it. For three days

209

they pressed home an attack upon a party of buffalo hunters at Adobe Walls, charge after charge, but were beaten off with heavy loss. Every war chief they had ever known seemed to be up; but now Washington at last had had enough. The Friends were out of the Agencies, and the military was in the saddle. A finish fight seemed cocked and primed. . . .

But they had had no news for weeks, the night they found Jaime Rosas.

They had come after dark into Puerto del Sol, a village with more people in it than most. It had no hacienda and no church, but it did have a two-acre corral with high adobe walls, loopholed, so that the corral could be fought as a fort. Several unnecessarily large adobe stores, with almost nothing for sale in them, looked a lot like warehouses. A Comanchero base, sure enough, Mart thought.

The place had two cantinas, each with more volunteer guitar singers than it needed, cadging for drinks. Amos picked the smaller and better of the two, and as they went in, Mart saw that in Puerta del Sol the cantinas actually did have señoritas, for a rarity. They had been overanticipated for a long time, due to Amos' original confusion of this country with a part of Old Mexico that was the whole length of Texas away. The territory dance girls had been disappointing, what few times they had seen any—just stolid-faced little women like squaws, either too fat or with a half-grown look. These of Puerto del Sol didn't look much better, at first.

Amos fell in at once with a smart-looking vaquero with leather lace on his hat. A haciendado, or the son

210

of one—if he wasn't one of the boss Comancheros. Mart bought a short glass of tequila and a tall glass of tepid water clouded with New Mexico Territory, and took them to a table in a corner. Amos didn't seem to like Mart standing by when he was angling for information. Sooner or later he was likely to include Mart in the conversation by some remark such as: "What the devil you haunting me for?" Or: "What in all hell you want now?" Since the dreams of Debbie had stopped, Mart was beginning to have a hard time remembering why he was still riding with Amos. Most days it was a matter of habit. He kept on because he had no plans of his own, nor any idea of where to head for if he split off.

The vaquero with the expensive hat went away, and came back with a shabby old man. Amos sat with these two, buying them drinks, but he seemed to have lost interest. All three seemed bored with the whole thing. They sat gazing idly about, with the placid vacuity common to the country, seeming to be trying to forget each other, as much as anything. Mart saw Amos make a Spanish joke he had worked out, something about the many flies drinking his liquor up, and the other two laughed politely. Amos wasn't finding out anything, Mart judged.

Mart's attention went back to the girls. There were five or six of them in here, but not the same ones all the time. They flirted with the vaqueros, and danced for them, and with them; and now and then a girl disappeared with one, whereupon another wandered in to take her place. They drank wine, but smelled mostly of vanilla-bean perfume and musk. These girls carried a sudden danger with them, as if death must be a he-goat, and liked to follow them around. Mart himself had seen one case of knife-in-the-belly, and had heard of a good many more. A girl let her eyes wander once too often, and the knives jumped with no warning at all. In the next two seconds there was liable to be a man on the dirt floor, and a surprised new face in hell. The girl screamed, and yammered, and had to be dragged away in a hollering tizzy; but was back the next night, with her eyes wandering just as much. Mart wondered if a girl got famous, and had songs made about her, if people pointed her out and said, "Five men are dead for that little one."

So he was watching for it, and able to handle it, when it almost happened to him. The tequila had an unpleasant taste, hard to get used to, as if somebody had washed his sox in it, but it hid a flame. As it warmed his brain, everything looked a lot prettier; and a new girl who came in looked different from all the others he had seen out here—or anywhere, maybe.

This girl was pert and trim, and her skirts flared in a whirl of color when she turned. Her Spanish-heeled shoes must have been a gift brought a long way, perhaps from Mexico City. The shoes set her apart from the others, who wore moccasins, at best, when they weren't barefoot altogether. She had a nose-shaped nose, instead of a flat one, and carried her head with defiance. Or anyhow, that was the way Mart saw her now, and always remembered her.

A lot of eyes looked this one up and down with appreciation, as if her dress were no more barrier to appraisal than harness on a filly. Martin Pauley dropped his eyes to his hands. He had a tall glass in one hand and a short glass in the other, and he studied this situation stupidly for a few moments before he swallowed a slug of warmish chalky water, and tossed off the rest of his tequila. He had drunk slowly, but a good many. And now the tequila looked up, fastened eyes upon the girl, and held without self-consciousness, wherever she went. There is a great independence, and a confident immunity to risk, in all drinks made out of cactus.

An old saying said itself in his mind. "Indian takes drink; drink takes drink; drink takes Indian; all chase squaw." It had a plausible, thoughtful sound, but no practical meaning. Presently the girl noticed him, and looked at him steadily for some moments, trying to make up her mind about him in the bad light. Nothing came of this immediately; a peonish fellow, dressed like a vaquero, but not a good one, took hold of her and made her dance with him. Mart sucked his teeth and thought nothing of it. He had no plans.

The girl had, though, and steered her partner toward Mart's table. She fixed her eyes on Mart, swung close, and kicked him in the shin. One way to do it, Mart thought. And here it comes. He drained a last drop from his tequila glass, and let his right hand come to rest on his leg under the table. Sure enough. The vaquero turned and looked him over across the table. His shirt was open to the waist, showing the brown chest to be smooth and hairless.

"Your eye is of a nasty color," the vaquero said poetically in Chihuahua Spanish. "Of a sameness to the

213

belly of a carp."

Mart leaned forward with a smile, eyebrows up, as if in response to a greeting he had not quite caught. "And you?" he returned courteously, also in Spanish. "We have a drink, no?"

"No," said the vaquero, looking puzzled.

"We have a drink, yes," the girl changed his mind. "You know why? The gun of this man is in his right hand under the table. He blows your bowels out the door in one moment. This is necessary."

She extended an imperious palm, and Mart slid a silver dollar across the table to her. The vaquero was looking thoughtful as she led him away. Mart never knew what manner of drink she got into the fellow, but she was back almost at once. The vaquero was already to be seen snoring on the mud floor. A compadre dragged him out by the feet, and laid him tenderly in the road.

She said her name was Estrellita, which he did not believe; it had a picked-out sound to him. She sat beside him and sang at him with a guitar. The tequila was thinking in Spanish now, so that the words of the sad, sad song made sense without having to be translated in his head.

> I see a stranger passing,
>   His heart is dark with sorrows,
> Another such as I am,
>   Behind him his tomorrows . . .

This song was a great epic tragedy in about a hundred stanzas, each ending on a suspended note, to keep the listener on the hook. But she hadn't got through more than half a dozen when she stopped and leaned forward to peer into his eyes. Perhaps she saw signs of his bursting into tears, for she got him up and danced with him. A whole battery of guitars had begun whaling out a *baile* as soon as she stopped singing, and the tequila was just as ready to romp and stomp as to bawl into the empty glasses. As she came close to him, her musk-heavy perfume wrapped around him, strong enough to lift him off his feet with one hand. The tequila thought it was wonderful. No grabbing of arms in dancing with this one—you swung the girl by taking hold of the girl. The round neckline of her dress was quite modest, almost up to her throat, and her sleeves were tied at her elbows. But what he found out was that this was a very thin dress.

"I think it is time to go home now," she said.

"I have no home," he said blankly.

"My house is your house," she told him.

He remembered to speak to Amos about it. The young well-dressed vaquero was gone, and Amos sat head to head with the shabby old man, talking softly and earnestly. "All right if I take a walk?" Mart interrupted them.

"Where you going to be?" Amos asked the girl in Spanish.

She described a turn or two and counted doors on her fingers. Amos went back to his powwow, and Mart guessed he was dismissed. "Wait a minute," Amos called him back. He gave Mart a handful of silver dol-

215

lars without looking up. Good thing he did. Running out of *dinero* is another first-class way to get in trouble around a cantina señorita.

Her *casa* turned out to be the scrubbiest horse stall of a jacal he had seen yet. She lighted a candle, and the place looked a little better inside, mostly because of a striped serape on the dirt floor and a couple tied on the walls to cover holes where the mud had fallen out of the woven twigs. The candle stood in a little shrine sheltering a pottery Virgin of Tiburon, and this reminded Mart of something, but he couldn't remember what. He blinked as he watched Estrellita cross herself and kneel briefly in obeisance. Then she came to him and presented her back to be unbuttoned.

All through this whole thing, Mart showed the dexterity and finesse of a hog in a sand boil, and even the tequila knew it. It was very young tequila at best, as its raw bite had attested, and it couldn't help him much after a point. One moment he was afraid to touch her, and in the next, when he did take her in his arms, he almost broke her in two. The girl was first astonished, then angry; but finally her sense of humor returned, and she felt sorry for him. She turned patient, soothing and gentling him; and when at last he slept he was in such a state of relaxation that even his toe nails must have been limp.

So now, of course, he had to get up again.

Amos came striding down the narrow *calle*, banging his heels on the hard dirt. One of his spurs had a loose wheel; it had always been that way. It never whispered when he rode, but afoot this spur made some different

216

complaint at every step. Thug, ding, thug, clank, thug, bingle, went Amos as he walked; and the familiar sound woke Mart from a hundred feet away.

"Get your clothes on," Amos said, as soon as the door was open. "We're on our way."

Except for a slight queerness of balance as he first stood up, Mart felt fine. There is no cleaner liquor than tequila when it is made right, however awful it may taste. "Right now? In the middle of the night?"

"Look at the sky."

Mart saw that the east was turning light. "I suppose that old man seen Jaime Rosas some far-fetched place. Maybe last year, or the year before."

"That old man is Jaime Rosas."

Mart stared at Amos' silhouette, then stamped into his boots.

"He says Bluebonnet has a young white girl," Amos told him. "One with yaller hair and green eyes."

"Where at?"

"Rosas is taking us to him. We'll be there before night."

They had been in New Mexico more than two years and a half.

27

They sat in a circle in the shade of a tepee eighteen feet across, three white men and seven war chiefs around a charred spot that would have been a council fire if a fire had been tolerable that day.

The scraped buffalo hide of the tepee had been rolled up for a couple of feet, and the hot wind crept under, sometimes raising miniature dust devils on the hard dirt floor.

Bluebonnet, the elusive ghost they had followed for so long, sat opposite the entrance flap. Mart had long since stopped trying to believe there was any Comanche named Bluebonnnet, or the Flower, or whatever his damned name meant in words. He judged Bluebonnet to be a myth, the work of an all-Indian conspiracy. Every savage in creation had probably heard of the two searchers by this time, and stood ready to join in the sport of sending them hither and yon in chase of a chief who did not exist. Yet there he was; and on the outside of the tepee, large as a shield, the oft-described, never-seen symbol of the Flower was drawn in faded antelope blood.

An oddly shimmering light, a reflection from the sun-blasted surface of the earth outside, played over the old chief's face. It was the broad, flat face common to one type of Comanche, round and yellow as a moon. Age was crinkling its surface in fine-lined patterns, into which the opaque eyes were set flush, without hollows.

The other six war chiefs weren't needed here. Bluebonnet had them as a courtesy—and to reassure his village that he wasn't making foolish trades behind the backs of his people. It wasn't much of a village. It numbered only fourteen lodges, able to turn out perhaps thirty or forty warriors by counting all boys over twelve. But it was what he had. His pride and his special notion of his honor were still very great, far though he was on his road to oblivion.

Jaime Rosas had four vaqueros with him, but he hadn't brought them into council. They were tall Indian-looking men, good prairie Comancheros, but he owed them no courtesies. The vaqueros had pitched a shade-fly of their own a little way off. Three of them slept most of the time, but one was always awake, day or night, whatever the time might be. Whenever several were awake at once they were to be heard laughing a good deal, or else singing a sad long song that might last a couple of hours; then all but one would go back to sleep again.

What was going on in the tepee was in the nature of a horse trade. The evening of their arrival had been devoted to a meager feast without dancing, the atmosphere considerably dampened by the fact that Rosas had brought no rum. The council began the next morning. It was a slow thing, with long stillnesses between irrelevant remarks conveyed in sign language. One thing about it, no one was likely to go off half cocked in a session like that. From time to time the pipe, furnished by Bluebonnet, was filled with a pinch of tobacco, furnished by Rosas, and passed from hand to hand, as a sort of punctuation.

They were in that tepee three days, the councils running from forenoon to sundown. Even a cowboy's back can get busted, sitting cross-legged as long as that. Jaime Rosas did all the talking done on the white men's side. This old man's face was weathered much darker than Bluebonnet's; his dirty gray mustache looked whiter than it was against that skin. His eyes had brown veins in the whites and red-rimmed lids. All day long he chewed slowly on a grass stem with teeth worn to brown stubs; by night he would have a foot-long stem eaten down to an inch or two. He could sit quiet as long as Bluebonnet could, and maybe a little longer; and when he unlimbered his sign language it ran as smoothly as Bluebonnet's, though this chief prided himself on the grace of his sign talk. The unpunctuated flow of compound signs made the conversation all but impossible to follow.

Rosas' hands might say, "Horse-dig-hole-slow-buffalo-chase-catch-no-enemy-run-chase-catch-no-sad." Mart read that to mean, "The horse is worthless—too slow for hunting or for war; it's too bad."

And Bluebonnet's answer, in signs of smooth speed and great delicacy: "Stiff-neck-beat-enemy-far-run-still-neck-horse-ride-leave-tepee-warriors-pile-up." They had him there, Mart admitted to himself. He believed Bluebonnet had said, "When a chief has run his enemies out of the country, he wants a horse he can ride with pride, like to a council." But he didn't know. Here came the pipe again.

"I'll never get no place in this dang country," he said to Amos. "It's a good thing we'll soon be heading home."

"Shut up." It was the first remark Amos had made that day.

Toward sundown of the first day Bluebonnet admitted he had a young white girl, blonde and blue-eyed, in his lodge.

220

"May not be the one," Amos said in Spanish.

"Who knows?" Rosas answered. "Man is the hands of God."

Around noon of the second day, Rosas presented Bluebonnet with the horse they had talked about most of the first day. It was a show-off palomino, with a stud-horse neck and ripples in its silver mane and tail. About what the old dons would have called a palfrey once. Mart wouldn't have wanted it. But the saddle on it, sheltered under a tied-down canvas until the moment of presentation, was heavily crusted with silver, and probably worth two hundred dollars. Rosas gave the old chief horse and rig upon condition that no present would be accepted in return. Bluebonnet turned wary for a while after that, as if the gift might have done more harm than good; but his eyes showed a gleam toward the end of the day, for what they talked about all afternoon was rifles.

Sundown was near on the third day when they came to the end at last. The abruptness of the finish caught Mart off guard. Rosas and Bluebonnet had been going through an interminable discussion of percussion caps, as near as Mart could make out. He had given up trying to follow it, and had let his eyes lose focus in the glow of the leveling sun upon the dust. He took a brief puff as the pipe passed him again, and was aware that one of the warriors got up and went out.

Amos said, "He's sent for her, Mart."

The desert air seemed to press inward upon the tepee with an unbelievable weight. His head swam, and he could not recognize a single familiar symbol among the next posturings of Bluebonnet's hands.

"He says she's well and strong," Amos told him.

Mart returned his eyes to Bluebonnet's hands. His head cleared, and he saw plainly the next thing the hands said. He turned to Amos in appeal, unwilling to believe he had properly understood.

"The girl is his wife," Amos interpreted.

"It doesn't matter." His mouth was so dry that the thick words were not understandable at all. Mart cleared his throat, and tried to spit, but could not. "It doesn't matter," he said again.

The warrior who had left the lodge now returned. As he entered, he spoke a Comanche phrase over his shoulder, and a young woman appeared. Her form was not that of a little girl; it hardly could have been after the lost years. This was a woman, thin, and not very tall, but grown. Her face and the color of her hair were hidden by a shawl that must once have been red, but now was dulled by the perpetually blowing dust.

His eyes dropped. She wore heel-fringed moccasins, a prerogative of warriors, permitted to squaws only as a high honor. But her feet were narrow and high-arched, unlike the short, splayed feet of Comanches. The ankles were tanned, and speckles of the everlasting dust clung to them, too, as if they were sprinkled with cinnamon; yet he could see the blue veins under the thin skin. She followed the warrior into the lodge with a step as light and tense as that of a stalking wolf. He realized with a sinking of the heart that the girl was afraid—not of the Flower, or his warriors, but of her own people.

222

Bluebonnet said in the Comanche tongue, "Come stand beside me."

The young woman obeyed. Beside Bluebonnet she turned reluctantly toward the council circle, still clutching the shawl that hid her face so that nothing was visible but the whitened knuckles of one hand. On one side of Mart, Amos sat, an immovable lump. On his other side, Rosas had thrown down his grass stem. His eyes were slitted, but his glance flickered back and forth between the girl and Amos' face, while he moved no other muscle. Over and over, white girls captured as children and raised by the Comanches have been ashamed to look white men in the face.

"Show them your head," Bluebonnet said in Comanche, Mart thought; though perhaps he had said "hair" instead of "head."

The white girl's head bowed lower, and she uncovered the top of it, to let them see the color of her hair. It was cropped short in the manner of the Comanches, among whom only the men wore long hair, but it was blonde. Not a bright blonde; a mousy shade. But blonde.

"Show your face," came Bluebonnet's Comanche words, and the girl let the shawl fall, though her face remained averted. The old chief spoke sharply at last. "Hold up your head! Obey!"

The girl's head raised. For a full minute the silence held while Mart stared, praying, trying to persuade himself of—what? The tanned but once white face was broad and flat, the forehead low, the nose shapeless, the mouth pinched yet loose. The eyes were green, all right, but small and set close together; they darted like an animal's, craving escape. Mart's mind moved again. Stare an hour, he told himself. Stare a year. You'll never get any different answer. Nor find room for any possible mistake.

This girl was not Debbie.

Mart got up, and blundered out into the reddening horizontal rays of the sunset. Behind him he heard Amos say harshly, "You speak English?" The girl did not answer. Mart never asked Amos what else was said. He walked away from the tepee of the Flower, out of the village, a long way out onto the thin-grassed flats. Finally he just stood, alone in the twilight.

28

Once more they went around the Staked Plains, passing to the south; but this time as they turned north they were headed home. They traveled by listless stages, feeling nothing much ahead to reach for now. Home, for them, was more of a direction than a place. It was like a surveyor's marker that is on the map but not on the ground: You're south of it, and you ride toward it, and after a while you're north of it, but you're never exactly there, because there isn't any such thing, except in the mind. They were nothing more than beaten men, straggling back down the long, long way they had traveled to their final defeat.

Fort Concho was deserted as they came to it, except for a token guard. But for once the emptiness had a difference. This was one garrison that had not been with-drawn by the fatheaded wishfulness that had disarmed more American troops than any other enemy. Three regiments under the colonel were on the march, riding northwest into the heart of the Comanche country. And these were part of a broad campaign, planned with thoroughness, and activated by a total resolution. For General Sheridan was in the saddle again, this time with a latitude of action that would let him put an end to rewarded murder once and for all.

North of Mackenzie's column, Colonel Buell was advancing; Colonel Nelson A. Miles was marching south from Fort Supply; Major William Price was coming into it from Fort Union beyond the Staked Plains. And at Fort Sill, Colonel Davidson, with per-haps the strongest force of all, to judge by the rumors they heard, hung poised until the other columns should be advantageously advanced. Under Sheridan there would be no more of the old chase, charge, scatter 'em and go home. These troops would dog and follow, fighting if the Indians stood, but always coming on again. Once a column fastened upon a Comanche band, that band would be followed without turnoff, regardless of what more tempting quarry crossed between. And this would go on until no hostile could find a way to stay out and live.

When they had learned the scope of what was hap-pening, Mart knew without need of words what Amos, with all his heart, would want to do now. It was the same thing he himself wanted, more than women, more than love, more than food or drink. They made a close study of their horses—a study about as needful as a close count of the fingers on their hands. Each horse had served as his rider's very muscles, day in and day out, for months. The two men were trying to persuade themselves that their horses were wiry, and wise in tricks for saving their strength, instead of just gaunted and low of head. But it couldn't be done, and not a horse was left at Fort Concho worth saddling.

Finally the two rode out and sat looking at the trail, stale and all but effaced, that the cavalry had made as it rode away. Up that trail hundreds of men were riding to what seemed a final kill—yet riding virtually blind for lack of just such scouts as Mart and Amos had become. But the column had so great a start it might as well have been on another world. Amos was first to shrug and turn away. Mart still sat a little while more, staring up that vacant trail; but at last drew a deep breath, let it all out again, and followed Amos.

They plodded north and east through a desolate land, for this year the country looked the worst they had ever seen it. The summer had been wickedly hot and totally dry; and on top of the drought great swarms of grasshoppers had come to chop what feed there was into blowing dust. The few bands of cattle they saw were all bones, and wild as deer. Only the aged cattle showed brands, for no one had worked the border ranges in a long time. Yet, if above all you wanted the cavalry to succeed, you had to look at the drought-ravaged range with a grim satisfaction. The cavalry carried horse corn, something no Indian would ever do, and the drought had given the grain-fed mounts an advan-

226

tage that not even Comanche horsemanship could overcome this one year.

Toward noon of a colorless November day they raised the Edwards layout—"the old Edwards place," people called it now, if they knew what it was at all. And now came an experience worth forgetting altogether, except for the way it blew up on them later on. A thread of smoke rose straight up in the dead air from the central chimney of the house. They saw it from a great way off, and Mart looked at Amos, but they did not change the pace of their horses. Riding nearer, they saw a scratched-up half acre in front of the house, where Martha had meant to have a lawn and a garden someday. Here a bony rack of a mule was working on some runty corn stalks. It lifted its head and stood motionless, a rag of fodder hanging from its jaws, as it watched them steadily all the way in.

They saw other things to resent. Most of the corral poles were gone for firewood, along with a good many boards from the floors of the galleries. The whole homestead had the trashy look of a place where nothing is ever taken care of.

"Got a sodbuster in here," Amos said as they came up.

"Or a Mex," Mart suggested.

"Sodbuster," Amos repeated.

"I guess I'll ride on," Mart said. "I got no craving to see how the house looks now."

"If you hear shots," Amos said, "tell the Mathisons I ain't coming."

"Looking for trouble?"

"Fixing to make some."

That settled that. They tied their ponies to the gallery posts. The latch string whipped out of sight into its little hole in the door as Amos crossed the gallery. He kicked the door twice, once to test it, and once to drive it in. The bar brackets never had been repaired very well since the dreadful night when they were broken.

By the woodbox, as if he wanted to take cover behind the stove, a gaunt turkey-necked man was trying to load a shotgun with rattling hands. Automatically Mart and Amos moved apart, and their six-guns came out. "Put that thing down," Amos said.

"You got no right bustin' in on—"

Amos fired, and splinters jumped at the squatter's feet. The shotgun clattered on the floor, and they had time to take a look at what else was in the room. Five dirty children stood goggle-eyed as far back as they could get, and a malarial woman was frying jack rabbit; the strong grease smelled as if fur had got into it. A dress that had been Martha's dress hung loose on the woman's frame, and some of the children's clothes were Debbie's. He might have been sorry for all these saucer eyes except for that.

"You're in my house," Amos said.

"Wasn't nobody using it. We ain't hurting your—"

"Shut up!" Amos said. There was quiet, and Mart noticed the dirt, and some big holes in the chimney, the walls, the window reveals, where adobe bricks had been prized out.

"Been looking for something, I see," Amos said. "Let's see if you found it. Hold 'em steady, Mart."

Amos picked up a mattock, and went into a bedroom, where he could be heard chunking a hole in the adobe with heavy strokes. He came back with an adobe-dusted tin box, and let them watch him pour gold pieces from it into a side pocket; Mart guessed there must be about four hundred dollars.

"I'll be back in a week," Amos said. "I want this place scrubbed out, and the walls patched and whitewashed. Fix them gallery floors out there, and start hauling poles for them corrals. Make all as it was, and might be I'll leave you stay till spring."

"I got no time for—"

"Then you better be long gone when I come!"

They walked out of there and rode on.

29

Nothing ever changed much at the Mathisons. The old, well-made things never wore out; if they broke they were mended stronger than they were before. Pump handles wore down to a high polish, door sills showed deeper hollows. But nothing was allowed to gather the slow grime of age. Only when you had been gone a couple of years could you see that the place was growing old. Then it looked smaller than you remembered it, and kind of rounded at the corners everywhere. Mart rode toward it this time with a feeling that the whole place belonged to the past that he was done with, like the long search that had seemed to have no end, but had finally run out anyway.

They didn't mean to be here long. Amos meant to ride on to Austin at once, to clear up the killings at Lost Mule Creek; and if he got held up, Mart meant to go there alone, and get it over. He didn't know what he was going to do after that, but it sure would be someplace else. He believed that he was approaching the Mathisons for the last time. Maybe when he looked over his shoulder at this place, knowing he would never see it again, then he would feel something about it, but he felt nothing now. None of it was a part of him any more.

The people had aged like the house, except a little faster and a little plainer to be seen. Mart saw at first glance that Aaron was almost totally blind. Tobe and Abner were grown men. And Mrs. Mathison was a little old lady, who came out of the kitchen into the cold to take him by both hands. "My, my, Martie! It's been so long! You've been gone five—no, it's more. Why, it's coming on six years! Did you know that?" No; he hadn't known that. Not to count it all up together that way. Seemingly she didn't remember they had been home twice in the meantime.

But the surprise was that Laurie was still here. He had assumed she would have gone off and married Charlie MacCorry long ago, and she had quit haunting him once he swallowed that. She didn't come out of the house as he unsaddled, but as he came into the kitchen she crossed to him, drying her hands. Why did she always have to be at either the stove or the sink? Well, because it was always coming time to eat again, actually. They were close onto suppertime right now.

She didn't kiss him, or take hold of him in any way.

230

"Did you—have you ever—" Resignation showed in her eyes, but they were widened by an awareness of tragedy, as if she knew the answer before she spoke. And his face confirmed it for her. "Not anything? No least trace of her at all?"

He drew a deep breath, wondering what part of their long try needed to be told. "Nothing," he said, finally, and judged that covered it all.

"You've been out so long," she said slowly, marveling. "I suppose you talk Comanche like an Indian. Do they call you Indian names?"

"I sure wouldn't dast interpret the most of the names they call us," he answered automatically. But he added, "Amos is known to 'em as 'Bull Shoulders.' "

"And you?"

"Oh—I'm just the 'Other.' "

"I suppose you'll be going right out again, Other?"

"No. I think now she was dead from the first week we rode."

"I'm sorry, Martie." She turned away, and for a few minutes went through slow motions, changing the setting of the table, moving things that didn't need to be moved. Something besides what she was doing was going through her mind, so plainly you could almost hear it tick. Abruptly, she left her work and got her coat, spinning it over her shoulders like a cape.

Her mother said, "Supper's almost on. Won't be but a few minutes."

"All right, Ma." Laurie gave Mart one expressionless glance, and he followed her, putting his sheepskin on, as she went out the door to the dog-trot.

231

"Where's Charlie?" he asked, flat-footed, once they were outside.

"He's still in the Rangers. He's stationed over at Harper's, now; he's done well enough so he could politic that. But we don't see him too much. Seems like Rangers live on the hard run nowadays." She met his eyes directly, without shyness, but without lighting up much, either.

A small wind was stirring now, shifting the high overcast. At the horizon a line of blood-bright sunset light broke through, turning the whole prairie red. They walked in silence, well apart, until they had crossed a rise and were out of sight of the house. Laurie said, "I suppose you'll be going on to Austin soon."

"We've got to. Amos put up a thousand head—Of course, the Rangers can't collect until a judge or somebody declares Debbie dead. But they'll do that now. We got to go there, and straighten it out."

"Are you coming back, Martie?"

The direct question took him off guard. He had thought some of working his way up toward Montana, if the Rangers didn't lock him up, or anything. They were having big Indian trouble up there, and Mart believed himself well qualified to scout against the Sioux. But it didn't make much sense to head north into the teeth of winter, and spring was far away. So he said something he hadn't meant to say. "Do you want me to come back, Laurie?"

"I won't be here."

He thought he understood that. "I figured you'd be married long before now."

"It might have happened. Once. But Pa never could stand Charlie. Pa's had so much trouble come down on him—he always blamed himself for what happened to your folks. Did you know that? I didn't want to bring on one thing more, and break his heart. Not then. If I had it to do over—I don't know. But I don't want to stay here now. I know that. I'm going to get out of Texas, Mart."

He looked stupid, and said, "Oh?"

"This is a dreadful country. I've come to hate these prairies, every inch of 'em—and I bet they stretch a million miles. Nothing to look forward to—or back at, either—I want to go to Memphis. Or Vicksburg, or New Orleans."

"You got kinfolk back there?"

"No. I don't know anybody."

"Now, you know you can't do that! You never been in a settlement bigger'n Fort Worth in your life. Any gol dang awful thing is liable to happen to you in a place like them!"

"I'm twenty-four years old," she said bitterly. "Time something happened."

He searched for something to say, and came up with the most stilted remark he had ever heard. "I wouldn't want anything untoward to happen to you, Laurie," he said.

"Wouldn't you?"

"I've been long gone. But I was doing what I had to do, Laurie. You know that."

"For five long years," she reminded him.

He wanted to let her know it wasn't true that he

233

hadn't cared what happened to her. But he couldn't explain the way hope had led him on, dancing down the prairie like a fox fire, always just ahead. It didn't seem real any more. So finally he just put an arm around her waist as they walked, pulling her closer to his side.

The result astonished him. Laurie stopped short, and for a moment stood rigid; then she turned toward him, and came into his arms. "Martie, Martie, Martie," she whispered, her mouth against his. She had on a lot of winter clothes, but the girl was there inside them, solider than Estrellita, but slim and warm. And now somebody began hammering on a triangle back at the house, calling them in.

"Oh, damn," he said, "damn, damn—"

She put her fingers on his lips to make him listen. "Start coughing soon's we go in the house. Make out you're coming down with a lung chill."

"Me? What for?"

"The boys put your stuff in the bunkhouse. But I'll work it out so you're moved to the grandmother room. Just you, by yourself. Late tonight, when they're all settled in, I'll come to you there."

Jingle-jangle-bang went the triangle again.

30 _____

That night Lije Powers came back.

They were still at the supper table as they heard his horse; and the men glanced at each other, for the plodding hoofs seemed to wander instead of coming straight on up to the door. And next they heard his curiously weak hail. Abner and Tobe Mathison went out. Lije swayed in the saddle, then lost balance and buckled as he tried to dismount, so that Tobe had to catch him in his arms.

"Drunker than a spinner wolf," Tobe announced.

"Drunk, hell," Abner disagreed. "The man's got a bullet in him!"

"No, I ain't," Lije said, and went into a coughing fit that made a fool of Mart's effort to fake a bad chest. Tobe and Abner were both wrong; Lije was as ill a man as had ever got where he was going on a horse. At the door he tottered against the jamb, and clung to it feebly, preventing them from closing it against the rising wind, until the coughing fit passed off.

"I found her," Lije said, still blocking the door. I found Deb'rie Edwards." He slid down the side of the door and collapsed.

They carried him into the grandmother room and put him to bed. "He's out of his head," Aaron Mathison said, pulling off Lije Powers' boots.

"I got a bad cold," Lije wheezed at them. He was glassy-eyed, and his skin burned their fingers. "But I'm no more out of my mind than you. I talked to her. She spoke her name. I seen her as close as from here to you. . . ."

"Where?" Amos demanded.

"She's with a chief named Yellow Buckle. Amos—you mind the Seven Fingers?"

Amos looked blank. The names meant nothing to him.

235

Aaron Mathison said, "Will you leave the man be? He's in delirium!"

"Be still!" Mart snapped at Aaron.

"I got a cold," Lije repeated, and his voice turned pleading. "Ain't anybody ever heard of the Seven Fingers?"

"Seems like there's a bunch of cricks," Mart said, groping for a memory, "west of the Wichita Mountains. . . . No, farther—beyond the Little Rainies. I think they run into the North Fork of the Red. Lije, ain't Seven Fingers the Kiowa name for them little rivers?"

"That's it! That's it!" Lije cried out eagerly. "Do this get me my rocking chai', Amos?"

"Sure, Lije. Now take it easy."

They piled blankets on him, and wrapped a hot stove lid to put at his feet, then spooned a little soup into him. It was what Mrs. Mathison called her "apron-string soup," because it had noodles in it. But Lije kept on talking, as if he feared he might lose hold and never be able to tell them once he let down.

"Yellow Buckle's squaws was feeding us. One comes behind me and she puts this calabash in my lap. Full of stewed gut tripe. . . . She bends down, and makes out like she picks a stick out of it with her fingers. And she whispers in my ear. 'I'm Deb'rie,' she says. 'I'm Deb'rie Edwards.' "

"Couldn't you get a look at her?"

"I snuck a quick look over my shoulder. Her head was covered. But I seen these here green eyes. Green-er'n a wild grape peeled out . . ."

"Was that all?" Amos asked as the old man trailed off.

"I didn't see her no more. And I didn't dast say nothing, or ask."

"Who's Yellow Buckle with?" The answer was so long in coming that Mart started to repeat, but the sick man had heard him.

"I seen . . . Fox Moon . . . and Bull Eagle . . . Singin' Dog . . . Hunts-His-Horse—I think it was him. Some more'll come back to me. Do it get me my chai' by the stove?"

"You're never going to want for anything," Amos said.

Lije Powers rolled to the edge of the bunk in a spasm of coughing, and the blood he brought up dribbled on the floor.

"Lije," Mart raised his voice, "do you know if—"

"Leave be now," Aaron Mathison commanded them. "Get out of this room, and leave be! Or I put you out!"

"Just one more thing," Mart persisted. "Is Yellow Buckle ever called any other name?"

Aaron took a step toward him, but the thin voice spoke once more. "I think—" Lije said, "I think—some call him Cut-face."

"Get out!" Aaron roared, and moved upon them. This time they obeyed. Mrs. Mathison stayed with the very ill old man, while Laurie fetched and carried for her.

"It upsets a man," Aaron said, all quietness again, when the door had closed upon the grandmother

237

room. "But I find no word in it to believe."

Mart spoke up sharply. "I think he's telling the truth!"

"There's a whole lot wrong with it, Mart," Amos said. "Like: 'I'm Deb'rie,' she says. Nobody in our family ever called her 'Deb'rie' in her life. She never heard the word."

"Lije says 'Debrie' for the same reason he says 'prairuh,' " Mart disputed him. "He'd talk the same if he was telling what you said, or me."

"And them Indians. Fox Moon is a Kotsetaka, and so is Singing Dog. But Bull Eagle is a Quohada, and never run with no Kotsetakas. I question if he ever seen one!"

"Can't a sick old man get one name wrong without you knock apart everything he done?"

"We was all through them Kotsetakas—"

"And maybe passed her within twenty feet!"

"All right. But how come we never heard of any Yellow Buckle?"

"We sure as hell heard of Scar!"

"Sure," Amos said wearily. "Lije was the same places we been, Martie. And heard the same things. That's all."

"But he saw her," Mart insisted, circling back to where they had begun.

"Old Lije has been a liar all his life," Amos said with finality. "You know that well as me."

Mart fell silent.

"You see, Martin," Aaron Mathison said gently, "yon lies a foolish old man. When you've said that, you've

238

said all; and there's the end on it."

"Except for one thing," Amos said, and his low voice sounded very tired. They looked at him, and waited, while for several moments he seemed lost in thought. "We've made some far casts, looking for a chief called Scar. We never found him. And Aaron, I believe like you: We never will. But suppose there's just one chance in a million that Lije is right, and I am wrong? That one slim shadow of a doubt would give me no rest forever; not even in my grave." He turned his head, and rested heavy eyes on Mart. "Better go make up the packs. Then catch the horses up. We got a long way more to go."

Mart ran for the bunkhouse.

31 ─────────────────────────────

In the bunkhouse Mart lighted a lamp. They had cracked their bedrolls open to get out clean shirts, and some of their stuff had got spread around. He started throwing their things together. Then he heard a scamper of light boots, and a whisk of wind made the lamp flutter as the door was thrown open. Laurie appeared against the dark, and she showed a tension that promised trouble.

"Shut the door," he told her.

She pressed it shut and stood against it. "I want the truth," she said. "If you start off again, after all this time—Oh, Mart, what's it supposed to mean?"

"It means, I see a chance she's there."

"Well, you're not going!"

"Who isn't?"

"I've dallied around this god-forsaken wind-scour for nearly six long years—waiting for you to see fit to come back! You're not going gallivanting off again now!"

It was the wrong tone to take with him. He no more than glanced at her. "I sure don't know who can stop me."

"You're a wanted man," she reminded him. "And Charlie MacCorry is less than half an hour away. If it takes all the Rangers in Texas to put handcuffs on you—they'll come when he hollers!"

He had no time to fool with this kind of an ambuscade, but he took time. He was clawing for a way to make her see what he was up against, why he had no choice. Uncertainly he dug out the doeskin packet in which he carried Debbie's miniature. The once-white leather was stained to the color of burlap, and its stiffened folds cracked as he unwrapped it; he had not dug it out for a long time. Laurie came to look as he opened the little plush case and held it to the light. Debbie's portrait was very dim. The dust had worked into it finally, and the colors had faded to shades of brown stain. No effect of life, or pertness, looked out from it any more. The little kitty-cat face had receded from him, losing itself behind the years.

Laurie hardened. "That's no picture of her," she said.

He looked up, appalled by the bitterness of her tone.

"It might have been once," she conceded. "But now it's nothing but a chromo of a small child. Can't you count up time at all?"

"She was coming ten," Mart said. "This was made before."

"She was eleven," Laurie said with certainty. "We've got the Edwards' family Bible, and I looked it up. Eleven—and it's been more than five years! She's sixteen and coming seventeen right now."

He had known that Debbie was growing up during all the long time they had hunted for her; but he had never been able to realize it, or picture it. No matter what counting on his fingers told him, he had always been hunting for a little child. But he had no reason to doubt Laurie. He could easily have lost a year in the reckoning some way, so that she had been a year older than he had supposed all the time.

"Deborah Edwards is a woman grown," Laurie said. "If she's alive at all."

He said, "If she's alive, I've got to fetch her home."

"Fetch what home? She won't come with you if you find her. They never do."

Her face was dead white; he stared at it with disbelief. He still thought it to be a good face, finely made, with beautiful eyes. But now the face was hard as quartz, and the eyes were lighted with the same fires of war he had seen in Amos' eyes the times he had stomped Comanche scalps into the dirt.

"She's had time to be with half the Comanche bucks in creation by now." Laurie's voice was cold, but not so brutal as her words. "Sold time and again to the highest bidder—and you know it! She's got savage brats of her own, most like. What are you going to do with them—fetch them home, too? Well, you won't. Because she won't let you. She'll kill herself before she'll even look you in the face. If you knew anything at all about a woman, you'd know that much!"

"Why, Laurie—" he faltered. "Why, Laurie—"

"You're not bringing anything back," she said, and her contempt whipped him across the face. "It's too late by many years. If they've got anything left to sell you, it's nothing but a—a rag of a female—the leavings of Comanche bucks—"

He turned on her with such a blaze in his eyes that she moved back half a step. But she stood her ground then, and faced up to him; and after a while he looked away. He had hold of himself before he answered her. "I'll have to see what Amos wants to do."

"You know what he wants to do. He wants to lead the yellowlegs down on 'em, and punish 'em off the face of creation. He's never wanted anything else, no matter how he's held back or pretended. Amos has leaned way backwards for love of his brother's dead wife—and not from regard for anything else on this earth or beyond it!"

He knew that was true. "That's why I've stayed with him. I told you that a long time ago."

"Amos has had enough of all this. I knew it the minute he stepped in the house. He's very patiently gone through all the motions Martha could have asked of him—and way over and beyond. But he's done."

"I know that, too," he said.

She heard the fight go out of his voice, and she changed, softening, but without taking hope. "I wanted you, Mart. I tried to give you everything I've got to give. It's not my fault it wasn't any good."

She had shaken him up, so that he felt sick. He couldn't lay hands on the purposes by which he had lived for so long, or any purpose instead. His eyes ran along the walls, looking for escape from the blind end that had trapped him.

A calendar was there on the wall. It had a strange look, because it picked up beyond the lost years his life had skipped. But as he looked at it he remembered another calendar that hadn't looked just right. It was a calendar a little child had made for him with a mistake in it, so that her work was wasted; only he hadn't noticed that then. And he heard the little girl's voice, saying again the words that he had never really heard her say, but only had been told, and imagined: "He didn't care. . . . He didn't care at all. . . ."

"Do you know," Laurie said, "what Amos will do if he finds Deborah Edwards? It will be a right thing, a good thing—and I tell you Martha would want it now. He'll put a bullet in her brain."

He said, "Only if I'm dead."

"You think you can outride the yellowlegs—and Amos, too," she read his mind again. "I suppose you can. And get to Yellow Buckle with a warning. But you can't outride the Rangers! You've been on their list anyway for a long time! Charlie MacCorry is only seven miles away. And I'm going to fetch him now!"

"You so much as reach down a saddle," he told her,

"and I'll be on my way in the same half minute. You think there's a man alive can give me a fourteen-mile start? Get back in that house!"

She stared at him a moment more, then slammed her way out. When she was gone Mart put Debbie's miniature in his pocket, then retied his packs to be ready for a fast departure in case Laurie carried out her threat; and he left the lamp burning in the bunkhouse as he went back to the kitchen.

Laurie did not ride for Charlie MacCorry. As it turned out, she didn't need to. MacCorry arrived at the Mathisons in the next fifteen minutes, stirred up by the squatter to whom Amos had laid down the law in the Edwards house.

32

If you'd come in and faced it out, like you said," Charlie MacCorry told them, "I don't believe there'd ever been any case against you at all."

Four years in the Rangers had done Charlie good. He seemed to know his limitations better now, and accepted them, instead of noisily spreading himself over all creation. Within those limits, which he no longer tried to overreach, he was very sure of himself, and quietly so, which was a new thing for Charlie.

"I said I'd come in when I could. I was on my way to Austin now. Until I run into Lije as I stopped over."

"He spoke of that," Aaron Mathison confirmed.

Resentment kept thickening Amos' neck. He

shouldn't have been asked to put up with this in front of the whole Mathison family. Mrs. Mathison came and went, staying with Lije Powers mostly. But there had been no way to get rid of Tobe and Abner, who kept their mouths shut in the background, but were there, as was Laurie, making herself as inconspicuous as she could.

"And you had my bond of a thousand head of cattle, in token I'd come back," Amos said. "Or did you pick them up?"

"We couldn't, very well, because you didn't own them. Not until the courts declared Deborah Edwards dead, which hasn't been done. I don't think Captain Clinton ever meant to pick them up. He was satisfied with your word. Then."

"Captain, huh?" Amos took note of the promotion. "What are you—a colonel?"

"Sergeant," MacCorry said without annoyance. "You've been close to three years. Had to come and find you on a tip. Your reputation hasn't improved any in that time, Mr. Edwards."

"What's the matter with my reputation?" Amos was angering again.

"I'll answer that if you want. So you can see what us fellers is up against. Mark you, I don't say it's true." No rancor could be heard in MacCorry's tone. He sat relaxed, elbows on the table, and looked Amos in the eye. "They say it's funny you leave a good ranch, well stocked, to be worked by other men, while you sky-hoot the country from the Nations to Mexico on no reasonable business so far as known. They say

245

you're almighty free with the scalping knife, and that's a thing brings costly trouble on Texas. They say you're a squaw man, who'd sooner booger around with the Wild Tribes than work your own stock; and an owlhoot that will murder to rob."

"You dare set there and say——"

"I do not. I tell you what's said. But all that builds up pressure on us. Half the Indian trouble we get nowadays is stirred up by quick-trigger thieves and squaw men poking around where they don't belong. And your name—names—are a couple that come up when the citizens holler to know why we don't do nothing. I tell you all this in hopes you'll see why I got to do my job. After all, this is a murder case."

"There ain't any such murder case," Amos said flatly.

"I hope you're right. But that's not my business. All I know, you stand charged with the robbery and murder of Walker Finch, alias Jerem Futterman. And two other deceased——"

"What's supposed to become of Yellow Buckle, while——"

"That's up to Captain Clinton. Maybe he wants to throw the Rangers at Yellow Buckle, with you for guide. You'll have to talk to him."

Watching Amos, Mart saw his mind lock, slowly turning him into the inert lump Mart remembered from long ago. He couldn't believe it at first, it was so long since he had seen Amos look like that.

"I'll ride there with you, Amos," Aaron Mathison said. "Sol Clinton will listen to me. We'll clear this thing once and for all."

Amos' eyes were on his empty hands, and he seemed incapable of speech.

"I'm not going in," Mart said to Charlie MacCorry.

"What?" The young Ranger looked startled.

"I don't know what Amos is of a mind to do," Mart said. "I'm going to Yellow Buckle."

"That there's maybe the worst thing I could hear you say!"

"All I want to do is get her out of there," Mart said, "before you hit him, or the cavalry hits. Once you jump him, it'll be too late."

"Allowing she's alive," Charlie MacCorry said, "which I don't—you haven't got a chance in a million to buy her, or steal her, either!"

"I've seen a white girl I could buy from an Indian."

"This one can talk. Letting her go would be like suicide for half a tribe!"

"I got to try, Charlie. You see that."

"I see no such thing. Damn it, Mart, will you get it through your head—you're under arrest!"

"What if I walk out that door?"

Charlie glanced past Aaron at Laurie Mathison before he answered. "Now, you ought to know the answer to that."

Laurie said distinctly, "He means he'll put a bullet in your back."

Charlie MacCorry thought about that a moment. "If he's particular about getting his bullets in front," he said to her, "he can walk out backwards, can't he?"

A heavy silence held for some moments before Amos spoke, "It's up to Sol Clinton, Mart."

"That's what I told you," Charlie said.

Amos asked, "You want to get started?"

"We'll wait for daylight. Seeing there's two of you. And allowing for the attitude you take." He spoke to Aaron. "I'll take 'em out to the bunkhouse; they can get some sleep if they want. I'll set up with 'em. And don't get a gleam in your eye," he finished to Mart. "I was in the bunkhouse before I come in here—and I put your guns where they won't be fell over. Now stand up, and walk ahead of me slow."

The lamp was still burning in the bunkhouse, but the fire in the stove was cold. Charlie watched them, quietly wary but without tension, while he lighted a lantern for a second light, and set it on the floor well out of the way. He wasn't going to be left in the dark with a fight on his hands by one of them throwing his hat at the lamp. Amos sat heavily on his bunk; he looked tired and old.

"Pull your boots if you want," Charlie MacCorry said. "I ain't going to stamp on your feet, or nothing. I only come for you by myself because we been neighbors from a long way back. I want this as friendly as you'll let it be." He found a chair with the back broken off, moved it nearer the stove with his foot, and sat down facing the bunks.

"Mind if I build the fire up?" Mart asked.

"Good idea."

Mart pawed in the woodbox, stirring the split wood so that a piece he could get a grip on came to the top.

Charlie spoke sharply to Amos. "What you doing with that stick?"

From the corner of his eye, Mart saw that Amos was working an arm under the mattress on his bunk. "Thought I heard a mouse," Amos said.

Charlie stood up suddenly, so that the broken chair overturned. His gun came out, but it was not cocked or pointed. "Move slow," he said to Amos, "and bring that hand out empty." For that one moment, while Amos drew his hand slowly from under the tick, Charlie MacCorry was turned three-quarters away from Mart, his attention undivided upon Amos.

Mart's piece of cordwood swung, and caught Mac-Corry hard behind the ear. He rattled to the floor bonily, and lay limp. Amos was kneeling beside him instantly, empty-handed; he hadn't had anything under the mattress. He rolled Charlie over, got his gun from under him, and had a look at his eyes.

"You like to tore his noggin' off," he said. "Lucky he ain't dead."

"Guess I got excited."

"Fetch something to make a gag. And my light *reata*."

33

They didn't know where the Seven Fingers were as well as they thought they did. West of the Rainy Mountains lay any number of watersheds, according to how far west you went. No creek had exactly seven tributaries. Mart had hoped to get hold of an Indian or two as they drew near. With luck they would have found a guide to take them within sight of Yellow Buckle's Camp. But Sheridan's long-awaited campaign had cleared the prairies; the country beyond the North Fork of the Red was deserted. They judged, though, that the Seven Fingers had to be one of two systems of creeks.

Leaving the North Fork they tried the Little Horsethief first. It had nine tributaries, but who could tell how many a Kiowa medicine man would count? This whole thing drained only seventy or eighty square miles; a few long swings, cutting for sign, disposed of it in two days.

They crossed the Walking Wolf Ridge to the Elkhorn. This was their other bet—a system of creeks draining an area perhaps thirty miles square. On the maps it looks like a tree. You could say it has thirty or forty run-ins if you followed all the branches out to their ends; or you could say it has eight, or four, or two. You could say it has seven.

The country had the right feel as they came into it; they believed this to be the place Lije had meant. But now both time and country were running out, and very fast. The murder charge against them might be a silly one, and liable to be laughed out of court. But they had resisted arrest by violence, in the course of which Mart had assaulted an officer with a deadly weapon, intending great bodily harm. Actually all he had done was to swing on that damn fool Charlie MacCorry, but such things take time to cool off, and they didn't have it. No question now whether they wanted to quit this long search; the search was quitting them. One way or the other, it would end here, and this time forever.

Sometimes they had sighted a distant dust far back on their trail, losing them when they changed direction, picking them up again when they straightened out. They hadn't seen it now for four days, but they didn't fool themselves. Their destination was known, within limits, and they would be come for. Not that they had any thought of escape; they would turn on their accusers when their work was done—if they got it done. But they must work fast now with what horse-flesh they had left.

The Elkhorn Country is a land of low ridges between its many dust-and-flood-water streams. You can't see far, and what is worse, it is known as a medicine country full of dust drifts and sudden hazes. You can ride toward what looks like the smoke of many fires, and follow it as it recedes across the ridges, and finally lose it without finding any fire at all. Under war conditions this was a very slow-going job of riding indeed. Each swale had to be scouted from its high borders before you dared cut for sign; while you yourself could be scouted very easily, at any time or all the time, if the Indians you sought were at all wary of your approach.

Yet this whole complex was within three days military march from Fort Sill itself, at the pace the yellowlegs would ride now. No commander alive was likely to search his own doorstep with painful care, endlessly cordoning close to home, while the other columns were striking hundreds of miles into the fastnesses of the Staked Plains. Yellow Buckle had shown an unexampled craftiness in picking this hole-up in which to lie low, while the military storm blew over. Here he was almost certain to be by-passed in the first hours of the campaign, and thereafter could sit out the war unmolested, until the exhaustion of both sides brought peace. When the yellowlegs eventually went home, as they always did, his warriors and his ponies would be fresh and strong, ready for such a year of raids and victories as would make him legendary. By shrewdly setting aside the Comanche reliance upon speed and space, he had opened himself a way to become the all-time greatest war chief of the Comanches.

Would it have worked, except for a wobbly old man, whose dimming eyes saw no more glorious vision than that of a chair by a hot stove?

"We need a week there," Mart said.

"We're lucky if we've got two days."

They didn't like it. Like most prairie men, they had great belief in their abilities, but a total faith in their bad luck.

Then one day at daylight they got their break. It came as the result of a mistake, though of a kind no plainsman would own to; it could happen to anybody, and most it had happened to were dead. They had camped after dark, a long way past the place where they had built their cooking fire. Before that, though, they had studied the little valley very carefully in the last light, making sure they would bed down in the security of emptiness and space. They slept only after all reasonable precautions had been taken, with the skill of long-practiced men.

But as they broke out in the darkness before dawn, they rode at once upon the warm ashes of a fire where a single Indian had camped. They had been within less than a furlong of him all night.

He must have been a very tired Indian. Though they caught no glimpse of him, they knew they almost stepped on him, for they accidentally cut him off from his hobbled horse. They chased and roped the Indian pony, catching him very easily in so short a distance that Mart's back was full of prickles in expectation of an arrow in it. None came, however. They retired to a bald swell commanding the situation, and lay flat to wait for better light.

Slowly the sun came up, cleared the horizon haze, and leveled clean sunlight across the uneven land.

"You think he's took out on us?"

"I hope not," Amos answered. "We need the bugger. We need him bad."

An hour passed. "I figured he'd stalk us," Mart said. "He must be stalking us. Some long way round. I can't see him leaving without any try for the horses."

"We got to wait him out."

"Might be he figures to foller and try us tonight."

"We got to wait him out anyway," Amos said.

Still another hour, and the sun was high.

"I think it's the odds," Mart believed now. "We're two to one. Till he gets one clean shot. Then it's even."

Amos said with sarcasm, "One of us can go away."

"Yes," Mart said. He got his boots from the aparejos, and changed them for the worn moccasins in which he had been scouting for many days.

"What's that for?" Amos demanded.

"So's he'll hear me."

"Hear you doing what? Kicking yourself in the head?"

"Look where I say." Mart flattened to the ground beside Amos again. "Straight ahead, down by the crick, you see a little willer."

"He ain't under that. Boughs don't touch down."

"No, and he ain't up it neither—I can see through the leaves. Left of the willer, you see a hundred-foot strip of saw grass about knee high. Left of that, a great long slew of buckbrush against the water. About belt deep. No way out of there without yielding a shot. I figure we got him pinned in there."

"No way to comb him out if that's where he is," Amos said; but he studied the buckbrush a long time.

Mart got up, and took the canteens from the saddles.

"He'll put an arrow through you so fast it'll fall free on the far side, you go down to that crick!"

"Not without raising up, he won't."

"That's a seventy-five yard shot from here—maybe more. I ain't using you for bait on no such—"

"You never drew back from it before!" Mart went jauntily down the slope to the creek, swinging the canteens. Behind him he could hear Amos rumbling curses to himself for a while; then the morning was quiet except for the sound of his own boots.

He walked directly, unhurrying, to the point where the firm ground under the buckbrush mushed off into the shallow water at the saw-grass roots. He sloshed

254

through ten yards of this muck, skirting the brush; and now his hackles crawled at the back of his neck, for he smelled Indian—a faint sunburnt smell of woodfires, of sage smoke, of long-used buffalo robes.

He came to the water, and stopped. Still standing straight up he floated the two canteens, letting them fill themselves at the end of their long slings. This was the time, as he stood motionless here, pretending to look at the water. He dared not look at the buckbrush, lest his own purpose be spoiled. But he let his head turn a little bit downstream, so that he could hold the buckbrush in the corner of his eye. He was certain nothing moved.

Amos' bullet yowled so close to him it seemed Amos must have fired at his back, and a spout of water jumped in the river straight beyond. Mart threw himself backward, turning, as he fell, so that he came down on his belly in the muck. He didn't know how his six-gun came cocked into his hand, but it was there.

"Stay down!" Amos bellowed. "Hold still, damn it! I don't think I got him!" Mart could hear him running down the slope, chambering a fresh cartridge with a metallic clank. He flattened, trying to suck himself into the mud, and for a few moments lay quiet, all things out of his hands.

Amos came splashing into the saw grass so close by that Mart thought he was coming directly to where Mart lay.

"Yes, I did," Amos said. "Come looky this here!"

"Watch out for him!" Mart yelled. "Your bullet went in the crick!"

"I creased him across the back. Prettiest shot you

255

ever see in your life!"

Mart got up then. Amos was standing less than six yards away, looking down into the grass. Two steps toward him and Mart could see part of the dark, naked body, prone in the saw grass. He stopped, and moved backward a little; he had no desire to see anything more. Amos reached for the Indian's knife, and spun it into the creek.

"Get his bow," Mart said.

"Bow, hell! This here's a Spencer he's got here." Amos picked it up. "He threw down on you from fifteen feet!"

"I never even heard the safety click—"

"That's what saved you. It's still on."

Amos threw the rifle after the knife, far out into the water.

"Is he in shape to talk?"

"He'll talk, all right. Now get your horse, quick!"

"What?"

"There's two Rangers coming up the crick. I got one quick sight of 'em at a mile—down by the far bend. Get on down there, and hold 'em off!"

"You mean fight?"

"No-no-no! Talk to 'em—say anything that comes in your head—"

"What if they try to arrest me?"

"Let' em! Only keep 'em off me while I question this Comanch'!"

Mart ran for his horse.

34

No Rangers were in sight a mile down the creek when Mart got there. None at two miles, either. By this time he knew what had happened. He had been sent on a fool's errand because Amos wanted to work on the Indian alone. He turned back, letting his horse loiter; and Amos met him at the half mile, coming downstream at a brisk trot. He looked grim, and very ugly, but satisfied with his results.

"He talked," Mart assumed.

"Yeah. We know how to get to Yellow Buckle now. He's got the girl Lije Powers saw, all right."

"Far?"

"We'll be there against night. And it's a good thing. There's a party of more than forty Rangers, with sixty-seventy Tonkawas along with 'em, on 'the hill by the Beaver'—that'll be old Camp Radziminski—and two companies of yellowlegs, by God, more'n a hundred of 'em, camped right alongside!"

"That's no way possible! Your Indian lied."

"He didn't lie." Amos seemed entirely certain. Mart saw now that a drop of fresh blood had trickled down the outside of Amos' scalping-knife sheath.

"Where is he now?"

"In the crick. I weighted him down good with rocks."

"I don't understand this," Mart said. He had learned to guess the general nature of the truth behind some kinds of Indian lies, but he couldn't see through this story. "I never heard of Rangers and cavalry working together before. Not in Indian territory, anyway. My guess is Sill sent out a patrol to chase the Rangers back."

Amos shrugged. "Maybe so. But the Rangers will make a deal now—they'll have to. Give the soldiers Yellow Buckle on a plate in return for not getting run back to Texas."

"Bound to," Mart said glumly, "I suppose."

"Them yellowlegs come within an ace of leaving a big fat pocket of Comanch' in their rear. Why, Yellow Buckle could have moved right into Fort Sill soon as Davidson marches! They'll blow sky high once they see what they nearly done. They can hit that village in two days—tomorrow, if the Rangers set the pace. And no more Yellow Buckle! We got to get over there."

They reset their saddles, and pressed on at a good long trot, loping one mile in three.

"There's something I got to say," Mart told Amos as they rode. "I want to ask one thing. If we find the village—"

"We'll find it. And it'll still be there. That one Comanche was the only scout they had out between them and Fort Sill."

"I want to ask one thing—"

"Finding Yellow Buckle isn't the hard part. Not now." Amos seemed to sense a reason for putting Mart off from what he wanted to say. "Digging the girl out of that village is going to be the hard thing in what little time we got."

"I know. Amos, will you do me one favor? When we find the village—Now, don't go off half cocked. I want to walk in there alone."

"You want—what?"

"I want to go in and talk to Yellow Buckle by myself."

Amos did not speak for so long that Mart thought he was not going to answer him at all. "I had it in mind," he said at last, "the other way round. Leave you stay back, so set you can get clear, if worst goes wrong. Whilst I walk in and test what their temper be."

Mart shook his head. "I'm asking you. This one time—will you do it my way?"

Another silence before Amos asked, "Why?"

Mart had foreseen this moment, and worked it over in his mind a hundred times without thinking of any story that had a chance to work. "I got to tell you the truth. I see no other way."

"You mean," Amos said sardonically, "you'd come up with a lie now if you had one to suit."

"That's right. But I got no lie for this. It's because I'm scared of something. Suppose this. Suppose some one Comanche stood in front of you. And you knew for certain in your own mind—he was the one killed Martha?"

Mart watched Amos' face gray, then darken. "Well?" Amos said.

"You'd kill him. And right there'd be the end of Debbie, and all hunting for Debbie. I know that as well as you."

Amos said thickly, "Forget all this. And you best lay clear like I tell you, too—if you don't want Yellow

259

Buckle to get away clean! Because I'm going in."

"I got to be with you, then. In hopes I can stop you when that minute comes."

"You know what that would take?"

"Yes; I do know. I've known for a long time."

Amos turned in the saddle to look at him. "I believe you'd do it," he decided. "I believe you'd kill me in the bat of an eye if it come to that."

Mart said nothing. They rode in silence for a furlong more.

"Oh, by the way," Amos said. I got something for you here. I believe you better have it now. If so happens you feel I got to be gunned down, you might's well have some practical reason. One everybody's liable to understand."

He rummaged in various pockets, and finally found a bit of paper, grease-marked and worn at the folds. He opened it to see if it was the right one; and the wind whipped at it as he handed it to Mart. The writing upon it was in ink.

Now know all men: I, Amos Edwards, being of sound mind, and without any known blood kin, do will that upon my death my just debts do first be paid. Whereafter, all else I own, be it in property, money, livestock, or rights to range, shall go to my foster nephew Martin Pauley, in rightful token of the help he has been to me, in these the last days of my life.

AMOS EDWARDS

Beside the signature was a squiggle representing a

seal, and the signatures of the witnesses, Aaron Mathison and Laura E. Mathison. He didn't know what the "E" stood for; he had never even known Laurie had a middle name. But he knew Amos had fixed him. This act of kindness, with living witnesses to it, could be Mart's damnation if he had to turn on Amos. He held out the paper to Amos for him to take back.

"Keep hold of it," Amos said. "Come in handy if the Comanches go through my pockets before you."

"It don't change anything," Mart said bleakly. "I'll do what I have to do."

"I know."

They rode four hours more. At mid-afternoon Amos held up his hand, and they stopped. The rolling ground hid whatever was ahead but now they heard the far-off barking of dogs.

35

Yellow Buckle's village was strung out for a considerable distance along a shallow river as yet unnamed by white men, but called by Indians the Wild Dog. The village was a lot bigger than the Texans had expected. Counting at a glance, as cattle are counted, Mart believed he saw sixty-two lodges. Probably it would be able to turn out somewhere between a hundred fifty and two hundred warriors, counting old men and youths.

They were seen at a great distance, and the usual scurrying about resulted all down the length of the village. Soon a party of warriors began to build up just outside. They rode bareback, with single-rope war bridles on the jaws of their ponies, and their weapons were in their hands. A few headdresses and medicine shields showed among them, but none had tied up the tails of their ponies, as they did when a fight was expected. This group milled about, but not excitedly, until twenty or so had assembled, then flowed into a fairly well-dressed line, and advanced at a walk to meet the white men. Meanwhile three or four scouts on fast ponies swung wide, and streaked in the direction from which Mart and Amos had come to make sure that the two riders were alone.

"Seem kind of easy spooked," Mart said, "don't they?"

"I wouldn't say so. Times have changed. They're getting fought back at now. Seems to me they act right cocky, and sure."

The mounted line halted fifty yards in front of them. A warrior in a buffalo-horn headdress drew out two lengths, and questioned them in sign language: "Where have you come from? What do you want? What do you bring?" The conventional things.

And Amos gave conventional answers. "I come very far, from beyond the Staked Plains. I want to make talk. I have a message for Yellow Buckle. I have gifts."

A Comanche raced his pony back into the village, and the spokesman faked other questions, meaninglessly, while he waited for instructions. By the time his runner was back from the village, the scouts had signaled from far out that the strangers appeared to be alone, and all was well up to here. The two riders were escorted into the village through a clamoring horde of cur dogs, all with small heads and the souls of gadflies; and halted before a tepee with the black smoke flaps of a chief's lodge.

Presently a stocky, middle-aged Comanche came out, wrapped himself in a blanket, and stood looking them over. He was weaponless, but had put on no headdress or decoration of any kind. This was a bad sign, and the slouchy way he stood was another. Amos' gestures were brusque as he asked if this man called himself Yellow Buckle and the chief gave the least possible acknowledgment.

Visitors were supposed to stay in the saddle until invited to dismount, but Yellow Buckle did not give the sign. He's making this too plain, Mart thought. He wants us out of here, and in a hurry, but he ought to cover up better than this. Mart felt Amos anger. The tension increased until it seemed to ring as Amos dismounted without invitation, walked within two paces of the chief, and looked him up and down.

Yellow Buckle looked undersized with Amos looming over him. He had the short bandy legs that made most Comanches unimpressive on the ground, however effective they might be when once they put hands to their horses. He remained expressionless, and met Amos' eyes steadily. Mart stepped down and stood a little in back of Amos, and to the side. Getting a closer look at this chief, Mart felt his scalp stir. A thin line, like a crease, ran from the corner of the Comanche's left eye to the line of the jaw, where no natural wrinkle would be. They were standing before the mythical, the long-hunted, the forever elusive Chief Scar!

The Indian freed one arm, and made an abrupt sign that asked what they wanted. Amos' short answer was all but contemptuous. "I do not stand talking in the wind," his hands said.

For a moment more the Comanche chief stood like a post. Amos had taken a serious gamble in that he had left himself no alternatives. If Yellow Buckle—Scar—told him to get out, Amos would have no way to stay, and no excuse for coming back. After that he could only ride to meet the Rangers, and guide them to the battle that would destroy Scar and most of the people with him. It's what he wants, Mart thought. I have to stay if Amos rides out of here. I have to make what try I can, never mind what Amos does.

But now Scar smiled faintly, with a gleam in his eye that Mart neither understood nor liked, but which might have contained derision. He motioned Amos to follow him, and went into the tepee.

"See they keep their hands off the mule packs," Amos said, tossing Mart his reins.

Mart let the split reins fall. "Guard these," he said in Comanche to the warrior who had been spokesman. The Comanche looked blank but Mart turned his back on him, and followed Amos. The door flap dropped in his face; he struck it aside with annoyance, and went inside.

A flicker of fire in the middle of the lodge, plus a seepage of daylight from the smoke flap at the peak, left the lodge shadowy. The close air carried a sting of wood smoke, scented with wild-game stew, buffalo hides, and the faintly musky robe smell of Indians. Two chunky squaws and three younger females had been stirred into a flurry by Amos' entrance, but they were settling down as Mart came in. Mart gave the smallest of these, a half-grown girl, a brief flick of attention, without looking directly at her but even out of the corner of his eye he could see that her shingled thatch was black, and as coarse as a pony's tail.

Women were supposed to keep out of the councils of warriors, unless called to wait on the men. But the two squaws now squatted on their piled robes on the honor side of the lodge, where Scar's grown sons should have been, and the three younger ones huddled deep in the shadows opposite. Mart realized that they must have jumped up to get out of there, and that Scar had told them to stay. This was pretty close to insult, the more so since Scar did not invite the white men to sit down.

Scar himself stood opposite the door beyond the fire. He shifted his blanket, wrapping it skirtlike around his waist; and his open buckskin shirt exposed a gold brooch in the form of a bow of ribbon, hung around his neck on a chain. In all likelihood his present name, assumed midway of his career, commemorated some exploit with which this brooch was associated.

Amos waited stolidly, and finally Scar was forced to address them. He knew them now, he told them in smooth-running sign language. "You," he said, indicating Amos, "are called Bull Shoulders. And this boy," he dismissed Mart, "is The Other."

265

Amos' hands lied fluently in answer. He had heard of a white man called Bull Shoulders, but the Chickasaws said Bull Shoulders was dead. He himself was called Plenty Mules. His friends, the Quohadas, so named him. He was a subchief among the Comanchero traders beyond the Staked Plains. His boss was called the Rich One. Real name—"Jaime Rosas," Amos used his voice for the first time.

"You are Plenty Mules," Yellow Buckle's hands conceded, while his smile expressed a contrary opinion. "A Comanchero. This—" he indicated Mart— "is still The Other. His eyes are made of mussel shells, and he sees in the dark."

"This—" Amos contradicted him again—"is my son. His Indian name is No-Speak."

Mart supposed this last was meant to convey an order.

The Rich One, Amos went on in sign language, had many-heap rifles. (It was that sign itself, descriptive of piles and piles, that gave Indians the word "heap" for any big quantity, when they picked up white men's words.) He wanted horses, mules, horned stock, for his rifles. He had heard of Yellow Buckle. He had been told—here Amos descended to flattery—that Yellow Buckle was a great horse thief, a great cow thief—a fine sneak thief of every kind. Yellow Buckle's friend had said that.

"What friend?" Scar's hands demanded.

"The Flower," Amos signed.

"The Flower," Scar said, "has a white wife."

No change of pace or mood showed in the movement of Scar's hands, drawing classically accurate pictographs in the air, as he said that. But Mart's hair stirred and all but crackled; the smoky air in the lodge had suddenly become charged, like a thunderhead. Out of the corner of his eye Mart watched the squaws to see if Scar's remark meant anything to them in their own lives, here. But the eyes of the Comanche women were on the ground; he could not see their down-turned faces, and they had not seen the sign.

White wife. Amos made the throw-away sign. The Rich One did not trade for squaws. If the Yellow Buckle wanted rifles, he must bring horses. Many-heaps horses. No small deals. Or maybe—and this was sarcasm—Yellow Buckle did not need rifles. Plenty Mules could go find somebody else. . . . Amos was giving a very poor imitation of a man trying to make a trade with an Indian. But perhaps it was a good imitation of a man who had been sent with this offer, but who would prefer to make his deal elsewhere to his own purposes.

Scar seemed puzzled; he did not at once reply. Behind the Comanche, Mart could see the details of trophies and accoutrements, now that his eyes were accustomed to the gloom. Scar's medicine shield was there. Mart wondered if it bore, under its masking cover, a design he had seen at the Fight at the Cat-tails long ago. Above the shield hung Scar's short lance, slung horizontally from the lodgepoles. Almost a dozen scalps were displayed upon it, and less than half of them looked like the scalps of Indians. The third scalp from the tip of the lance had long wavy hair of a deep red-bronze. It was a white woman's scalp, and the woman it had belonged to must have been beautiful. The squaws had kept this scalp brushed and oiled, so that it caught red glints from the wavering fire. But Scar's lance bore none of the pale fine hair that had been Martha's, nor the bright gold that had been Lucy's hair.

Scar turned his back on them while he took two slow, thoughtful steps toward the back of the lodge and in that moment, while Scar was turned away from them, Mart felt eyes upon his face, as definitely as if a finger touched his cheek. His glance flicked to the younger squaws on the women's side of the lodge.

He saw her then. One of the young squaws wore a black head cloth, covering all of her hair and tied under her chin; it was a commonplace thing for a squaw to wear, but it had sufficed to make her look black-headed like the others in the uncertain light. Now this one had looked up, and her eyes were on his face in an unwavering stare, as a cat stares; and the eyes were green and slanted, lighter than the deeply tanned face. They were the most startling eyes he had ever seen in his life, strangely cold, impersonal yet inimical, and as hard as glass. But this girl was Debbie.

The green eyes dropped as Scar turned toward the strangers again and Mart's own eyes were straight ahead when the Comanche chief looked toward them.

Where were the rifles? Scar's question came at last.

Beyond the Staked Plains, Amos answered him. Trading must be there.

Another wait, while Mart listened to the ringing in

268

his ears.

Too far, Scar said. Let the Rich One bring his rifles here.

Amos filled his lungs, stood tall, and laughed in Scar's face. Mart saw the Comanche's eyes narrow but after a moment he seated himself cross-legged on his buffalo robes under the dangling scalps and the shield. "Sit down," he said in Comanche, combining the words with the sign.

Amos ignored the invitation. "I speak no more now," he said, using his voice for the second time. His Comanche phrasings were slow and awkward but easily understood. "Below this village I saw a spring. I camp there, close by the Wild Dog River. Tomorrow, if you wish to talk, find me there. I sleep one night wait one day. Then I go."

"You spoke of gifts," Yellow Buckle reminded him.

"They will be there." He turned and, without concession to courtesy, he said in English, "Come on, No-Speak." And Mart followed him out.

36

Pringles ran up and down Mart's back as they rode out of that village with the cur dogs bawling and blaspheming again all around them, just beyond kick-range of their horses' feet. But until they were out of there they had to move unhurriedly, as if at peace and expecting peace. Even their eyes held straight ahead, lest so much as an exchange of glances be misread as a trigger for trouble.

Amos spoke first, well past the last of the lodges. "Did you see her? . . . Yeah," he answered himself. "I see you did." His reaction to the sudden climax of their search seemed to be the opposite of what Mart had expected. Amos seemed steadied, and turned cool.

"She's alive," Mart said. It seemed about the only thing his mind was able to think. "Can you realize it? Can you believe it? We found her, Amos!"

"Better start figuring how to stay alive yourself. Or finding her won't do anybody much good."

That was what was taking all the glory, all the exultation, out of their victory. They had walked into a hundred camps where they could have handled this situation, dangerous though it must always be. White captives had been bought and sold before time and again. Any Indian on earth but Scar would have concealed the girl, and played for time, until they found a way to deal.

"How in God's name," Mart asked him, "can this thing be? How could he let us walk into the lodge where she was? And keep her there before our eyes?"

"He meant for us to see her, that's all!"

"This is a strange Comanche," Mart said.

"This whole hunt has been a strange thing. And now we know why. Mart, did you see—there's scarce a Comanch' in that whole village we haven't seen before."

"I know."

"We've even stood in that same one lodge before. Do you know where?"

"When we talked to Singing Dog on the Little Boggy."

"That's right. We talked to Singing Dog in Scar's own lodge—while Scar took the girl and hid out. That's how they've kept us on a wild-goose chase five years long. They've covered up, and decoyed for him, every time we come near."

"We've caught up to him now!"

"Because he let us. Scar's learned something few Indians ever know: He's learned there's such a thing as a critter that never quits follering or gives up. So he's had enough. If we stood in the same lodge with her, and didn't know her, well and good. But if we were going to find her, he wanted to see us do it."

"So he saw—I suppose."

"I think so. He has to kill us, Mart."

"Bluebonnet didn't think he had to kill us."

"He never owned to having a white girl until Jaime Rosas made him a safe deal. And down there below the Llanos we was two men alone. Up here, we got Rangers, we got yellowlegs, to pull down on Scar. We rode square into the pocket where he was figuring to set until Davidson marched, and all soldiers was long gone. Scar don't dast let us ride loose with the word."

"Why'd he let us walk out of there at all?"

"I don't know," Amos said honestly. "Something tied his hands. If we knew what it was we could stretch it. But we don't know." Amos bent low over the horn to look back at the village under his arm. "They're holding fast so far. Might even let us make a pass at settling down at the spring. . . ."

271

But neither believed the Comanches would wait for night. Scar was a smart Indian, and a bitter one. The reason his squaws were on the honor side of the lodge where his sons should be was that Scar's sons were dead, killed in war raids upon the likes of Mart and Amos. He would take no chances of a slip-up in the dark.

"We'll make no two mistakes," Amos said, and his tone was thoughtful. "They got some fast horses there. You saw them scouts whip up when they took a look at our back trail. Them's racing ponies. And they got nigh two hours of daylight left."

They reached the spring without sign of pursuit, and dismounted. Here they had a good three-furlong start, and would be able to see horses start from the village when the Comanches made their move. They would not, of course, be able to see warriors who ran crouching on foot, snaking on their bellies across open ground. But the Comanches hated action afoot. More probably they would try to close for the kill under pretense of bringing fresh meat, perhaps with squaws along as a blind. Or the Comanches might simply make a horse race of it. The fast war ponies would close their three-eighths-mile lead very easily, with even half an hour of daylight left. Some Indians were going to be killed but there could hardly be but one end.

They set to work on the one thin ruse they could think of. Mart kicked a fire together first—about the least token of a fire that would pass for one at all—and set it alight. Then they stripped saddles and packs. They would have to abandon these, in order to look as though they were not going any place. Bridles were left on the horses, and halters on the mules.

"We'll lead out," Amos said, "like hunting for the best grass. Try to get as much more lead as we can without stirring 'em up. First minute any leave the village, we'll ease over a ridge, mount bareback—stampede the mules. Split up, of course—ride two ways—"

"We'll put up a better fight if we stay together," Mart objected.

"Yeah. We'd kill more Indians that way. There's no doubt of it. But a whole lot more than that will be killed if one of us stays alive until dark—and makes Camp Radziminski."

"Wait a minute," Mart said. "If we lead the yellowlegs on 'em—or even the Rangers, with the Tonkawas they got—there'll be a massacre, Amos! This village will be gutted out."

"Yes," Amos said.

"They'll kill her—you know that! You saw it at Deadhorse Bend!"

"If I didn't think so," Amos said, "I'd have killed her myself."

There was the substance of their victory after all this long time: One bitter taste of death, and then nothing more, forever.

"I won't do this," Mart said.

"What?"

"She's alive. That means everything to me. Better she's alive and living with Indians than her brains bashed out."

A blaze of hatred lighted Amos' eyes, while his face

was still a mask of disbelief. "I can't believe my own ears," he said.

"I say there'll be no massacre while she's in that village! Not while I can stop it, or put it off!"

Amos got control of his voice. "What do you want to do?"

"First we got to live out the night. That I know and agree to. Beyond that, I don't know. Maybe we got to come at Scar some far way round. But we stay together. Because I'm not running to the troops, Amos. And neither are you."

Amos' voice was half choked by the congestion of blood in his neck, "You think the likes of you could stop me?"

Mart pulled out the bit of paper upon which the will was written, in which Amos left Mart all he had. He tore it slowly into shreds, and laid them on the fire. "Yes," he said, "I'll stop you."

Amos was silent for a long time. He stood with his shoulders slack, and his big hands hanging loose by his thighs, and he stared into space. When finally he spoke his voice was tired. "All right. We'll stay together through the night. After that, we'll see. I can't promise no more."

"That's better. Now let's get at it!"

"I'm going to tell you something," Amos said. "I wasn't going to speak of it. But if we fight, you got to murder all of 'em you can. So I'll tell you now. Did you notice them scalps strung on Scar's lance?"

"I was in there, wasn't I?"

"They ain't there," Mart said. "Not Martha's. Not

Lucy's. Not even Brad's. Let's—"

"Did you see the third scalp from the point of the lance?"

"I saw it."

"Long, wavy. A red shine to it—"

"I saw it, I told you! You're wasting—"

"You didn't remember it. But I remember." Amos' voice was harsh, and his eyes bored into Mart's eyes, as if to drive the words into his brain. "That was your mother's scalp!"

No reason for Mart to doubt him. His mother's scalp was somewhere in a Comanche lodge, if a living Indian still possessed it. Certainly it was not in her grave. Amos let him stand there a moment, while his unremembered people became real to him—his mother, with the pretty hair, his father, from whom he got his light eyes, his young sisters, Ethel and Becky, who were just names. He knew what kind of thing their massacre had been, because he had seen the Edwards place, and the people who had raised him, after the same thing happened there.

"Let's lead off," Amos said.

But before they had gone a rod, the unexpected stopped them. A figure slipped out the willows by the creek, and a voice spoke. Debbie was there—alone, so far as they could see she had materialized as an Indian does, without telltale sound of approach.

She moved a few halting steps out of the willow scrub, but stopped as Mart came toward her. He walked carefully, watchful for movement in the thicket behind her. Behind him he heard the metallic crash as

275

Amos chambered a cartridge. Amos had sprung onto a hummock, exposing himself recklessly while his eyes swept the terrain.

Mart was at four paces when Debbie spoke, urgently, in Comanche. "Don't come too close. Don't touch me! I have warriors with me."

He had remembered the voice of a child, but what he was hearing was the soft-husky voice of a grown woman. Her Comanche was fluent, indistinguishable from that of the Indians, yet he thought he had never heard that harsh and ugly tongue sound uglier. He stopped six feet from her; one more inch, he felt, and she would have bolted. "Where are they, then?" he demanded. "Let 'em stand up and be counted, if they're not afraid!"

Mystification came into her face; she stared at him with blank eyes. Suddenly he realized that he had spoken in a rush of English—and she no longer understood. The lost years had left an invisible mutilation as definite as if fingers were missing from her hand. "How many warriors?" he asked in gruff Comanche; and everything they said to each other was in Comanche after that.

"Four men are with me."

His eyes jumped then, and swept wide; and though he saw nothing at all, he knew she might be telling the truth. If she had not come alone, he had to find out what was happening here, and quick. Their lives might easily depend upon their next guess. "What are you doing here?" he asked harshly.

"My—" He heard a wary hesitancy, a testing of

276

words before they were spoken. "My—father—told me come."

"Your *what?*"

"Yellow Buckle is my father."

While he stared at her, sure he must have misunderstood the Comanche words, Amos put in. "Keep at her! Scar sent her all right. We got to know why!"

Watching her, Mart was sure Debbie had understood none of Amos' Texan English. She tried to hurry her stumbling tale. "My father—he believes you. But some others—they know. They tell him—you were my people once."

"What did *you* tell him?"

"I tell him I don't know. I must come here. Make sure. I tell him I must come."

"You told him nothing like that," he contradicted her in Comanche. "He smash your mouth, you say 'must' to him!"

She shook her head. "No. No. You don't know my father."

"We know him. We call him Scar."

"My father—Scar—" she accepted his name for the chief. "He believes you. He says you are Comancheros. Like you say. But soon—" she faltered—"soon he knows."

"He knows now," he contradicted her again. "You are lying to me!"

Her eyes dropped, and her hands hid themselves in her ragged wash-leather sleeves. "He says you are Comancheros," she repeated. "He believes you. He told me. He—"

He had an exasperated impulse to grab her and shake her; but he saw her body tense. If he made a move toward her she would be gone in the same instant. *"Debbie,* listen to me! I'm *Mart!* Don't you remember me?" He spoke just the names in English, and it was obvious that these two words were familiar to her.

"I remember you," she said gravely, slowly, across the gulf between them. "I remember. From always."

"Then stop lying to me! You got Comanches with you—so you say. What do you want here if you're not alone?"

"I come to tell you, go away! Go tonight. As soon as dark. They can stop you. They can kill you. But this one night—I make him let you go."

"Make him?" He was so furious he stammered. *"You* make him? No squaw alive can move Scar a hand span—you least of all!"

"I can," she said evenly, meeting his eyes. "I am—bought. I am bought for—to be—for marriage. My—man—he pays sixty ponies. Nobody ever paid so much. I'm worth sixty ponies."

"We'll overcall that," he said. "Sixty ponies! We'll pay a hundred for you—a hundred and a half—"

She shook her head.

"My man—his family—"

"You own five times that many ponies yourself—you know that? We can bring them—many as he wants—and enough cattle to feed the whole tribe from here to—"

"My man would fight. His people would fight. They

278

are very many. Scar would lose—lose everything."

Comanche thoughts, Comanche words—a white woman's voice and form . . . the meeting toward which he had worked for years had turned into a nightmare. Her face was Debbie's face, delicately made, and now in the first bloom of maturity; but all expression was locked away from it. She held it wooden, facing him impassively, as an Indian faces a stranger. Behind the surface of this long-loved face was a Comanche squaw.

He spoke savagely, trying to break through to the Debbie of long ago. "Sixty ponies," he said with contempt. "What good is that? One sleep with Indians—you're a mare—a sow—they take what they want of you. Nothing you can do would turn Scar!"

"I can kill myself," she said.

In the moment of silence, Amos spoke again. "String it out. No move from the village yet. Every minute helps."

Mart looked into the hard green eyes that should have been lovely and dear to him; and he believed her. She was capable of killing herself, and would do it if she said she would. And Scar must know that. Was this the mysterious thing that had tied Scar's hands when he let them walk away? An accident to a sold but undelivered squaw could cost Scar more than sixty ponies. It could cost him his chiefship, and perhaps his life.

"That is why you can go now," she said, "and be safe. I have told him—my father—"

His temper flared up. "Stop calling that brute your father!"

"You must get away from here," she said again,

279

monotonously, almost dropping into a ritual Comanche singsong. "You must go away quick. Soon he will know. You will be killed—"

"You bet I'm getting out of here," he said, breaking into English. "And I got no notion of getting killed, neither! Amos! Grab holt that black mule! She's got to ride that!"

He heard leather creak as Amos swung up a saddle. No chance of deception now, from here on; they had to take her and run.

Debbie said, "What—?"

He returned to Comanche. "You're going with us now! You hear me?"

"No," Debbie said. "Not now. Not ever."

"I don't know what they have done to you. But it makes no difference!" He wouldn't have wasted time fumbling Comanche words if he had seen half a chance of taking her by main force. "You must come with me. I take you to—"

"They have done nothing to me. They take care of me. These are my people."

"Debbie, Debbie—these—these Nemenna murdered our family!"

"You lie." A flash of heat-lightning in her eyes let him see an underlying hatred, unexpected and dreadful.

"These are the ones! They killed your mother, cut her arm off—killed your own real father, slit his belly open—killed Hunter, killed Ben—"

"Wichitas killed them! Wichitas and white men! To steal cows—"

"*What?*"

"These people saved me. They drove off the whites and the Wichitas. I ran in the brush. Scar picked me up on his pony. They have told me it all many times!" He was blanked again, helpless against lies drilled into her over the years.

Amos had both saddles cinched up. "Watch your chance," he said. "You know now what we got to do."

Debbie's eyes went to Amos in quick suspicion, but Mart was still trying. "Lucy was with you. You know what happened to her!"

"Lucy—went mad. They—we—gave her a pony—"

"Pony! They—they—" He could not think of the word for rape. "They cut her up! Amos—Bull Shoulders—he found her, buried her—"

"You lie," she answered, her tone monotonous again, without heat. "All white men lie. Always."

"Listen! Listen to me! I saw my own mother's scalp on Scar's lance—there in the lodge where you live!"

"Lies," she said, and looked at him sullenly, untouched. "You Long Knives—you are the evil ones. You came in the night, and started killing us. There by the river."

At first he didn't know what she was talking about; then he remembered Deadhorse Bend and Debbie's locket that had seemed to tell them she had been there. He wondered if she had seen the old woman cut down, who wore her locket, and the old man sabered, as he tried to save his squaw.

"I saw it all," she said, as if answering his thought.

Mart changed his tone. "I found your locket," he said gently. "Do you remember your little locket? Do you remember who gave it to you? So long ago. . . ."

Her eyes faltered for the first time; and for a moment he saw in this alien woman the little girl of the miniature, the child of the shrine in the dream.

"At first—I prayed to you," she said.

"You what?"

"At first—I cried. Every night. For a long time. I cried to you—come and get me. Take me home. You didn't come." Her voice was dead, all feeling washed out of it.

"I've come now," he said.

She shook her head. "These are my people. You—you are Long Knives. We hate you—fight you—always, till we die."

Amos said sharply, "They're mounting up now, up there. We got to go." He came over to them in long, quick strides, and spoke in Comanche, but loudly, as some people speak to foreigners. "You know Yellow Buckle thing?" he demanded, backing his words with signs. "Buckle, Scar wear?"

"The medicine buckle," she said clearly.

"Get your hands on it. Turn it over. Can you still read? On the back it says white man's words 'Ethan to Judith.' Scratched in the gold. Because Scar tore it off Mart's mother when he killed and scalped her!"

"Lies," Debbie repeated in Comanche.

"Look and see for yourself!"

Amos had been trying to work around Debbie, to cut her off from the willows and the river, but she was watching him, moving enough to keep clear. "I go back now," she said. "To my father's lodge. I can do nothing here." Her movements brought her no closer to Mart, but suddenly his nostrils caught the distinct, unmistakable Indian odor, alive, immediate, near. For an instant the unreasoning fear that this smell had brought him, all through his early years, came back with a sickening chill of revulsion. He looked at the girl with horror.

Amos brought him out of it. "Keep your rifle on her, Mart! If she breaks, stun her with the butt!" He swayed forward, then lunged to grab her.

She wasn't there. She cried out a brief phrase in Comanche as she dodged him, then was into the brush, running like a fox. "Git down!" Amos yelled, and fired his rifle from belt level, though not at her; while simultaneously another rifle fired through the space in which Debbie had stood. Its bullet whipped past Mart's ear as he flung himself to the ground. The Comanche who had fired on him sprang up, face to the sky, surprisingly close to them, then fell back into the thin grass in which he had hidden.

Dirt jumped in Mart's face, and a ricochet yowled over. He swiveled on his belt buckle, and snap-fired at a wisp of gunsmoke sixty yards away in the brush. He saw a rifle fall and slide clear of the cover. Amos was standing straight up, trading shots with a third sniper. "Got him," he said, and instantly spun half around, his right leg knocked from under him. A Comanche sprang from an invisible depression less than thirty yards away, and rushed with drawn knife. Mart fired, and the Indian's legs pumped grotesquely as he fell, sliding him on his face another two yards before he was still. All guns were silent then; and Mart went to Amos.

"Go on, God damn it!" Blood pumped in spurts from a wound just above Amos' knee. "Ride, you fool! They're coming down on us!"

The deep thrumming of numberless hoofs upon the prairie turf came to them plainly from a quarter mile away. Mart sliced off a pack strap, and twisted it into a tourniquet. Amos cuffed him heavily alongside the head, pleading desperately. "For God's sake, Mart, will you ride? Go on! Go on!"

The Comanches weren't yelling yet, perhaps wouldn't until they struck. Of all the Wild Tribes, the Comanches were the last to start whooping, the first to come to close grips. Mart took precious seconds more to make an excuse for a bandage. "Get up here!" he grunted, stubborn to the bitter last; and he lifted Amos.

One of the mules was down, back broken by a bullet never meant for it. It made continual groaning, whistling noises as it clawed out with its fore hoofs, trying to drag up its dead hindquarters. The other mules had stampeded, but the horses still stood, snorting and sidestepping, tied to the ground by their long reins. Mart got Amos across his shoulders, and heaved him bodily into the saddle. "Get your foot in the stirrup! Gimme that!" He took Amos' rifle, and slung it into the brush. "See can you tie yourself on with the saddle strings as we ride!"

He grabbed his own pony, and made a flying mount as both animals bolted. Sweat ran down Amos' face; the bullet shock was wearing off, but he rode straight up, his wounded leg dangling free. Mart leaned low on the neck, and his spurs raked deep. Both horses stretched their bellies low to the ground, and dug out for their lives, as the first bullets from the pursuit buzzed over. The slow dusk was closing now. If they could have had another half hour, night would have covered them before they were overtaken.

They didn't have it. But now the Comanches did another unpredictable, Indian kind of a thing. With their quarry in full view, certain to be flanked and forced to a stand within the mile, the Comanches stopped. Repeated signals passed forward, calling the leaders in; the long straggle of running ponies lost momentum, and sucked back upon itself. The Comanches bunched up, and sat their bareback ponies in a close mass—seemingly in argument.

Things like that had happened before that Mart knew about, though never twice quite the same. Sometimes the horse Indians would fight a brilliant battle, using the fast-breaking cavalry tactics at which they were the best on earth—and seem to be winning; then unexpectedly turn and run. If you asked them later why they ran, they would say they ran because they had fought enough. Pursued, they might turn abruptly and fight again as tenaciously as before—and explain they fought then because they had run enough. . . .

This time they came on again after another twenty-five minutes; or, at least, a picked party of them did. Looking back as he topped a ridge, Mart saw what looked like a string of perhaps ten warriors, barely visible in the last of the light, coming on fast at three miles. He turned at a right angle, covered by the ridge, and loped in the new direction for two miles more. The dusk had blackened to almost solid dark when he dismounted to see what he could do for Amos.

"Never try to guess an Indian," Amos said thickly, and slumped unconscious. He hung to the side of the horse by the saddle strings he had tied into his belt, until Mart cut him down.

Camp Radziminski was twenty miles away.

37

Martin Pauley sprawled on a pile of sacked grain in Ranger Captain Sol Clinton's tent, and waited. With Amos safe under medical care, of sorts, Mart saw a good chance to get some sleep; but the fits and starts of a wakeful doze seemed to be the best he could make of it. The Ranger was still wrangling with Brevet-Colonel Chester C. Greenhill over what they were about to do, if anything at all. He had been over there for two hours, and it ought to be almost enough. When he got back, Mart would hear whether or not five years' search could succeed, and yet be altogether wasted.

Camp Radziminski was a flattish sag in the hills looking down upon Otter Creek—a place, not an installation. It had been a cavalry outpost, briefly, long ago; and an outfit of Rangers had wintered here once after that. In the deep grass you could still fall over the crumbling footings of mud-and-wattle walls and the precise rows of stones that had bordered military pathways; but the stockaded defenses were long gone.

Mart had been forced to transport Amos on a travois. This contraption was nothing but two long poles dragged from the saddle. The attached horse had shown confusion and some tendency to kick Amos' head off, but it hadn't happened. Mart found Radziminski before noon to his own considerable surprise. And the dead Comanche scout was proved to have told the truth with considerable exactness under Amos' peculiarly effective methods of questioning.

Here were the "more than forty" Rangers, their wagon-sheet beds scattered haphazardly over the best of the flat ground, with a single tent to serve every form of administration and supply. Here, too, were the two short-handed companies of cavalry—about a hundred and twenty men—with a wagon train, an officer's tent, a noncom's tent, a supply tent, and a complement of pup tents sheltering two men each. This part of the encampment was inconveniently placed, the Rangers having been here first; but the lines of tents ran perfectly straight anyway, defying the broken terrain.

And here, scattered up and down the slopes at random, were the brush wickiups of the "sixty or seventy" Tonkawas, almost the last of their breed. These were tall, clean, good-looking Indians, but said to be cannibals, and trusted by few; now come to fight beside the Rangers in a last doomed, expiring effort to win the good will of the white men who had conquered them.

As Mart had suspected, the Army and the Rangers were not working together at all. Colonel Greenhill had not, actually, come out to intercept the Rangers.

Hadn't known they were there. But, having run smack into them, he conceived his next duty to be that of sending them back where they belonged. He had been trying to get this done without too much untowardness for several days; and all concerned were now fit to be tied.

In consequence, Mart found Captain Sol Clinton in no mood to discuss the murder charge hanging over Mart and Amos, by reason of the killings at Lost Mule Creek. From this standpoint, Clinton told Mart, he had been frankly hopeful of never seeing either one of them again. Seeing's they saw fit to thrust themselves upon him, he supposed he would have to do something technical about them later. But now he had other fish to fry—and by God, they seemed to have brought him the skillet! Come along here, and if you can't walk any faster than that you can run, can't you?

He took Mart to Colonel Greenhill who spent an hour questioning him in what seemed a lot like an effort to break his story; and sent him to wait in Clinton's tent after. Sol Clinton had spoken with restraint while Mart was with them, but as Mart walked away he heard the opening guns of Sol's argument roar like a blue norther, shaking the tent walls. "I'm sick and tired of war parties murdering the be-Jesus out of Texas families, then skedaddling to hide behind you yellowlegs! What are you fellers running, a damn Wild Indian sanctuary up here? The chief purpose of this here Union is to protect Texas—that's how *we* understood it! Yonder's a passel of murderers, complete with Texican scalps and white girl captive! I say

288

it's up to you to protect us from them varmints by step-ping the hell to one side while I—"

They had been at it for a long time, and they were still at it, though with reduced carrying power. Mart dozed a little, but was broad awake instantly as Sergeant Charlie MacCorry came in. Charlie seemed to have worked up to the position of right-hand man, or something, for he had stood around while Captain Clinton first talked to Mart, and he had been in Colonel Greenhill's tent during Mart's session there as well. His attitude toward Mart had seemed noncom-mittal—neither friendly nor stand-offish but quiet, rather, and abstracted. It seemed to Mart an odd and overkindly attitude for a Ranger sergeant to take toward a former prisoner who had slugged him down and got away. And now Charlie seemed to have some-thing he wanted to say to Mart, without knowing how to bring it up. He warmed up by offering his views on the military situation.

"Trouble with the Army," Charlie had it figured, "there's always some damn fool don't get the word. A fort sends some colonel chasing all over creation after a bunch of hostiles; and he finds 'em, and jumps 'em, and makes *that* bunch a thing of the past; and what does he find out then? Them hostiles was already coming into a different fort under full-agreed truce. Picked 'em off right on the doorstep, by God. Done away with them peaceful Indians all unawares. Well! Now what you got? Investigations—boards—court-martials—and wham! Back goes the colonel so many files he's virtually in short pants. Happens every time."

He paced the tent a few moments, two steps one way, two steps back, watching Mart covertly, as if expecting him to speak.

"Yeah," Mart said at last.

Charlie seemed freed to say what he had on his mind. "Mart . . . I got a piece of news."

"Oh?"

"Me and Laurie—we got married. Just before I left."

Mart let his eyes drop while he thought it over. There had been a time, and it had gone on for years, when Laurie was always in his mind. She was the only girl he had ever known very well except those in the family. Or perhaps he had never known her, or any girl, at all. He reached for memories that would bring back her meaning to him. Laurie in a pretty dress, with her shoulders bare. Laurie joking about her floursack all-overs that had once read "Steamboat Mills" across her little bottom. Laurie in his arms, promising to come to him in the night . . .

All that should have mattered to him, but he couldn't seem to feel it. The whole thing seemed empty, and dried out, without any real substance for him any more. As if it never could have come to anything, no matter what.

"Did you hear me?" Charlie asked. "I say, I married Laurie."

"Yeah. Good for you. Got yourself a great girl."

"No hard feelings?"

"No."

They shook hands, briefly, as they always did; and Charlie changed the subject briskly. "You sure fooled

290

me, scouting up this attack on Scar. I'd have swore that was the last thing you wanted. Unless you got Debbie out of there first. Being's they're so liable to brain their captives when they're jumped. You think they won't now?"

"Might not," Mart said dully. He stirred restlessly. "What's happened to them king-pins over there? They both died, or something?"

Charlie looked at him thoughtfully, unwilling to be diverted. "Is she—Have they—" He didn't know how to put it, so that Mart would not be riled. "What I'm driving at—has she been with the bucks?"

Mart said, "Charlie, I don't know. I don't think so. It's more like—like they've done something to her mind."

"You mean she's crazy?"

"No—that isn't it, rightly. Only—she takes their part now. She believes them, not us. Like as if they took out her brain, and put in an Indian brain instead. So that she's an Indian now inside."

Charlie believed he saw it now. "Doesn't want to leave 'em, huh?"

"Almost seems like she's an Indian herself now. Inside."

"I see." Charlie was satisfied. If she wanted to stay, she'd been with the bucks all right. Had Comanche brats of her own most likely.

"I see something now," Mart said, "I never used to understand. I see now why the Comanches murder our women when they raid—brain our babies even— what ones they don't pick to steal. It's so we won't

291

breed. They want us off the earth. I understand that, because that's what I want for them. I want them dead. All of them. I want them cleaned off the face of the world."

Charlie shut up. Mart sounded touched in the head, and maybe dangerous. He wouldn't have slapped Mart's face again for thirty-seven dollars.

Sol Clinton came in, now, at last. He looked angry, yet satisfied and triumphant all at once. "I had to put us under his command," the Ranger captain said. "I don't even know if I legally can—but it's done. Won't matter, once we're out ahead. We're going to tie into 'em, boys!"

"The Tonks, too?"

"Tonkawas and all. Mart, you're on pay as civilian guide. Can you find 'em again in the dark? Can you, hell—you've got to! I want to hit before sunrise—leave Greenhill come up as he can. You going to get us there?"

"That I am," Mart said; and smiled for the first time that day.

38

Scouting ahead, Mart Pauley found Scar's village still where he had seen it last. Its swarming cur dogs yammered a great part of every night, and their noise placed the village for him now. The Comanches claimed they could always tell what the dogs were barking at—wolves, Indians, white men, or spooks—and though Mart only partly believed this he reconnoitered the place from a great way out, taking no chances. He galloped back, and met Captain Sol Clinton's fast-traveling Rangers less than an hour before dawn.

"We're coming in," he said to Captain Clinton, turning his horse alongside. "I should judge we're within—" he hesitated. He had started to say they were within three to five miles, but he had been to very few measured horse races, and had only a vague idea of a mile. "Within twenty minutes trot and ten minutes walk," he put it. "There you top a low hogback, looking across flat ground; and the village is in sight beyond."

"In sight from how far?"

There it was again. Mart thought the hogback was about a mile from the village, but what's a mile? "Close enough to see trees, too far to see branches," he described it.

That was good enough. "Just about what we want," Sol accepted it. Everything else had been where Mart had said it would be throughout the long night's ride. The captain halted his forty-two Rangers, passing the word back quietly along the loose column of twos.

His men dismounted without further command, loosened cinches, and relieved themselves without military precision. They looked unhurried, but wasted no motions. These men supplied their own clothes, saddles, and weapons, and very often their own horses; what you had here was a bunch of individuals, each a tough and weathered fighting man in his own right, but also in his own manner.

Behind them the sixty-odd Tonkawas pulled up at an orderly interval, a body of riders even more quiet than the Rangers. They stepped down and looked to their saddles, which included every form of museum piece from discarded McClellans to Indian-craft rigs with elkhorn trees. Each dug a little hole in which to urinate, and covered it over when he was done.

A word from Clinton sent a young Ranger lacing forward to halt the point, riding a furlong or so ahead in the dark. They were in their last hour before action, but the Ranger captain made no inspection. He had inspected these men to their roots when he signed them on, and straightened them out from time to time after, as needed; they knew their business if they were ever going to.

Clinton sharpened a twig, picked his teeth with it, and looked smug. He had made a good march, and he knew it, and judged that the yellowlegs would be along in about a week. He cast an eye about him for the two cavalry troopers who had ridden with them as runner-links with Colonel Greenhill. They didn't seem to be in earshot. Captain Clinton spoke to Lieutenant Bart Lester, a shadowy figure in the last of the night. "Looks like we might get this thing cleaned up by breakfast," he said, "against something different goes wrong." Before Colonel Greenhill comes up, he meant. "Of course, when's breakfast is largely up to Scar. You can't—Who's this?"

Charlie MacCorry had come galloping up from the rear, where he had been riding tail. Now he pulled up, leaning low to peer at individuals, looking for Captain Clinton.

"Here, Charlie," Sol spoke.

"Hey, they're on top of us!"

"Who is?"

"The yellowlegs! They're not more than seven minutes behind!"

The toothpick broke between Sol Clinton's teeth, and he spit it out explosively as he jumped for his horse. "Damn you, Charlie, if you've let—"

"Heck, Sol, we didn't hear a thing until the halt. It's only just this minute we—"

"Bart!" Clinton snapped. "Take 'em on forward, and quick! Lope 'em out a little—but a lope, you hear me, not a run! I'll be up in a couple of minutes!" He went into his loose-cinched saddle with a vault, like a Comanche. He was cussing smokily, and tightening the cinch with one hand as he started hell-for-leather to the rear. The word had run fast down the column, without any shouting, and some of the Rangers were already stepping into their saddles. Charlie ducked his head between his shoulders. "Knew I'd never git far in the Rangers." Mart followed as Charlie spurred after Clinton who was riding to the Tonkawas.

"We can run for it," Charlie offered hopefully as Sol pulled up. "I believe if we hold the Tonks at a slow gait behind us—"

"Oh, shut up," Clinton said. He had to send the Tonkawas on, so that his own men would be between the Tonkawas and the cavalry when they went into action. The Cavalry couldn't be expected to tell one Indian from another, Clinton supposed, in the heat of action. The Tonks would race forward, anyway, pretty soon. No power on earth could hold those fools once the enemy was sighted.

"Hey, Spots!" Clinton called. "Where are you?"

Spotted Hog, the war chief commanding the Tonkawas, sprang onto his pony to ride the twenty yards to Clinton. "Yes, sir," he said in English of a strong Texan accent.

"Tell you what you do," Clinton said. "We're pretty close now; I'm sending you on in. I want—"

Spotted Hog whistled softly, a complicated phrase, and they heard it repeated and answered some distance to the rear.

"Wait a minute, will you? Damn it, Spots, I'm telling you what I want—and nothing no different!"

"Sure, Captain—I'm listening."

"The village is still there, right where it was supposed to be. So—"

"I know," Spotted Hog said.

"—so swing wide, and find out which side the crick they're holding their horses. Soon as you know—"

"The west side," the Tonkawa said. "The ponies are on the west side. Across from the village."

"Who told you to put your own scouts out? Damnation, if you've waked up that village—Well, never mind. You go hit that horse herd. The hell with scalps—run off that herd, and you can have the horses."

"We'll run 'em!"

"All right—get ahead with it."

"Yes, sir!" Spotted Hog jumped his pony off into the dark where a brisk stir of preparation could be heard among the Tonkawas.

"I got to send Greenhill some damn word," Clinton began; and one of the cavalry troopers was beside him instantly.

"You want me, sir?"

"God forbid!" Clinton exploded. "Git forward where you belong!" The trooper scampered, and Clinton turned to MacCorry. "Charlie . . . No. No. What we need's a civilian—and we got one. Here, Mart! You go tell Greenhill where he's at."

"What when he asks where you are?"

"I'm up ahead. That's all. I'm up ahead. And make this stupid, will you? If he gives you orders for me, don't try to get loose without hearing 'em; he'll only send somebody else. But you can lose your way, can't you? You're the one found it!"

"Yes, sir," Mart said with mental reservations.

"Go on and meet him. Come on, Charlie." They were gone from there, and in a hurry.

Galloping to the rear, past the Tonkawas, Mart saw that they were throwing aside their saddles, and all gear but their weapons, and tying up the tails of their ponies. No war paint had been seen on them until now, but as they stripped their shirts their torsos proved to be prepainted with big circles and stripes of raw colors. Great, many-couped war bonnets were flowering like turkey tails among them. Each set off, bareback, as soon as he was ready, moving up at the lope; there would be no semblance of formation. The Tonkawas rode well, and would fight well. Only they would fight from the backs of their horses, while the Comanches would be all over their ponies, fighting from under the necks, under the bellies—and still would run their horses the harder.

Once clear of the Tonkawas, Mart could hear the cavalry plainly. The noise they made came to him as a steady metallic whispering, made up of innumerable clinks, rattles, and squeaks of leather, perhaps five minutes away. Darkness still held as he reached them, and described the position of the enemy to Colonel Greenhill. The hundred and twenty cavalrymen wheeled twos into line.

"Has Clinton halted?" Greenhill asked.

"Yes, sir." Well . . . he had.

Some restrained shouting went on in the dark. The cavalry prepared to dismount, bringing even numbers forward one horse length; dismounted; reset saddles; and dressed the line. Colonel Greenhill observed that he remembered this country now; he had been over every foot of it, and would have recognized it to begin with, had he been booned with any decent kind of description. He would be glad to bet a barrel of forty-rod that he could fix the co-ordinates of that village within a dozen miles. If he had had so much as a single artillery piece, he would have shown them how to scatter that village before Scar knew they were in the country.

Mart was glad he didn't have one, scattering the Comanches being the last thing wanted. In his belief, the pony herd was the key. A Comanche afoot was a beaten critter; but let him get to a horse and he was a long gone Comanche—and a deadly threat besides. He felt no call, however, to expound these views to a brevet-colonel.

"Tell Captain Clinton I'll be up directly," Greenhill ordered him; and went briskly about his inspection.

Mart started on, but made a U-turn, and loped to the rear, behind the cavalry lines. At the far end of the dismounted formation stood four narrow-bowed covered wagons, their drivers at attention by the bridles of the nigh leaders. Second wagon was the ambulance; a single trooper, at attention by a front wheel, was the present sanitary detail. Martin Pauley rode to the tail gate, stepped over it from the saddle, and struck a shielded match. Amos lay heavily blanketed, his body looking to be of great length but little substance, upon a narrow litter. By his heavy breathing he seemed asleep, but his eyes opened to the light of the match.

"Mart? Where are we?"

"Pretty close on Scar's village. I was to it. Within dog-bark, anyway. Sol sent the Tonks to make a try at their horses, and took the Rangers on up. He wants to hit before Greenhill finds what he's up to. How you feel?"

Amos stared straight upward, his eyes bleak and unforgiving upon the unseen night above the canvas; but the question brought a glint of irony into them, so that Mart was ashamed of having asked it.

"My stuff's rolled up down there by my feet," Amos said. "Get me my gun from it."

If he had been supposed to have it, the sanitary detail would have given it to him, but it was a long time since they had gone by what other people supposed for them. Mart brought Amos his six-gun, and his cartridge belt, and checked the loading. Amos lifted a shaking hand, and hid the gun under his blankets. Outside they heard the "Prepare to mount!"

"I got to get on up there." Mart groped for Amos' hand. He felt a tremor in its grip, but considerable strength.

"Get my share of 'em," Amos whispered.

"You want scalps, Amos?"

"Yeah. . . . No. Just stomp 'em—like I always done—"

Men and horses were beginning to show, black and solid against a general grayness. You could see them now without stooping to outline them against the stars, as Mart stepped from the wagon bed into the saddle. The cavalry had wheeled into column of twos and was in motion at the walk. Mart cleared the head of the column, and lifted his horse into a run.

39

Sol Clinton's forty-two Rangers were dismounted behind the last ridge below Scar's village as Mart came up. They had plenty of light now—more than they had wanted or intended. Captain Clinton lay on the crest of the ridge, studying the view without visible delight. Mart went up there, but Clinton turned on him before he got a look beyond.

"God damn you, Pauley, I—"

"Greenhill says, tell you he's coming," Mart got in hastily. "And that's all he says."

But Clinton was thinking about something else. "Take a look at this thing here!"

Mart crawled up beside Clinton, and got a shock. The fresh light of approaching sunrise showed Scar's village in clear detail, a scant mile from where they lay. Half the lodges were down, and between them swarmed great numbers of horses and people, the whole thing busy as a hoof-busted ant hill. This village was packing to march.

A hundred yards in front of the village a few dozen mounted warriors had interposed themselves. They sat about in idle groups, blanket-wrapped upon their standing ponies. They looked a little like the Comanche idea of vedettes, but more were riding out from the village as Mart and Sol Clinton watched. What they had here was the start of a battle build-up. Clinton seemed unsurprised by Scar's readiness. You could expect to find a war chief paying attention to his business once in a while, and you had to allow for it. But— "What the hell's the matter with you people? Can't you count? That band will mount close to three hundred bucks!"

"I told you he might want this fight. So he's got himself reinforced, that's all."

A rise of dust beyond the village and west of the Wild Dog showed where the Comanche horse herd had been put in motion. All animals not in use as travois horses or battle ponies—the main wealth of the village—were being driven upstream and away. But the movement was orderly. Where were the Tonkawas? They might be waiting upstream, to take the horses away from the small-boy herders; they might have gone home. One thing they certainly were not doing was what they had been told. Captain Clinton had no comment to waste on that, either.

He pulled back down the hill, moving slowly, to give himself time to think. Lieutenant Bart Lester came forward, dogged by the two uniformed orderlies. "Flog on back, boy," Clinton told one of them. "Tell Colonel Greenhill I am now demonstrating in front of the village to develop the enemy strength, and expedite his commitment.... Guess that ought to hold him. Mount 'em up, Bart."

The Rangers mounted and drifted into line casually, but once they were formed the line was a good one. These men might shun precision of movement for themselves, but they habitually exacted it from their horses, whether the horses agreed to it or not. Mart placed himself near the middle of the line and watched Clinton stoically. He knew the Ranger would be justified in ordering a retreat.

Clinton stepped aboard his horse, looked up and down the line of Rangers, and addressed them conversationally. "Well, us boys was lucky again," he said. "For once we got enough Comanches to go around. Might run as high as a dozen apiece, if we don't lose too many. I trust you boys will be glad to hear this is a fight, not a surprise. They're forming in front of the village, at about a mile. I should judge we won't have to go all the way; they'll come to meet us. What I'd like to do is bust through their middle, and on into the village; give Greenhill a chance to hit 'em behind, as they turn after us. This is liable to be prevented. In which case we'll handle the situation after we see what it is."

Some of the youngsters—and most of the Rangers were young—must have been fretting over the time Clinton was taking. The Cavalry would be up pretty quick, and Colonel Greenhill would take over; probably order a retirement according to plan, they supposed, without a dead Comanche to show. Clinton knew what he was doing, however. In broad daylight, lacking surprise, and with unexpected odds against him, he wanted the cavalry as close as it could get without telling him what to do. And he did not believe Greenhill would consider retreat for a second.

"In case you wonder what become of them antic Tonks," Clinton said, "I don't know. And don't pay them Comanches no mind, neither—just keep your eye on me. I'm the hard case you're up against around here—not them childish savages. If you don't hear me first time I holler, you better by God read my mind—I don't aim to raise no two hollers on any one subject in hand."

He pretended to look them over, but actually he was listening. The line stood steady and perfectly straight. Fidgety horses moved no muscle, and tired old nags gathered themselves to spring like lions upon demand, before a worse thing happened. And now they heard the first faint, far-off rustle of the bell-metal scabbards as the cavalry came on.

"I guess this sloppy-looking row of hay-doodles is what you fellers call a line," Sol criticized them. "Guide center! On Joe, here. Joe, you just follow me." Deliberately he got out a plug of tobacco, bit off a chew, and rolled it into his cheek. It was the first tobacco Mart had ever seen him use. "Leave us go amongst them," the captain said.

He wheeled his horse, and moved up the slope at a walk. The first direct rays of the sun were striking across the rolling ground as they breasted the crest, bringing Scar's village into full view a mile away. A curious sound of breathing could be heard briefly along the line of Rangers as they got their first look at what they were going against. A good two hundred mounted Comanches were now strung out in front of the village, where only the vedettes had stood before; and more were coming from the village in a stream. The war ponies milled a bit, and an increased stir built up in the village beyond, in reaction to the Ranger advance.

Clinton turned in his saddle. "Hey, you—orderly!"

"Yes, sir!"

"Ride back and tell Colonel Greenhill: Captain Clinton, of the Texas Rangers, presents his respects—"

"Yes, sir!" The rattled trooper whirled his horse.

"Come back here! Where the hell you going? Tell him the Comanches are in battle line east of the crick, facing south—and don't say you seen a million of 'em! Tell him I say there's a couple hundred. If he wants to know what I'm doing, I'm keeping an eye on 'em. All right, go find him."

They were at a thousand yards, and the stream of Comanches from the village had dwindled to a straggle. It was about time; their number was going to break three hundred easily. A line was forming in a practiced manner, without confusion, and it was going to be a straight one. It looked about a mile long, but it wasn't; it wouldn't be much longer than a quarter of a mile if the Comanches rode knee to knee. Still, Mart expected a quarter mile of Comanches to be enough for forty-two men.

Clinton waved an arm, and stepped up the pace to a sharp trot. He was riding directly toward the village itself, which would bring them against the Comanche center. A single stocky warrior, wearing a horn headdress, loped slowly across the front of the Comanche line. Mart recognized Scar first by his short lance, stripped of its trophy scalps for combat. Incredibly, in the face of advancing Rangers, Scar was having himself an inspection! At the end of the line he turned, and loped back toward the center, unhurrying. When he reached the center he would bring the Comanche line to meet them, and all this spooky orderliness would be over.

Captain Clinton let his horse break into a hand-lope, and the forty behind him followed suit in the same stride. Their speed was little increased, but the line moved in an easier rhythm. Scar's line still stood quiet, unfretting. The beef-up from the village had stopped at last; Scar's force stood at more than three hundred and fifty Comanches.

They were within the half mile. They could see the tall fan-feathered bonnets of the war chiefs, now, and the clubbed tails of the battle ponies. The warriors were in full paint; individual patterns could not yet be made out, but the bright stripes and splotches on the naked bodies gave the Comanche line an oddly broken color.

Now Scar turned in front of his center; the line moved, advancing evenly at a walk. Some of the veteran Indian fighters among the Rangers must have felt a chill down their backs as they saw that. This Indian was too cool, held his people in too hard a grip; his battle would lack the helter-skelter horserace quality that gave a smaller and better disciplined force its best opportunities. And he wasn't using a Comanche plan of attack at all. The famous Comanche grinding-wheel attack made use of horsemanship and mobility, and preserved the option to disengage intact. The head-on smash for which Scar was forming was all but unknown among Comanches. Scar would never have elected close grips to a finish if he had not been sure of what he had. And he had reason. Coolly led, this many hostiles could mass five deep in front of Clinton, yet still wrap round his flanks, roll him up, enfold him. The Rangers watched Sol, but he gave no order, and the easy rating of his horse did not change.

They were at the quarter mile. A great swarm of squaws, children, and old people had come out from the village. They stood motionless, on foot, a long, dense line of them—spectators, waiting to see the Rangers eaten alive. Scar's line still walked, unflustered, and Clinton still came on, loping easily. Surely he must have been expecting some break, some turn in his favor; perhaps he had supposed the cavalry would show itself by this time, but it had not. What he would have done without any break, whether he would have galloped steadily into that engulfing destruction, was something they were never going to know. For now the break came.

Out of the ground across the river the Tonkawas appeared, as if rising out of the earth. Nothing over there, not a ridge, not an arroyo, looked as though it would hide a mounted man, let alone seventy; yet, by some medicine of wits and skill, they appeared with no warning at all. The tall Tonkawas came in no semblance of a line; they rode singly, and in loose bunches, a rabble. But they moved fast, and as if they knew what they were doing, as they poured over the low swell that had somehow hidden them on the flank of the Comanches. A sudden gabble ran along Scar's line, and his right bunched upon itself in a confused effort to regroup.

And now the Tonkawas did another unpredictable thing that no Comanche could have expected because he never would have done it. On the open slope to the river the Tonkawas pulled up sliding, and dropped from their horses. They turned the animals broadside, rested their firearms across the withers, and opened fire. In enfilade, at four hundred yards, the effect was murderous. Ragged gaps opened in the Comanche right where riderless ponies bolted. Some of the bonneted war chiefs—Hungry Horse, Stiff Leg, Standing Elk, Many Trees—were among the first to go down, as crack shots picked off the marked leaders. A few great buffalo guns slammed, and these killed horses. Scar shouted unheard as his whole right, a third of his force, broke ranks to charge splashing through the river.

The Tonkawas disintegrated at once. Some faded upstream after the horse herd, but scattered shots and war cries could be heard among the lodges as others filtered into the village itself. More gaps opened in Scar's line as small groups turned back to defend the village and the horses.

"I'll be a son-of-a-bitch," Clinton said.

He gave the long yell, and they charged; and Scar, rallying his hundreds, rode hard to meet them. The converging lines were at a hundred feet when Clinton fired. Forty carbines crashed behind him, ripping the Comanche center. The Rangers shifted their carbines to their rein hands, drew their pistols. Immediately the horses cannoned together.

It was Mart's first mounted close action, and what he saw of it was all hell coming at him, personally. A war pony went down under his horse at the first bone-cracking shock; his horse tripped, but got over the fallen pony with a floundering leap, and Comanches were all around him. Both lines disappeared in a yelling mix, into which Comanches seemed to lace endlessly from all directions. They rode low on the sides of their ponies, stabbing upward with their lances, and once within reach they never missed. If a man side-slipped in the saddle to avoid being gutted, a deep groin thrust lifted him, and dropped him to be trampled. Only chance was to pistol your enemy before his lance could reach you. The gun reached farther than the lance, and hit with a shock that was final; but every shot was a snapshot, and nobody missed twice. You had five bullets, and only five—the hammer being

308

carried on an empty cylinder—to get you through it all.

A horse screamed, close by, through the war whoops and the gun blasting. Beside Mart a Ranger's horse gave a great whistling cough as it stumbled, and another as its knees buckled, then broke its neck as it overended. The shoulder of a riderless pony smashed Mart's knee. Struggling to hold up his staggered horse, he pistol-whipped a lance at his throat; the splintered shaft gashed his neck, but he fired into a painted face. A whipping stirrup somehow caught him on the temple. An unearthly, inhuman sound was cidered out of a Ranger as his knocked-down horse rolled over him, crushing his chest with the saddle horn.

The Comanches became a mass, a horde, seeming to cover the prairie like a buffalo run. Then abruptly he was clear of it, popped out of it like a seed. The battle had broken up into running fights, and he saw that most of the Rangers were ahead of him into the village. One last Comanche overtook him. Mart turned without knowing what warned him, and fired so late that the lance fell across his back, where it balanced weirdly, teetering, before it fell off.

He looked back, letting his horse run free as he reloaded; and now he saw the stroke that finished the battle, and won his respect for the cavalry forever. Greenhill was coming in at the quarter mile, charging like all hell-fire, in so tight a line the horses might have been lashed together. Scar massed his Comanches, and he outnumbered his enemies still; he struck hard, and with all he had. Into the packed war ponies the cavalry smashed head on, in as hard a blow as cavalry ever struck, perhaps. A score of the light war ponies went down under the impact of the solid line, and the rest reeled, floundered backward, and broke. Into the unbalanced wreckage the cavalry plowed close-locked, sabering and trampling.

Most of the village had emptied, but at the far end a great number of Comanche people—squaws, children, and old folks, mostly—ran like wind-driven leaves in a bobbing scatter. The Rangers were riding through to join the Tonkawas in the running fight that could be heard far up the Wild Dog; but they made it their business to stamp out resistance as they went. The dreadful thing was that the fleeing people were armed, and fought as they ran, as dangerous as a torrent of rattlesnakes. Here and there lay the body of an old man, a squaw, or a half-grown boy, who had died rather than let an enemy pass unmolested; and sometimes there was a fallen Ranger. Mart had to go through these people; he had to hunt through them all, and keep on hunting through them, until he found Debbie, or they got him.

A squaw as broad as a horse's rump, with a doll-size papoose on her back, whirled on him at his stirrup. Her trade gun blasted so close that the powder burned his hand, yet somehow she missed him. And now he saw Amos.

He couldn't believe it, at first, and went through a moment of fright in which he thought his own mind had come apart. Amos looked like a dead man riding, his face ash-bloodless, but with a fever-craze burning in his eyes. It seemed a physical impossibility that he should have stayed on a horse to get here, even if some bribed soldier had lifted him into the saddle.

Actually, witnesses swore later, there had been no bribed soldier. Amos had pistol-whipped one guard, and had taken a horse at gunpoint from another . . .

He must have seen Mart, but he swept past with eyes ahead, picking his targets coolly, marking his path with Comanche dead. Mart called his name, but got no response. Mart's blown horse was beginning to wobble, so that Amos pulled away, gaining yards at every jump; and though Mart tried to overtake him, he could not.

Then, ahead of Amos, Mart believed he saw Debbie again. A young squaw, slim and shawl-headed, ran like a deer, dodging among the horses. She might have got away, but she checked, and retraced two steps, to snatch up a dead man's pistol; and in that moment Amos saw her. The whole set of his laboring body changed, and he pointed like a bird dog as he charged his horse upon her. The lithe figure twisted from under the hoofs, and ran between the lodges. Amos whirled his horse at the top of its stride, turning it as it did not know how to turn; it lost footing, almost went down, but he dragged it up by the same strength with which he rode. Its long bounds closed upon the slim runner, and Amos leaned low, his pistol reaching.

Mart yelled, "Amos—no!" He fired wild at Amos' back, missing from a distance at which he never missed. Then, unexpectedly, Amos raised his pistol without firing, and shifted it to his rein hand. He reached down to grab the girl as if to lift her onto his saddle.

311

The girl turned upon the rider, and Mart saw the broad brown face of a young Comanche woman, who could never possibly have been Debbie. Her teeth showed as she fired upward at Amos, the muzzle of her pistol almost against his jacket. He fell heavily; his body crumpled as it hit, and rolled over once, as shot game rolls, before it lay still.

40

O nly a handful of squaws, mostly with small children on their backs, had been taken prisoner. Mart talked to them, in their own tongue and in sign language, until the night grew old, without learning much that seemed of any value. Those who would talk at all admitted having known Debbie Edwards; they called her by a Comanche name meaning "Dry-Grass-Hair." But they said she had run away, or at least disappeared, three nights before—during the night following Mart and Amos' escape.

They supposed, or claimed to suppose, that she had run to the soldiers' camp on the Otter. Or maybe she had tried to follow Bull Shoulders and the Other, for she had gone the same way he himself had taken. Trackers had followed her for some distance in that direction, they said, before losing trace. They didn't know why she had gone. She had taken no pony nor anything else with her. If she hadn't found somebody to help her, they assumed she was dead; they didn't believe she would last long, alone and afoot, upon the prairie. Evidently they didn't think much of Dry-Grass-Hair in the role of an Indian.

"They're lying," Sol Clinton thought. "They've murdered her, is about the size of it."

"I don't think so," Mart said.

"Why?"

"I don't know. Maybe I just can't face up to it. Maybe I've forgot how after all this time."

"Well, then," Clinton humored him, "she must be between here and Camp Radziminski. On the way back we'll throw out a cordon. . . ."

Mart saw no hope in that, either, though he didn't say so, for he had nothing to suggest instead. He slept two hours, and when he awoke in the darkness before dawn he knew what he had to do. He got out of camp unnoticed, and rode northwest in a direction roughly opposite to that in which Camp Radziminski lay.

He had no real reason for doubting Clinton's conclusion that Debbie was dead. Of course, if it was true she was worth sixty horses, Scar might have sent her off to be hidden; but this did not jibe with Scar's bid for victory or destruction in open battle. The squaws' story didn't mean anything, either, even if they had tried to tell the truth, for they couldn't know what it was. The bucks never told them anything. His only excuse, actually, for assuming that Debbie had in truth run away, and perhaps still lived, was that only this assumption left him any course of action.

If she had run away it was on the spur of the moment, without plan, since she had taken nothing with her that would enable her to survive. This suggested that she had found herself under pressure of some sudden and deadly threat—as if she had been accused, for instance, of treachery in connection with his own escape. In such a case she might indeed have started after Mart and Amos, as the squaws claimed. But he had a feeling she wouldn't have gone far that way without recoiling; he didn't believe she would have wanted to come to him. Therefore, she must have wanted only to get away from Comanches; and, knowing them, she would perhaps choose a way, a direction, in which Comanches would be unlikely to follow. . . .

He recalled that the Comanches believed that the mutilated, whether in mind or body, never entered the land beyond the sunset, but wandered forever in an emptiness "between the winds." They seemed to place this emptiness to the northwest, in a general way; as if long-forgotten disasters or defeats in some ancient time had made this direction which Debbie, thinking like an Indian, might choose if she was trying to leave the world of the living behind her. He had it all figured out—or thought he did.

This way took him into a land of high barrens, without much game, grass, or water. About a million square miles of broken, empty country lay ahead of him, without trails, and he headed into the heart of the worst of it. "I went where no Comanche would go," he explained it a long time after. He thought by that time that he had really worked it out in this way, but he had not. All he actually had to go on was one more vagueness put together out of information unnoticed or forgotten, such as sometimes adds itself up to a hunch.

He drifted northwest almost aimlessly, letting his weariness, and sometimes his horse, follow lines of least resistance—which was what a fugitive, traveling blindly and afoot, would almost inevitably have done. After a few miles the country itself began to make the decisions. The terrain could be counted on to herd and funnel the fugitive as she tired.

Toward the end of that first day, he saw vultures circling, no more than specks in the sky over a range of hills many hours ahead. He picked up the pace of his pony, pushing as hard as he dared, while he watched them circling lower, their numbers increasing. They were still far off as night closed down, but in the first daylight he saw them again, and rode toward them. There were more of them now, and their circles were lower; but he was certain they were a little way farther on than they had been when first seen, What they were watching still moved, then, however slowly; or at least was still alive, for they had not yet landed. He loped his stumbling pony, willing to kill it now, and go on afoot, if only he could come to the end before daylight failed him.

Early in the afternoon he found her moccasin tracks, wavering pitifully across a sand patch for a little way, and he put the horse full out, its lungs laboring. The vultures were settling low, and though they were of little danger to a living thing, he could wait no longer for his answer.

And so he found her. She lay in a place of rocks and dust; the wind had swept her tracks away, and sifted the dust over her, making her nearly invisible. He over-

315

rode, passing within a few yards, and would have lost her forever without the vultures. He had always hated those carrion birds of gruesome prophecy, but he never hated them again. It was Mart who picked—or blundered into—the right quarter of the compass; but it was the vultures that found her with their hundred-mile eyes, and unwillingly guided him to her by their far-seen circles in the sky.

She was asleep, rather than unconscious, but the sleep was one of total exhaustion. He knew she would never have wakened from it of herself. Even so, there was a moment in which her eyes stared, and saw him with terror; she made a feeble effort to get up, as to escape him, but could not. She dropped into lethargy after that, unresisting as he worked over her. He gave her water first, slowly, in dribbles that ran down her chin from her parched lips. She went into a prolonged chill, during which he wrapped her in all his blankets, chafed her feet, and built a fire near them. Finally he stewed up shredded jerky, scraped the fibers to make a pulp, and fed it to her by slow spoonfuls. It was not true she smelled like a Comanche, any more than Mart, who had lived the same kind of life that she had.

When she was able to talk to him, the story of her runaway came out very slowly and in pieces, at first; then less haltingly, as she found he understood her better than she had expected. He kept questioning her as gently as he could, feeling he had to know what dreadful thing had frightened her, or what they had done to her. It no longer seemed unnatural to talk to her in Comanche.

They hadn't done anything to her. It wasn't that. It was the medicine buckle—the ornament, like a gold ribbon tied in a bow, that Scar always wore, and that had given him his change of name. She had believed Amos lied about its having belonged to Mart Pauley's mother. But the words that he had said were written on the back stayed in her mind. Ethan to Judith . . . The words were there or they weren't. If they were there, then Amos' whole story was true, and Scar had taken the medicine buckle from Mart's mother as she died under his knife.

That night she couldn't sleep; and when she had lain awake a long time she knew that somehow she was going to have to see the medicine buckle's back. Scar had been in council most of the night, but he slept at last. Mart had to imagine for himself, from her halting phrases, most of what had happened then. The slanting green eyes in the dark-tanned face were not cat's eyes as she told him, nor Indian's eyes, but the eyes of a small girl.

She had crawled out from between the squaws, where she always slept. With two twigs she picked a live coal out of the embers of the fire. Carrying this, she crept to the deep pile of buffalo robes that was Scar's bed. The chief lay sprawled on his back. His chest was bare, and the medicine buckle gleamed upon it in the light of the single ember. Horribly afraid, she got trembling fingers upon the bit of gold, and turned it over.

How had she been able to do that? It was a question he came back to more than once without entirely understanding her answer. She said that Mart himself had made her do it; he had forced her by his medicine. That was the part he didn't get. Long ago, in another world, he had been her dearest brother; he must have known that once. The truth was somewhere in that, if he could have got hold of it. Perhaps he should have known by this time that what the Indians call medicine is three-fourths the compelling ghosts of early associations, long forgotten. . . .

She had to lean close over the Comanche, so close that his breath was upon her face, before she could see the writing on the back of the medicine buckle. And then—she couldn't read it. Once, for a while, she had tried to teach Comanche children the white man's writing; but that was long ago, and now she herself had forgotten. But Amos had told her what the words were; so that presently the words seemed to fit the scratches on the gold: "Ethan to Judith . . ." Actually, the Rangers were able to tell Mart later, Amos had lied. The inscription said, "Made in England."

Then, as she drew back, she saw Scar's terrible eyes, wide open and upon her face, only inches away. For an instant she was unable to move. Then the coal dropped upon Scar's naked chest, and he sprang up with a snarl, grabbing for her.

After that she ran; in the direction Mart and Amos had gone, at first, as the squaws had said—but this was chance. She didn't know where she was going. Then, when they almost caught her, she had doubled back, like any hunted creature. Not in any chosen direction, but blindly, running away from everything, seeking space and emptiness. No thought of the limbo

318

"between the winds" had occurred to her.

"But you caught me. I don't know how. I was better off with them. There, where I was. If only I never looked—behind the buckle—"

Sometime, and perhaps better soon than late, he would have to tell her what had happened to Scar's village after she left it. But not now.

"Now I have no place," Debbie said. "No place to go, ever. I want to die now."

"I'm taking you back. Can't you understand that?"

"Back? Back where?"

"Home, Debbie—to our own people!"

"I have no people. They are dead. I have no place—"

"There's the ranch. It belongs to you now. Don't you want to—"

"It is empty. Nobody is there."

"I'll be there, Debbie."

She lifted her head to stare at him—wildly, he thought. He was frightened by what he took to be a light of madness in her eyes, before she lowered them. He said, "You used to like the ranch. Don't you remember it?"

She was perfectly still.

He said desperately, "Have you forgotten? Don't you remember anything about when you were a little girl, at all?"

Tears squeezed from her shut eyes, and she began to shiver again, hard, in the racking shake they called the ague. He had no doubt she was taking one of the dangerous fevers; perhaps pneumonia, or if the chill was from weakness alone, he feared that the most. The open prairie had ways to bite down hard and sure on any warm-blooded thing when its strength failed. Panic touched him as he realized he could lose her yet.

He knew only one more way to bring warmth to her, and that was to give her his own. He lay close beside her, and wrapped the blankets around them both, covering their heads, so that even his breath would warm her. Held tight against him she seemed terribly thin, as if worked to the very bone; he wondered despairingly if there was enough of her left ever to be warmed again. But the chill moderated as his body heat reached her; her breathing steadied, and finally became regular.

He thought she was asleep, until she spoke, a whisper against his chest. "I remember," she said in a strangely mixed tongue of Indian-English. "I remember it all. But you the most. I remember how hard I loved you." She held onto him with what strength she had left; but she seemed all right, he thought, as she went to sleep.

Center Point Publishing
600 Brooks Road • PO Box 1
Thorndike ME 04986-0001 USA

(207) 568-3717

US & Canada:
1 800 929-9108